OTHER BOOKS BY RHIANNON HELD

Silver
Tarnished
Reflected

Wolfsbane

Rhiannon Held

Printed in the United States of America

First Printing, 2015

ISBN 978-1-943545-00-1

Cover design by Kate Marshall
Paw icon by Mattijs Dekkers

www.rhiannonheld.com

To Kate
I tried to think of something cleverer than "without
her, this book wouldn't exist" ... but without her,
this book wouldn't exist.

ACKNOWLEDGEMENTS

journey. Corry Lee, Kate Marshall, the Fairwood Writers, and my agent, Cameron McClure, all offered suggestions on various drafts. In fact, I owe an immeasurable debt to Kate many times over, for the beautiful cover, the formatting, and for learning the scary and complicated world of self-publishing right along with me.

Andrea Howe of Blue Falcon Editing did an excellent job with the copy-editing of this book. Duane Wilkins at the University Bookstore has always been supportive, and was gracious enough to welcome me to read there once more. My fellow archaeologists, Seattle writers, choral singers, and MOO gamers have seen me through the emotional ups and downs, even when some of them didn't understand a single thing I was talking about. The king and queen of support-without-specific-knowledge have been my parents, and the sister is and always will be the brainstormer extraordinaire.

And last to thank are the fans—if people had not demanded it, often and enthusiastically, this book would never have seen the light of day.

Wolfsbane

1

Andrew Dare strode out of the pack house to meet his daughter and her boyfriend as they pulled into the driveway. Waiting for them to arrive had been enough to give him bald patches, tearing his metaphorical fur out. On the phone they'd claimed the timing would be tight but doable. He hadn't realized how tight. Felicia would barely be able to wash up before they had to leave for the airport to meet the Russian envoy. Assuming, of course, that she was willing to come, and assuming she agreed that the Russians were even a threat. He'd planned on having much more time to explain things to her.

Tom, Felicia's boyfriend, was driving. He was laughing as he jumped out of his battered pickup, but he must have caught the scent of Andrew's tension because he sobered and jogged around to open the passenger door. Felicia jumped out in wolf form and lifted her nose to test his scent herself.

They'd left to roam together only about six months ago, and visited briefly since, but seeing his daughter again still caught Andrew unexpectedly hard. Perhaps it was because she'd been kept from him for so much of her childhood. Her wolf form was black with hints of brown or red in the under fur, nothing like her mother's, but she *moved* like Andrew's late wife in some way he couldn't define.

"Since it's just off full, we were taking turns driving so neither would get too itchy in human," Tom said, apologetic as if Andrew had objected to the fact that his daughter was currently unable to converse with him.

That was the least of his worries, since it was easily fixed. Andrew gestured to the house. "Come on, I'll explain inside. The timing's Lady-damned tight." Felicia bounded in with a few loping strides, and Tom managed a similar gait even with human legs. Andrew followed with slightly more dignity to give Felicia time to shift.

He shut the door behind himself quickly when he saw Felicia shivering in human form. This afternoon, the March wind had a chill bite with a droplet or two left from earlier drizzle.

Tom shrugged off his jacket and Felicia pulled it over her shoulders. "What's the hurry?" she asked, frowning. The expression harkened back to her teen years, the ones Andrew had raised her through. The wobble away from the adult self she was steadily growing into made him smile and banished her mother from his mind.

"I know you said you wanted me here for some appointment, but you didn't say it was an emergency." Felicia looked around the foyer distractedly, attention more on the house

than him. The pair had stopped by to move their things into
the new pack house, but it had been decorated since then.

Felicia blanched,

"The Russians?" She'd held her arms loose, pretending she
wasn't cold, but now she hugged the borrowed coat around
herself. "You're kidding me."

Andrew hated to scare his daughter, but seeing her reaction eased a knot in his voice. His mate, Silver, believed
him about the Russians, but the other North Americans still
seemed dubious about the threat they presented. Two weeks
had passed since word had come about the envoy, so he'd had
plenty of time to start doubting himself.

Tom scrubbed a hand through perpetually overgrown
hair and eyed them both. "Third? What does that mean?"

Felicia answered before Andrew could. "It's a European thing. I've told you how much more formal they are over
there." She dropped her chin a moment later, abashed, as she
probably realized she'd been so disrespectful as to practically
interrupt her alpha. Andrew waved for her to continue. Roam-
ers lost the niceties out on their own. He trusted she'd get back
into the habit soon enough.

"For important meetings, you send an alpha, beta, and
third. And guards, of course, but they don't count. The third

is a translator, or family of the person they're meeting, or expert on the subject they're meeting about, or whatever." Felicia murmured something to herself in Spanish, then shook her head. "It sounds too literal translated into English. Maybe lieutenant would be better? It doesn't have to be literally the third of three people, it's the third level of status."

She eyed her father. "But it's not like I speak Russian, so I don't know why Dad wants me." She tossed him the flicker of a smile. "I'm only nineteen. Not about to wow them with my high rank."

Andrew brushed Felicia's dark waves of hair from her shoulder and nudged her to the stairs. "I want you because you were raised European and so you're the only other one around here besides Silver who actually believes the Russians are a threat. We have about twenty minutes before we have to leave for the airport, so shower fast and put on something formal if you're willing to come. We can figure out our strategy in the car." He squeezed her shoulder to substitute for the words of a proper welcome he didn't have time to give her.

That made her laugh for some reason. She twisted around and gave him a tight embrace. "Love you too, Papa." Her accent slipped back in even before the last word. She ran up the stairs.

That left Tom standing in the entryway, looking lost. He had the same lanky build as when Andrew had last seen him—by now in his mid-twenties, it wasn't like he'd grow any more—but he'd filled himself out with a little more confidence. He eyed Andrew from under slightly shaggy bangs. "Russians? I know there's a pack out there somewhere, but don't they keep to themselves?"

Andrew checked the cuff of his sport coat for lint, but it hadn't developed any in the past ten minutes. He was as ready

everyone knew,

whom in the ensuing infighting, but there were persistent rumors of a Russian visitor who happened to disappear in the chaos. That's the most recent example, but there are plenty of others over the centuries. For the Russians to suddenly take enough of an interest in us to send an envoy—that's very, very bad. I don't buy their story about an heirloom for a minute. When have Were ever kept heirlooms?"

Andrew's beta, John, entered the foyer from the hall leading to the kitchen, smell of his recently finished coffee clinging to him. "There's a difference between our situation and Warsaw's, though. It's this thing called the Pacific Ocean." John's carefully combed hair and formal jacket clashed with his easy, solid manner. Andrew usually appreciated that solidity in a beta, but not when it made him cling to wrong assumptions. "Whatever the Russians do in Europe, why would they care what we're up to on a completely different continent? In all those centuries, they've never bothered North Americans. The Roanoke pack, even before you took over, was far bigger than anything it sounds like Warsaw managed."

"If they were staying on that side of the ocean, I'd say you were right." Andrew took a deep breath, trying once more, as he had multiple times over these weeks, to set aside the instinctive dread his time in Europe had instilled in him. "But now they've made contact with us, and are sending someone over. I can't see how they could possibly have good intentions."

Silver followed her cousin out of the kitchen, licking the remains of some snack off her fingers. She was a great believer in food calming tempers, so she'd even convinced Andrew to eat something earlier. She smacked John upside the head with her good hand and advanced on Andrew next. He ducked out of the way. "No more snapping and snarling about that, remember? Roanoke presents one front. Whether they're a threat or not, it doesn't change the respect we offer the envoy."

Tom glanced from beta to alpha and started edging for the stairs. Andrew would have let him go, but Silver lifted a hand in a subtle gesture. Tom settled his weight back onto his heels. Andrew didn't know if Tom realized Silver was using his presence to keep John from further objections—John knew better than to disagree with the alpha more than he already had in front of other pack members—but Andrew was grateful to the young man anyway.

Silver approached Andrew, stopping a pace away to hold her good arm out, lips curved in dry amusement as she waited for him to check her appearance. She wore a tailored jacket over a less formal top, soft with a hint of lace, and she'd tucked her left hand into the pocket of her slacks to make her bad arm look natural. The illusion worked until she moved and the arm, dead weight from the shoulder, didn't respond right. Her white hair was braided back, minimizing the shock of the color from the front.

Not a very physically intimidating sight to offer the Russians, but Silver's intimidation had never been in her appear-

slightly damp hair. At first Andrew couldn't figure out what she was reacting to, since she'd seen Silver dressed formally before. A moment later he realized Felicia had seen his engagement ring on the hand over Silver's shoulder.

He dropped his hand and brought it forward to rotate the ring uncomfortably. He still hadn't gotten used to wearing one again, it had been so long since Felicia's mother's death. Before the Russians, he'd meant to find a way to break the news to Felicia gently, in case it made her uncomfortable. Now he had no idea what to say. "Felicia, we—"

Sadness laced Felicia's scent, but she smiled, and replaced it with amusement. "Finally!" She strode over and took his left hand to examine the ring Silver had chosen for him, stainless steel with circles on the top and bottom for the Lady at full and new. His fidgeting had turned the full to the side, and Felicia turned it to face his palm, as was traditional for luck. "You have good taste, Silver." She released Andrew's hand, and held hers out to Silver, who extended her right hand instead.

"I didn't want to wear it on my bad hand," Silver said. Andrew smelled her apprehension, sharper than his own, as Felicia examined the ring he'd chosen for her. She exhaled in relief when Felicia captured her in a quick hug.

"You have to tell me details later." Felicia stepped back, and spoke before Andrew could. "I know; we'll be late." She strode down the hall toward the garage, and John followed.

Andrew glanced at Tom. He could use the young man's help, but he didn't want to make him feel minimized. "It would be useful if you'd drop us off and pick us up so we don't have to deal with the hassle of parking."

Tom held up his hands. "Hey, you tell me I can stay with the car and don't have to navigate political shit, I'm not going to talk you out of it. I'm happy to help." He bounded after the others.

Andrew managed a chuckle, and Silver led the way after Tom. "Whatever the Russian pack's intentions, this will be one envoy. Meeting us in a place thronged with humans," she said without looking back. Andrew didn't know if she'd felt his tension through his touch or if she was just responding to all of his behavior lately.

"I know," Andrew said. He did know; some part of him just refused to quite believe it.

2

Tatiana let the stream of people from her plane carry her along until she spotted a sign about continuing to exit past that point. She slipped out of the flow, leaned against the wall, and rummaged in the top front pocket of her rolling carry-on case. Once she exited, she would be facing the North American alpha, and she wanted a few moments to gather her thoughts.

Tatiana retucked the leftover packet of pretzels from the flight, zipped the pocket, and straightened. Blue rocks and inset metal fish engravings sparkled in the floor at her feet. In general, the airport looked like most of the other big airports she'd been in, though some character seemed to have seeped into the air, despite herds of humans and numerous intervening vents. Maybe a hint of the sea, though not as much as in Anchorage. Much less than at home.

Tatiana smoothed her hair's careful golden waves, though they hadn't been disarranged, then slipped back into the stream of people, past the bored security guard at the exit point. She was well-prepared for this, she reminded herself. She'd spent several weeks in Anchorage practicing her English idiom and wasting her money on lubricating the voices of Alaskan Were in their favorite bar. Some of her siblings were better at fighting or killing, but she was the one with the best English, the most skill with her words. If anyone could convince the North American alpha to let the packs he'd united resume their independence, it would be her.

And if she failed, her alpha could send a different assassin. She'd told him she'd kill no more for him, and she would stand by that. It didn't matter if he increased her responsibilities stealthily—this mission was one to persuade and influence, when she'd only ever gathered information before now, after retiring from lethal duties—she'd still stop short of killing.

Tatiana felt a little easier for having reminded herself of all that. She relaxed into a more casual stride. *Lady guide my feet to run, my jaws to catch, my teeth to rend.*

"*For I am a tooth in Her jaws, and I will rend Her prey.*" Tatiana murmured the last part of the prayer in Old Were, then switched her thoughts resolutely to English. Any listener here would likely mistake it for Russian, but you never knew what snatches even a North American Were might recognize.

Even in a busy airport, nothing could disguise the Were waiting for her. They stood off to the side, in a quiet patch in front of a restaurant's windows, the entrance farther down. Four of them, standing two and two. Tatiana slowed as she tried to decipher them. The alpha should be in the back, but the sturdy, muscular man there kept his gaze on the ground like a guard

pha. She could see it in how tall he stood, though he was leaner than his beta. His dark hair was streaked with two white locks at the temples. *Lady-touched.* Tatiana heard her mother's priesthood-trained cadence for the term in her mind. But his mate was the one reputed to be Lady-touched, not him.

That was alpha, beta, and third, even if they'd switched places, so Tatiana supposed the remaining woman was the famous mate. The one who'd started this all, she suspected, though her alpha had only mentioned the threat of a united North America's fighting strength. Apparently he actually expected her to believe fighting strength was the worry, after rumors of a Lady-touched North American reached the Russian pack and he started seeking visions after a decade with no need for them. He'd even had the priestesses standing with him when he'd explained Tatiana's task to her, for the Lady's sake. Fighting strength indeed. Religious strength, more like.

As Tatiana neared, she saw the mate's hair, pulled tightly back, was pure white. It surprised Tatiana to discover that part was true. After the outrageous stories she'd collected from European packs and Alaskan Were, Tatiana had fully expected nothing more than a blond woman with a silver scar or two.

In Warsaw, they'd told her this woman had been slain with silver and risen from the dead, carrying the spirit of the Lady inside her. Like the Lady, she could heal others and grant visions. Tatiana had believed not a word, and she hoped her alpha hadn't either. There was being religiously observant, and there was being foolish. The Lady no longer walked this land with Her children.

She'd had higher hopes for the Alaskans, even drunk. Stubbornly independent, they weren't part of the united pack, but Tatiana had expected them to have contact with friends and family in it. But apparently they spent too much time in wolf to bother with facts. The most talkative one had told her of the mate's white hair and pale eyes, and how, though she maintained she couldn't shift, a ghostly white wolf had been seen among the trees at the full when she was near.

In person, the woman was beautiful, but in a way of clashing extremes. Her features were soft enough to be called pretty, but her white hair and confident posture could fit only with the word "striking." Tatiana quickly pulled her eyes away from tracing her neck to the line of her collarbone and lower. No time for distraction. The woman's eyes were a normal blue, tinged with a hint of gray, nothing pale or even striking there. Without thinking, Tatiana let her gaze settle on the woman's and found dominance, all the sharper for its unexpectedness. Another alpha.

Then Tatiana was in front of the Were, no more time to observe. "Sir," Tatiana said and bowed, marking a crescent on her forehead with the side of her thumb. It never hurt to pres-

ent yourself as low-ranked at the start when hunting information or applying influence. You could always switch to intimi-

strong enough to have won any fights. She held her left arm a
little stiffly, hand in her pocket. Perhaps from an injury that
formed the seed of the "slain by silver" part of the stories. She
smelled of silver in a diffuse way, but Tatiana expected that
would be from some concealed weapon, wrapped carefully and
carried to balance the fighting weakness the injury caused.

The pair of alphas certainly had confidence. The woman
pressed her thumb to her forehead, clearly answering Tatiana's
gesture, though she didn't mark a full moon to indicate her
rank. Tatiana had encountered that before with the Europeans,
at least. Then her mate just bowed his head and made no gesture at all. How was she supposed to take that?

"Roanoke Andrew Dare." The man offered his hand to
shake in the human fashion, and Tatiana accepted it carefully. "My mate, Roanoke Silver." She also shook Tatiana's hand.
Andrew tipped his head to indicate the others. "My beta, John
Powell, and my daughter, Felicia."

Tatiana didn't know why the alpha bothered noting that
the young woman was his daughter—her age made that obvious—but she was already hunting in a whiteout with every-

thing else, so she set that aside to chew over later. "I am Tatiana. May I have permission to enter your territory?"

Roanoke Andrew nodded formal assent, but Tatiana caught Felicia smiling. It sat well on her mobile features. She suspected it was her accent. She'd practiced her idiom in Anchorage, and she'd watched plenty of American TV at home, but she hadn't yet been able to soften her Russian accent.

Might as well use that, though. "Pleased to meet you, Mr. Bond," she said.

Felicia laughed, the sound infectious. The two men joined in, though Roanoke Silver looked blank. Everyone relaxed. Tatiana smiled. She'd found a sense of humor was an excellent way to gain people's trust.

"Do you have any luggage?" Roanoke Andrew waited for Tatiana's nod, then led the way toward an escalator. She didn't know where she was supposed to walk, but he adjusted his pace to keep her abreast of him in easy conversational distance, so she took the hint. She couldn't read anything specific about his mood in the close air of the terminal, so she supposed he wasn't worried about his scent.

After a few questions about her flight and banal comments about the weather, silence descended as they had to string out into a line on the escalator. At the bottom, Tatiana brought out her first real question. It wasn't anything likely to help her craft her suggestions to them about stepping down, but she'd found that if she indulged her idle curiosity at first, it lowered people's guard and they opened up more later. "Why Roanoke?"

"Since we don't live in that city, you mean?" Andrew dropped back and let his beta check the glowing flight numbers above the carousels while he focused on Tatiana.

She nodded. "All the European alphas I have met take

Tatiana's voice tried to tighten as she glanced over the slow parade of black cases sliding by. She caught herself and forced relaxation into her muscles before tension could reach her scent. The contents of her suitcase couldn't be a secret if she wanted to use them. "Black, but with a blue ribbon on the handle and a crescent moon key chain. Careful, there are some bottles of wine in it." Packed along with the wine glasses as carefully as a mother would cushion her cubs, so hopefully the baggage handlers hadn't destroyed her mission before she could even begin it.

Felicia nodded and wiggled her way to a place at the front of the crowd while Tatiana and the rest retired to a row of attached seats. The two alphas sat, so Tatiana joined them, though the beta remained standing. "Roanoke was the name of the colony that brought the first Were to North America." Andrew watched Tatiana's face as he explained, probably for any points of pronounced confusion. "And the Roanoke a generation ago was the first to unite the North American packs. It started with the ones in the east, and when Silver and I added the rest, we moved the Roanoke home pack here."

Tatiana had to smile at the cavalier way he said "added," like it was nothing more than inviting a few people to a party. That was the sort of boasting she expected from alphas. The real challenge would be finding out how they'd actually done it, and what weaknesses that might have introduced.

Silver seemed to realize the source of Tatiana's amusement, and snapped her fingers. "Just that easy, of course."

"What do you call your own alpha?" Andrew was trying to be nonchalant about the question, but Tatiana knew when someone was dying for an answer. She hadn't let it show that badly since she'd been practically a cub, out on her virgin mission, but she knew the feeling. She'd bet the question was also supposed to lead to her divulging where her alpha lived and what her place in the pack's hierarchy was.

"Father, generally," Tatiana said, and looked off into the crowd. Which was technically true, since she called him that out loud, whatever she thought of him privately. Besides, while she'd warned her alpha that she'd have to give the North Americans some information in return, and he'd reluctantly agreed, she planned to make them work for it.

"Ha!" Felicia came up, rolling Tatiana's case along with exaggerated smoothness. She gave the exclamation a laughing tone, pleased about Tatiana's answer for some reason. Tatiana couldn't see why. "Guess I'm an apt third after all."

Tatiana took the case and crouched to feel along the seams as she sniffed. No moisture, no scent of alcohol. The wine should be all right. "Thank you."

Andrew stood too and held his arm toward the door. "Shall we?"

Tatiana followed him promptly like the low mid-ranker she'd presented herself as. These North Americans were cer-

3

Silver didn't like the way the Russian looked at them, and she didn't like the way the envoy made Death laugh. She let her mate and his daughter do the talking as they left the place where humans gathered to travel. Silver knew she was the only one who could see both of a Were's selves at the same time, so while the envoy's tame self smiled at the others, Silver watched her wild self. The wild self was the dark gray of the beaches of Silver's childhood, liberally mixed with black, and with a dusting of white like snow at the tips of the fur. As it walked at the tame self's heels, it tried to look everywhere at once, ears locking onto the tiniest noise, and sometimes no noise at all. Watchful, not nervous. Watching for what? That was the question.

"So suspicious." Death paced wherever he liked, and at the

moment he was too gleeful to fall in beside Silver as he sometimes did, walking the steps that should have belonged to her

of that particular dead man when he was feeling particularly cruel. She took his point, however. The man who had killed her pack had been a stranger, one who had wormed his way into her pack's trust, but that would not happen here.

A human bumped into her, pulling Silver back to the present. She hated the human traveling place. When she wasn't concentrating, her mind tried to tell her it was a grove of trees, the canopy soaring high above. It caught the noise and cupped it around the hundreds of humans who trampled beneath. They, at least, were comprehensible in their ebb and flow whether she concentrated or not. But since this was a traveling place, that ebb and flow was fenced with rules she couldn't keep straight. Go here, not there. Do not pass that door. She could follow Dare, but she did not like knowing that should he or the others be called away, she would likely be ensnared by some forbidden passageway.

"You could have stayed back at the den." Death switched to his more habitual voice, a male Were Silver did not know. Perhaps it was the first Were to ever die. Death strode ahead, then turned to watch with an ironic flip of his tail. "Like a good alpha's mate. Did you see her surprise? She did not expect a woman to stand equally dominant."

Silver refused to be drawn into answering Death where the envoy would hear and think her crazy. Silver had seen the woman's face when their eyes met to measure dominance. She'd been surprised, certainly. But had there been more? Did she think Silver weak for her bad arm? Dare weak for the silver scars the white in his hair hinted at, even if they could not be seen beneath his clothes? Would she take that impression back to her alpha, her father, before they could show her differently? Silver did not doubt her own strength, but she knew she did not wear it splashed across her fur. Or was their appearance a good thing, likely to convince the Russians to leave them alone as no threat?

The group paused at the many river branches that surrounded the traveling place. Dare and the others watched the river, so Silver watched the envoy when the woman thought the tumbling water kept their attention from her. She had high cheekbones, giving her face an elegant, oval shape, but her body had more comfortable, rounded lines. Her hair was a warmer, deeper golden than the bleached color that human women seemed to favor. When she wasn't smiling, she looked more calculating, colder. Then Tom forded the river to meet them, and the envoy smiled once more.

"It will take time to make the arrangements, but in a week or so, we can gather the sub-alphas for you to meet," Dare said, smiling himself. Silver nodded. They'd discussed that at length, as part of the larger question of whether it would be better to minimize their strength. But in the end they'd decided that nothing could hide the fact that they'd united most of North America, and so it would be better to emphasize the fact they

been about nearly everything else. Confused about the customs, probably.

"Nor could we keep track of the concerns of every pack member the way a sub-alpha living with them can," Dare continued. "What does your father do?"

"Trusts to his betas." The envoy's expression sharpened with concentration, and Silver presumed she was picking her way through a thorn thicket of information she did not want to reveal. How many betas? How many Were did the Russian alpha lead? Did they live in one place, or in many? "There is only one alpha, in name and in power."

"Names have great power, but to bolster someone's strength, not create it out of nothing." That came out more acidic than Silver had intended. "And we would rather see our sub-alphas strong, in any case. Because we use their strength, we don't crush it before it threatens our own."

"Names will count for nothing when it is your teeth against this Russian alpha's." Death loped beside them with long, easy strides. "Do not forget that in your word battles with his envoy."

Silver clenched her hand to remind herself not to look at Death. This envoy would see her staring at nothing at all, and think her another kind of weak: weak-minded. Dare set his hand briefly over hers for a moment, and she relaxed it. This envoy was judging them, but together they had much strength to show her.

Anything else was useless worrying, but Silver indulged in it anyway.

The Russian envoy was not at all what Andrew had expected. She was considerably older than Felicia, of course, but Andrew couldn't imagine sending his daughter into possibly hostile territory. Not when he had an entire pack of Were to choose from. Or several packs' worth. He'd noticed the way she'd dodged that question.

When he pulled up in the driveway, Tom jumped out of the pack's minivan first to hold a door that was perfectly capable of staying open on its own for the envoy. Andrew circled around to the passenger side door and opened it for Silver, since she sometimes had trouble with handles.

The strange thing wasn't that the envoy was attractive— and she certainly was—it was that she seemed so determined to present herself as neutrally ranked, Andrew decided. She could have used her attractiveness aggressively, a mocking challenge to look at what you couldn't have. Or could have, if she decided to let you. But instead she was being so very careful. He'd thought Russia would be trying to threaten them, send them a warning about what waited for them if they expanded their

territory beyond their continent. Instead, she apparently was
going to be extremely polite at them. Perhaps she was simply

loom you're looking for, anyway?" he asked.

"It is an icon." Tatiana held up her hands, illustrating an
object about a foot or foot and a half square. "A painting, on
wood. We are not certain it is on this continent, but the family
who had it last immigrated here in the nineteenth century, so
perhaps we can track it to its final location from here."

Her accent threw off the rhythm of her words in places,
so Andrew had to concentrate to follow her, but her grammar
was certainly very good. "You came all this way for a piece of
human religious art?" A laugh bubbled up at the absurd image
of a Russian Were as a collector of human art, but Andrew suppressed it.

He ushered her inside the house and lingered in the foyer.
The staircase curled up grandly, the showpiece that was the living room to the side, taking up the full two stories. The soaring
architecture and sleek furniture oozed money in a way that he
hated, because the Roanoke he'd defeated had lived this way
too, but it was a quick way to impress people. The shiny new
feeling would wear off soon, he assumed. They'd moved in only
a few months ago. The last owners may have kept it like a mag-

azine, but Were children had a habit of gnawing on banister posts, and Were adults had a habit of roughhousing their way to dents in the walls.

"Human art?" Tatiana gazed around her in a satisfyingly impressed manner, and laced her fingers loosely together behind her back. She seemed slightly offended by his question. "Of course not. An icon of the Lady."

John and Felicia entered too late to understand the context, but Silver went pale—a beat late, after Death explained what an icon was, Andrew assumed—and even as an atheist, Andrew had to swallow his exclamation. He rounded on Tatiana. "How could you have made an *image* of the Lady? Are you all *insane*? Or is that why you want it back, for damage control? If they immigrated in the nineteenth century, you're Lady-damned late."

Tatiana rocked back a step and raised her eyebrows. She seemed genuinely taken aback. "I . . . don't understand. Are you not also followers of the Lady here?" She brought her thumb up to her forehead, but rather than press the pad to her skin, she drew a half circle with the side, as she had before.

"Yes, but we don't make *images*, or write things *down*, just waiting for a human to get their hands on it and get confused about this strange religion that they've never heard of before that has so much to do with wolves and shape-shifting." Andrew found himself gesturing violently, and he forced himself to drop his hands. How could the Russians be so stupid?

John only clenched his jaw, but Felicia muttered a scrap of prayer in Spanish. Silver voiced the religious objection for all of them. "When the Lady was forced to leave Her children, she took the memory of her image with Her, so that it would not cause them pain. To create some pale semblance of it from your imagination is to mock Her sacrifice." Silver's tone stayed

land? Fits your worldview, does it?" Were weren't native to the Americas, that much was clear, but it wasn't as if they had archaeologists to guess at their origins as humans did. Their stories began in deep forest, nothing clearer than that.

Tatiana said something with a prayer cadence in a language that might have been Russian, for all Andrew knew. "You say that, but you do not know our native tongue." She took a deep breath and seemed to gather herself, emotions smoothing away to the earlier neutral politeness. "I do not think we will settle religious questions in a few minutes standing in the hallway. Whatever the truth, isn't it better I take the icon home to Were hands, instead of leaving it for humans to find?"

"Better to find it," Silver agreed. Andrew shot her a look. He'd noticed that she hadn't said anything about sending it home with the Russian, but he hoped that omission had escaped the envoy.

"But right now, we can drop your things in the guesthouse." Andrew gestured through the house. To give themselves the space they needed for the pack, they'd taken down the fence where two properties adjoined, and landscaped a path between the back doors. They could have pulled into the other driveway and entered from the front door of the second house they'd turned into the guesthouse, but this route showed more of the sweep of the property.

Halfway down the hall, Felicia's stupid cat poked its head out of a doorway and trotted over to yowl at her feet. Tatiana stopped dead and stared at it, which reminded Andrew how unusual it was. It didn't look like much, lean and leggy, purple-gray with ghosts of tabby stripes, but it was perfectly at ease while surrounded by Were. Felicia gave it a few absent strokes, then tried to shoo it away with her foot.

"A house cat," Tatiana said, accent turning her incredulous statement into something exotic, like she'd accused them of having an endangered leopard.

"It's Felicia's," Silver said, at the same moment Felicia said, "It's Silver's."

Andrew exhaled his amusement. Tatiana was welcome to tell her alpha they kept a cat. Felicia had brought it home as an act of defiance a while back, but Silver had taken a liking to it and had been the one making sure it got fed while Felicia was roaming. Andrew himself found it amusing enough to not bother about. "Not enough meat on its bones to be worth hunting, and people *will* keep feeding it, so it hangs around." He shrugged, lifted the cat, and slung it out of their way. It landed gracefully and wandered off again, nonchalant.

Tatiana stared after the cat as she passed the doorway it had disappeared into, but didn't offer any other comment. Tom interrupted them next, before they could reach the back door. He put his hand on Andrew's arm and leaned close to speak.

The envoy would still hear, but the gesture would hopefully make her aware that she shouldn't ask prying questions about this piece of pack business. "Craig showed up while we were

the delay gracefully in front of the stranger.

Outside, the gravel path dragged at the suitcase's wheels, so Felicia hoisted the larger one up by the side handle. Tatiana did the same with her carry-on. The weather was almost cooperating today, so while it was cold, the clouds were thin, and patches of sunlight in the distance promised a brighter late afternoon.

The guesthouse was smaller, four bedrooms instead of seven, and the floor plan wasted less space on things like staircases and two-story rooms. Andrew opened the door to the sound of angry voices. Craig and . . . Sacramento, he supposed, as their only other houseguest at the moment, though she was supposed to have been out for the day.

Andrew tossed a glance to Felicia. She must have understood his message, because she set the envoy's suitcase down outside, delaying. Andrew strode forward through the kitchen to chase everyone out ahead of the envoy. Hopefully Tatiana would hang back with her luggage and give Silver and John a chance to distract her. He knew he didn't need to signal Silver for her to do that.

A shadow moved at the very edge of his vision as he reached the stairs. "And you thought everyone would behave," Death said, too deeply black in silhouette to seem quite real, like a blind spot or optical failing. Ever since Andrew had been injured, some kind of mental trick or subconscious worry made him imagine he saw Death occasionally. He ignored him as usual. Death remained. "Your naïve hope is adorable."

Andrew gritted his teeth. He shouldn't be surprised, he supposed. Since no one but Silver and now Felicia believed in the danger the Russians posed, they didn't really have the visceral motivation to be on their best behavior.

Andrew cleared his throat. "What's going on?"

Sacramento and Craig, facing off in the upstairs hall, both jumped and fell instantly silent. After a beat, Sacramento came down a couple steps toward him. She looked especially severe today, blond hair, brown at the roots, pulled into a tail high on the back of her head. The remains of her anger lent her features an angular cast. "Roanoke Dare. I got distracted on my way out. He . . ." She trailed off in the face of Andrew's expression and looked at the carpet.

Craig took a moment longer to shake off the argument. He had his head tipped down, square jaw clenched, apparently enduring but not accepting her earlier words. "The mistake I made was in the past. I have apologized for it." He lifted his head. "Directly to the one I wronged, not you."

Andrew started up the stairs, ready to rein Craig in more directly, but the man had apparently said his piece. He, too, looked at the floor. "Whatever brought you here, it's going to have to wait," Andrew said.

He stepped aside to let Craig by, but too late. Tatiana arrived at the bottom of the stairs, Silver and the others trailing her. Her expression showed slight curiosity and perhaps An

maybe with a little time alone together, she and Felicia could bond over being alphas' daughters.

Felicia led Tatiana away and Silver joined Andrew, attention tight on the combatants, probably trying to read their body language for what had set them off. John set the luggage ready to take upstairs when they were out of the way and leaned against the newel post.

Andrew drew a deep breath to calm his frustration and looked from one to the other. "All right." He nodded to Craig. "Why are you here?"

Craig held his hands up, nonthreatening. "I didn't come to cause trouble. I heard that you were making Sacramento interview betas. I have experience, and living alone isn't suiting me."

Andrew speared Sacramento with a glare when she opened her mouth to retort. Craig was perfectly correct, but a more astute beta wouldn't have phrased it that way. In the two years since Sacramento had been forced to dump her first beta, she hadn't managed to keep one for more than a few months. For the past nine months or so, she'd essentially stopped trying to find one, which wasn't healthy for an alpha. He and Silver had dragged her up here and told her she couldn't go home until she'd chosen one of the people they introduced her to. Until now, around Sacramento everyone had stuck to the polite fiction that Andrew and Silver were merely lending Sacramento their expertise.

Sacramento crossed her arms. "You tried to force your last alpha out of office."

Craig shook his head. "That carcass was buried long ago. I was wrong about what was best for her, and what was best for our child. I told Michelle that." He held his hands open, appealing more to his Roanokes than Sacramento, it seemed. "I'd never make the same mistake twice."

Silver padded over to Craig and set her hand on his arm. "You moved to your present home to be close to Portland and your son, didn't you? Has something changed?"

Craig shrugged, an awkward, minimal movement. "There's an easy commuter flight. It wouldn't take that much longer than driving does, with traffic. I could still see him every other weekend."

Something in his tone made Andrew turn to get a better read on his scent. His voice held the pain of someone who couldn't stand living without a pack any longer. At the moment, he lived in Vancouver, Washington, just across the river from Portland, but even living across the river from a pack you didn't really belong to was plenty lonely. Andrew knew that feeling, and remembered how it could twist so tight something in you started to tear.

"That's true, but are you sure you'd want to work with Sacramento, given your past disagreements over Portland and her baby?" Silver voiced the question on Andrew's mind, leaning in to Craig, keeping her calming touch on his arm.

"I can get past it if she can." Craig lifted his head, chin

leading madness. "You think apologies are still owed? I seem to recall he wasn't the only disrespectful one during that debate."

Sacramento's scent soured with embarrassment, and she stepped back up to the top of the stairs so she could dip to one knee. "Roanoke Silver. My apologies. I'll get out of your way." She looked over her shoulder at her room, and pushed back up to her feet at a nod from Silver.

Andrew turned back to Craig, and looked the man over in silence for a few moments. He sighed. "I doubt you'll ever talk her into it, and I would strongly recommend against trying, Craig. If you need a pack, we can help you some other way. But nothing's going to happen immediately. We've got the Russian envoy to deal with. We'll let you know when that's done, you can come back, and we can discuss it."

Curiosity seeped into Craig's scent, but he was smart enough this time not to ask. He nodded, and descended the stairs without saying anything else. John lifted the envoy's suit-cases again, and ferried them upstairs without comment.

Silver waited until they were alone, then sighed and set her forehead against Andrew's shoulder. "Their sense of timing for causing trouble would make Death proud."

"It'll be all right. The envoy didn't see much of it." Andrew tried to convince himself of the words as he said them. "Unless in Russia there would have been blood on the walls by now, and she judges us for that."

"So I'm not the only one who felt judged?" Silver led the way down the stairs, tone growing dry. "I forgot how little I look the part on the outside until I saw her expression." She stopped at the bottom and rolled her shoulder muscles on her bad side, making her dead arm fall in a slightly more open position.

Andrew caught her bad wrist and helped her tuck the hand back into her pocket. "Anyone would only have to speak to you to know different." He tried to make his tone as confident as possible, but he didn't like the envoy's manner either. She wasn't a fighter, but that didn't make her any less dangerous if she reported back to the Russians' fighters that they were juicy targets. She couldn't see the massive silver scars on his back, but the white in his hair certainly stood out.

He glanced through the back door's small beveled panes. They mostly caught a splash of low-slanting sunlight and an abstract bit of green from the lawn. He could imagine the path stretching away to the main house, however. "If she's so on her guard with us, maybe it would be better to stall and let Felicia see what she can get out of her. Then again, we don't want to make it seem like we need a long time to deal with a simple disagreement between our Were."

"We could walk back slowly. Let our scent be known in the den, so we're back but not interfering," Silver said.

"Good idea." Andrew led the way to the path. He offered Silver his arm so they could walk back in stately—and slow—style. Hopefully Felicia would get a better read on the ~~~~

4

Tatiana hid a smile as Felicia hustled her back to the main house. The young were so endearingly transparent sometimes. As if there was any doubt why they were leaving the guesthouse. In Felicia's place, she wouldn't have tried to pretend otherwise.

Felicia stopped close to the main house's back door and swept a hand to the backyard. "We haven't been moved in for too long, so we're still working on the landscaping. The previous owners had a water feature thing we might resurrect." She indicated an empty plastic tub set into the ground. "Except the cubs will probably get continually wet, so maybe not."

Tatiana didn't care about landscaping, so she tuned the rest of the babble out. That's all it was, too. She could smell the young woman's nervousness. It matched the sort of scent her

European contacts usually gave off, but it was nothing like the beta's scent. He'd seemed almost cavalier about her, which was unexpected. The alphas had control of themselves not to reveal

the guesthouse, just talking. Words had their place, certainly, but only when supported by strength.

Felicia's babbling paused as she led Tatiana inside the house, and Tatiana took the opportunity to slip in a few questions. The Roanokes had done her a favor. The argument in the guesthouse had already stopped by the time she had gotten close enough to hear details anyway, and now she could draw information out of Felicia alone. "How long has your father been with his mate? They look very comfortable together."

Voices murmured in the next room, but when they entered the kitchen, it was empty. Felicia scanned the room and dived on an empty mixing bowl and an abandoned spoon on the island. She tidied them into the sink. "Four or five years, I think. I wasn't around when they met."

Tatiana glanced around the kitchen, but it was mundane enough. Huge, shiny appliances and gleaming granite counters. Low-level heat radiated from the oven, presumably dinner cooking. It wasn't far enough along to give off much scent through the door yet.

Now she was back in the house, Tatiana kept getting hints

of a human scent too, worn in like the owner of the scent had lived here as long as the Were had. Why would a human live in a pack house?

Tatiana set that aside to consider later. Perhaps she could find some leverage in their sympathy for a human. That was weak, certainly. "How long have they been Roanokes?" That fact, at least, she trusted her sources about. Even the Alaskan Were had agreed with everyone else about when the North American packs had united, so the question would be a good gauge for Felicia's other answers.

Felicia hesitated, discomfort clear on her face. Oh, to be that young and unguarded again. Tatiana wondered if the Roanokes had neglected to brief her on what she should and shouldn't reveal. It certainly looked that way. If so, Tatiana would be happy to take advantage of it.

"Four years." Once she decided to answer, Felicia accessed the number instantly, without need to think back or count. Tatiana raised her brows to comment on the similarity of the numbers and Felicia laughed. "Yeah, it's kind of related. Partly because when Dad helped Silver, it exposed how incompetent the former Roanoke was, but also you've met them. Put those two together and they're too dominant *not* to lead something."

"Helped Silver?" According to the Alaskan, Andrew had saved Silver from *something*—probably not actual death—and he'd slaughtered, or she'd slaughtered, or they'd both slaughtered her enemies. And so she had been Lady-touched. Tatiana knew she'd probably have to get the truth of that story from someone, if she were to find Silver's weaknesses.

"You'll have to ask Silver about that." Felicia glanced one

more time around the kitchen, then led Tatiana to the dining room. The alpha's children clustered around a long, scarred but sturdy table, writing and reading busily. The youngest looked

She stared into space rather than at her textbook. The other children had been studying more seriously, but when their attention locked onto the stranger and Felicia, several squealed, and nearly all of them tumbled off their chairs. Their English was too sloppy, overlapping, and shrill for Tatiana to follow, but she caught Felicia's name, and anyone could see they were excited to see her.

Felicia hugged as many as she could at once, looking bemused. "I haven't been away that long. You just want to get out of homework, you little monsters."

The eldest young woman, clearly supposed to be in charge, growled at them. "She's right; homework time's not over yet." She had to glare at several of the children before they finally climbed back into their chairs and bent their heads over their work. Tatiana collected stares sidelong rather than outright.

Children were children—Tatiana had taken her turn watching her younger siblings when she was a teen—but she found it interesting that they would dare to be so ill-behaved in front of a stranger. Someone needed to instill a little healthy fear in them. Who knew who that stranger might be?

Following her own orders, the young woman looked down at her book, frowned in confusion, and turned back a few pages. Felicia threw her arms around the young woman's shoulders from behind. "Tracy! Senioritis?"

Tracy turned into the hug. "And how. But how are you doing? I didn't know you were coming back!"

After that inexplicable exchange, Felicia tipped her head to Tatiana. "I'm here because of the envoy. I'll let Dad do the official introductions to pack members. I'm just showing her the house."

After a last squeeze, Felicia pulled away from the hug. Before she could lead the way to the next room, a shaggy-headed five- or six-year-old burst out of a door onto the hallway. His trajectory suggested he'd run up the stairs from a basement. He was making staticky noises that Tatiana finally realized were weapons fire because of the bright red fighter jet or spaceship toy in his hand. He zoomed it through the air and pounded into the dining room, buzzing several of the kids' heads.

"Where's the squadron? We need backup! Pew, pew!" He dropped a handful of much smaller airplanes and toy cars on the table.

Tracy pushed her chair back with an exasperation that suggested this wasn't the first time. "Edmond, it's homework time. No one can play until it's done." She tried to give him all his toys back, but he snagged only two and ran away again.

"But I wanna say hi to Felicia!" He tackled her in a hug, then pressed an ambulance into her unresisting hand. He pulled away and handed Tatiana a metal jumbo jet branded on the side with the name of an American airline.

Felicia winced. Tatiana tried to resist, but he was so young, she found herself charmed by his disobedience. And why not interact with him a little? She wasn't likely to learn much, but you never knew, and it might further lower Felicia's guard. She

ship he twisted it in an acrobatic flight path back to the door he'd emerged from.

Felicia glanced from her ambulance to Tracy once Edmond was on the stairs. Tracy sighed. "Ever since he saw on TV that planes fight in packs, everyone has to play with him in his squadron." Tracy pointed to the door. "You're supposed to follow him everywhere until he gets bored of bossing you around."

"We'd better hurry, then." Tatiana zoomed her plane a little on the way down into the basement, but omitted the sound effects. Felicia followed, suspicion visibly fading into confusion.

Tatiana suspected the basement wouldn't have been on the regular tour. It was set up like it had been intended to be a home theater with a projector on the ceiling in front of a blank wall and floor cushions everywhere, but the children had taken over. A large bench that opened into a toy box sat in one corner so things could be tidied away, but the lid was up and it had hemorrhaged its contents over the floor.

Edmond smashed his ship into a LEGO tower with a resounding crash. "We got 'em!"

Felicia squeaked as the small bricks skittered over the floor in a wide radius. "Edmond!" She used a half-grown version of the tone Andrew had used earlier, and Edmond instantly put his ship down and hung his head. "Clean those up right now."

Felicia waited, glaring, until Edmond found a plastic bucket and started dumping handfuls of loose bricks inside. That lasted about a minute until he started making weapons noises again as he threw in the LEGO bricks. Felicia left him to it and went to shut the toy box lid so she could sit and supervise from there. She eyed Tatiana. "Uh. Sorry."

Tatiana sat down next to her and they both watched Edmond work. "I like kids." She only wished she could have her own, truly her own, but that wasn't something to think about at the moment. Tatiana set her mind carefully back on strategic paths.

Perhaps Felicia would be interested in playing chase. She was young for Tatiana's actual taste, but adult enough to be responsible for her choices. Tatiana had planned to lay enticing trails for whichever of the alpha pair seemed most susceptible, sowing pack-disintegrating chaos into their relationship, but she could already tell that wouldn't work.

A chase with someone else could still provide information, though. She could go after one of the pack's men, but while men often bounded into playing chase more easily, women tended to talk more. Easy enough to let slip one of the alpha's weaknesses, or sore points, without even realizing it.

Tatiana turned her head, tracing the curve of Felicia's neck with her eyes. She wondered, too. The way Andrew had singled out this one of his daughters made Tatiana think that perhaps he considered her alpha elect. Strange, to think of a female alpha, without even the support of being Lady-touched as Silver was, but across Europe everyone talked about how the North Americans liked that sort of thing

Felicia snorted. "With a five-year-old, sure." She frowned at Edmond, who'd gotten three-quarters of the LEGO into the bucket before stopping to build something with the remainder. Tatiana's scent must have reached her, because she threw Tatiana a quick glance, as if doubting she'd smelled right.

"Give it time." Tatiana set her hand over Felicia's.

Felicia shoved to her feet, awkwardness seeping into the air around her. "This isn't giving you a tour, though. C'mon. I can introduce you to my boyfriend. I think he's probably upstairs."

She took the basement stairs a little fast, and Tatiana trailed to allow plenty of space between them. That was a no, then. A more uncomfortable one than she'd expected—but then Felicia paused at the top of the stairs and checked her expression anxiously, and Tatiana understood. Felicia must be worried that refusing in the wrong way would offend the influential visitor. Tatiana suppressed a smile. She was far from hurt, but perhaps she should pretend to be. A frown in the right place, and she bet Felicia would be back to panicked babbling.

When they emerged from the basement into the main

hallway, a very professional-looking woman almost bumped into them. A human woman. She caught Felicia by the shoulders with a disrespectful abruptness that seemed intended to be affectionate. "Have you seen John around?"

Tatiana stepped back a little bit, trying to keep the shock off her face. She'd smelled that a human had been around the house, but she'd never have imagined that the North Americans would let the woman blunder around where Tatiana could see her.

The human looked normal enough, short brown hair and great ass—if you were into humans. Felicia summoned a friendly smile that made it nowhere near her scent, though of course the human didn't notice. "Hi, Susan. I think he's probably getting ready for the big dinner party tonight."

Susan looked over and brazenly caught Tatiana's eyes in the annoying human style of greeting. Tatiana avoided the gaze rather than teach the human a lesson in dominance.

"Oh, that's right. I didn't realize his guests would be getting here already." Susan nodded to Tatiana and smiled apologetically. "I'm afraid I never stick around for the boring shop talk. I never understand half of what he says about software." She patted Felicia's shoulder. "Well, I'm off home. Tell him to call me tomorrow, would you?"

As Susan passed Tatiana on the way to the door, she gave her another glance—she probably thought it was covert—with a mixture of curiosity and wariness like she was worried the curiosity would be taken wrong. Whatever she'd said about being happy to leave, it was clear she wasn't quite so sanguine.

Tatiana remembered that look, on another human woman's face. Another human woman who was wondering why Tatiana was taking an interest in her. She gritted mental teeth against the memory and reminded herself that Susan didn't

Lady's name was the woman doing here? "She's his girlfriend." Felicia shrugged, uncomfortable. "She's around sometimes, but by now everyone's used to making sure she doesn't find out anything." She eyed Tatiana defensively, but Tatiana raised her hands in a calming gesture. Susan was in no danger from her. She wasn't going to walk that trail again. If she got pregnant or stumbled onto something she shouldn't, that was the North Americans' problem.

Felicia strode a little too fast down the hall toward the stairs. "Let me show you upstairs. We have a deck with a pretty nice view down the hill."

Tatiana followed. After everything else, she wondered what would be hiding upstairs. A true wolf curled up in one of the bedrooms, perhaps?

5

While Felicia and the envoy were upstairs, Andrew supervised the table being set for dinner. The children had been shooed off to play in the basement. They'd have sandwiches down there while the adults sweated through the finer points of dining etiquette. Andrew envied them in many ways.

Silver snagged his wrist as he crossed back to the kitchen to check the chicken pot pies' progress in the oven. "They know what they're doing. Susan briefed them all before she had to leave. Having their alpha hovering won't help."

Andrew let himself be led around the other side of the kitchen island. With the oven light on, he could see the pot pies from here anyway. "I'm starting to think we should have served steaks after all. She's acting strange enough as it is, so maybe serving something with the meat small and well-cooked says weak and human to Russians."

Silver laced her fingers with his. "But it's not just the North Americans, is it? Don't Europeans also use that kind of food to

driving his own.

Things had been simple then, following orders from the middle of the pack. Maybe if things had been different, he'd still be there now, not alpha here. Andrew suspected that those Spanish fighters would be furious with him if they were here, for working so hard to avoid the need for such skirmishes. Lady knew if this would work. Perhaps nothing could prevent a clash with Russia at this point.

"What trail are your thoughts haring off on now?" Silver said with quiet humor, and brought up their joined hands to knock them against his side.

"A very old one." Andrew shook himself out of it. He didn't believe in the Lady, so it didn't matter what She knew. He'd continue doing everything he could to make sure the Russian went away satisfied and didn't return. "It smells like the food's almost done. We can probably get everyone seated."

Silver nodded and slipped into the dining room to help direct everyone. He and Silver usually allowed precedence seating to be loose, but it needed to be carefully executed tonight. Even with only the adults of the Roanoke home pack attending, it was a lot of people to juggle.

Andrew went the other way, out into the hall. He suspected that Felicia would be monitoring the smells. Sure enough, she was leading the way down the staircase as he approached. She'd collected Tom at some point, and they walked abreast down the stairs, Tom's arm slung over Felicia's shoulders.

Anger flashed through Andrew. He'd thought his daughter had better diplomatic instincts than to allow herself to be distracted from their guest by finding her boyfriend at the first opportunity.

But then he examined them more closely. Tom looked baffled and protective, leading Andrew to surmise that their posture was Felicia's idea, not his, and the reason for it was the root of his protectiveness. Felicia, on the other hand, looked clingy. Tom's arm had tousled her hair under it, but she hadn't done anything to smooth it. If she'd been cuddling for the sake of showing off her relationship, she'd have arranged her hair to fall just so.

Felicia pulled away from Tom at the bottom of the stairs and switched their connection to just interlaced fingers. "I showed her the deck and stuff," she said, head down and position apologetic.

Andrew nodded absently. "Dinner's ready if you'd like to join us," he told the envoy. She didn't look particularly bothered about Tom, at least. If anything, she seemed slightly amused. Andrew held out his arm toward the dining room.

"Thank you." Tatiana inclined her head and strode confidently that way. She presumably remembered the location from her tour with Felicia. Andrew had to suppress a punchy smile. She really did sound like a Bond girl.

"I chased Susan out, too." Felicia had her hand up against her shoulder, smoothing her hair. She briefly curled her fingers into a thumbs up, then returned smoothly to the original

see that as evidence of terrible judgment, a pack that needed to be taken out. Dangerous to her because if the Russians saw her as a danger to all Were, they might decide to take care of her themselves.

They couldn't erase her scent from the house, not without using enough cleaning products to scream that they had something to hide. So John and Susan had removed their wedding rings and everyone had agreed to the official story about the clueless girlfriend. Susan had been worried that after so long learning Were body language, she wouldn't be able to fake obliviousness anymore. Felicia seemed to be saying it had worked, though. Good.

Andrew strode for the dining room. One obstacle down, one dangerously awkward dinner to go.

Dinner began with introductions of everyone at the table to the envoy, then Silver and Dare received their portions of the meal. The others made conversation about nothing much as a young Were spooned out everyone else's portions in order of rank. Dare prompted her with light nods when necessary. Instead of beginning to eat, Silver watched the envoy's wild self. It had relaxed enough from its intense focus on her and Dare to sniff at Sacramento's wild self. Strict ranking placed the two women next to each other, much as Silver would have liked to avoid the reminder of the misbehaving pack member.

The snow-dusted color of the envoy's wild self stood out more clearly next to Sacramento's more uniform gray. The women also each called out different aspects of the other by comparison. Both were fair haired, but the envoy had stronger features and softer curves. And even that fair hair was different: Sacramento's was sharper, a lightened brown rather than a true gold.

"Everything straightened out with the pack now?" The envoy smiled without real warmth and took her first bite.

"Of course," Dare said, his smile just as empty. The exchange struck Silver as being like wild selves snapping at the air before a fight. Posturing, with no real effort to wound.

She didn't see him approach, but she felt Death as a brush of fur against her shin. He settled himself right on top of her feet. "The real fun comes later," he said, amused.

Sacramento flushed, radiating embarrassment. Interestingly, the envoy actually looked apologetic, and put out a hand to the other woman's arm.

"Craig—he was the one I was arguing with—he and I have history," Sacramento murmured, low.

"I got to meet your son while you were gone," the envoy told Dare with the air of someone changing the subject. For Sacramento's sake? "He's a delightful child."

Silver couldn't help herself, she glanced at Dare, even though she knew perfectly well Felicia was his only child. His matching confusion was clear. "My son?" He directed the

wouldn't have guessed he was carefully avoiding any mention of Edmond's mother. That was Susan, the human who really should not have been around. "I only have Felicia."

"Edmond is your . . . beta's son. All other children, they are not yours?" The envoy spoke very slowly. If she had not had such a command of the language before, Silver would have thought she understood only a few words of it now, by her reaction. She seemed utterly lost, stumbling through a snowstorm in the new.

Dare remained silent, trying to figure out the situation before he committed himself to words, and Silver followed his lead. Clearly, the envoy needed time to organize her thoughts before she asked any more questions. Felicia stepped up to fill the void. "Yep, I get the fun of being alpha's child all to myself." She smiled awkwardly.

The envoy rebuilt a smile piece by piece, ending before it reached her eyes. "The boy had such an alpha's air," she said, and everyone laughed lightly. In her case, Silver did it more to reassure the envoy than to appreciate the thin joke.

"Do you have any siblings?" Sacramento tilted her head

as she asked it. Her wild self laid its muzzle over the envoy's wild self's neck. Interesting, that when everyone was thinking about the abstract of alphas' children, her question seemed to indicate an interest in the envoy personally.

Sacramento seemed to have a real talent for falling for the wrong woman. Silver would have to discuss with Dare whether they should meddle, or even just warn Sacramento.

"If you want her to chase the Russian all the harder, you should definitely speak to her." Death's fur brushed against Silver's legs as he settled himself more comfortably. "Or do you actually think you could keep her away?"

"I—" The envoy looked down at her food, and seemed to realize that the real purpose of a meal was to eat. She gathered up a bite, but did not raise it. "I am my mother's only child." She started eating, deliberately. Silver wondered what other children her father had. That phrasing had been too careful, and the envoy had clearly been tipped off-balance about something. Something to do with Edmond.

"Do you have any children of your own?" the envoy asked Sacramento. Silver didn't know if the envoy had planned it that way, but Sacramento's startled laughter helped ease the atmosphere.

"Someday, I'd like a few. All the better to show how a woman can be an alpha and a mother." Sacramento grinned and nodded to Dare, then Silver. "Witness their self-control in not commenting on the idea, though. I'm too young and care-free at the moment."

Silver made her silence more pointed, by way of playing along. She didn't think Sacramento would be a bad mother,

far from it. But raising cubs was about working together, with
a partner, with family, and Sacramento wasn't so consistent
about that. Or about not making having cubs so far to held

seemed a likely place to start looking for them, but I might
need to expand back up into British Columbia." The envoy was
calm now, so Silver's attention widened enough that she caught
a flicker of movement farther down the table. Tom had jerked
his head up, surprised by something in her remark. He opened
his mouth, then dropped his head, frowning.

"Yes?" Silver said, raising her eyebrows at him. He was
right to read the situation as tense enough not to jump in without prompting, but information about the truth of this woman's story would be useful. Was there really such an heirloom as
she'd described? "You know where to find the trail of the family
she seeks?"

Tom flicked a glance at the envoy, then spoke toward Silver instead. "When Felicia and I weren't speaking last year,
you remember how I went roaming alone? I did some tracing
of ancestors in eastern Washington. And I found this family
burial plot where they had tombstones, and some of them did
have Cyrillic characters. And they had pictures of wolves and
all sorts of stupid shit carved on them for everyone to see."

Only belatedly did Tom seem to consider Tatiana's reaction to that judgment, but she stayed neutral, undoubtedly because of her encounter with good sense earlier. Silver wanted to shake her head. Writing and painting Were secrets on everything. Unforgivably dangerous.

"Perhaps I can visit this plot," Tatiana said, and offered Tom a small smile. He didn't seem to know what to do with it.

"We can certainly escort you anywhere you want," Dare said with a dip of his head. "Or if you will give us names, we can search for them in that town's human records. It's very difficult to avoid those." He lifted a hand in the approximate direction of the exit from their den. "But for tonight, perhaps you'd like to come hunting with us?"

"Certainly. I am very curious to see a North American hunt. A chase to clear the mind." The envoy looked at Sacramento as she said it, with the smallest hint of a smile. Silver had to suppress the urge to put her face in her hand. She could feel Death's smugness radiating into her skin, though he remained silent. At times like these, he didn't even need to laugh.

6

Evergreens grew taller and thicker along the roads as they drove toward the pack's hunting lands, but Tatiana could still see the development behind them. She suspected that once she was out of the car, this forest would smell completely different than those at home, too. It would be full of glass and concrete and exhaust and garbage and humans—an instantly recognizable mixture that said "city" for some distance, even as the houses thinned out.

Tatiana stared out the window and focused part of her attention on memorizing the route, as she had the one from the airport to the pack house. With the rest of her attention, she tried to decide if she was being self-indulgent. The blond woman who'd fought in the guesthouse and been seated next to her at dinner had been introduced as Sacramento, one of that strange class of sub-alphas. In practice, she seemed ranked just below the beta. Cultivating her could give Tatiana valuable information, much as she could have gotten if she'd been successful with Felicia. But Sacramento was also gorgeous. A little uptight in how she carried herself, and her hair and clothes, but that just made Tatiana ache to be the one who coaxed her into letting go.

And Felicia really was the alpha's daughter. And no one else was. Tatiana's mind bounced from thought to thought like she was on her first mission. She could hardly conceive of the idea. North Americans knew their parents. From birth. Everyone *acknowledged* their parents.

At home, every cub was called the alpha's, to pretend the pack was like one of true wolves, though Lady knew Were had enough other differences from their animal ancestors. That explanation read to Tatiana more like an excuse for an ancient tradition that had lost its original purpose. The cubs were all raised together in the knowledge that they belonged to the alpha pair, though in practice everyone knew their mother. It was a little hard to hide who had nursed you. If your mother had a mate, the conclusion was obvious, but Tatiana's mother had never had a mate, or even a steady lover.

Lady. If she'd been born in North America, she would have known who her father was.

She wondered if her alpha had had any conception of the cultural differences when he'd sent her here. She certainly hadn't. She'd assumed that since she knew Europe well, she knew North America. And it might even be that she didn't know Europe properly, either. She'd never been invited into a European pack house, never met their children to think to ask about their parentage. She'd always talked with adults in neutral locations. Perhaps the Europeans acknowledged the

humans to hunt, and forests that weren't. The idea of owning a patch of trees, fenced and taxed in the human manner, seemed too constrained to her, but eminently logical for Were living where wildernesses rarely lacked humans anymore, and those that did had few opportunities for Were on two legs to make a living.

The road narrowed and grew steeper, trees pressing close on both sides. The houses drew back, set away from the road up winding gravel driveways. Tatiana sat straighter to get a wider range of view out the window, which suddenly rolled down, along with the others in the vehicle. She glanced over to see Andrew just taking his hand from the driver's controls. She wasn't going to hang her head out the window, but she did draw in lungfuls of the scents. She craved immersion in a place with growing things and a chance to run on four legs after the plane ride.

Their SUV, leading a minivan with the rest of the pack adults, pulled up a driveway to a gate. Felicia's boyfriend hopped out and opened it, then stood back and motioned everyone through with a grinning flourish. The vegetation on the other side of the gate showed evidence of repeated flattening under tires, and both vehicles pulled off onto it as if settling into habitual parking spots.

Everything was boisterous chaos for a few minutes as everyone undressed and shifted. Andrew edged to the back of the group before pulling off his clothes, which only made Tatiana curious what he was trying to hide. She slipped after him in time to catch a glimpse of the knotted scar tissue across his lower back as he partially turned to reply to someone. Odd. North American alphas must sometimes keep their scars to boast about past battles, though she would have expected Andrew to show them off in that case.

Tatiana also noticed red tinting on several of the wolf forms, something she'd never seen at home. Andrew was within the gray Russian spectrum, though with a patch of coarser, white fur over his back, probably from the injury that caused his scars, but Felicia was red-tinted black and her boyfriend was a sandy brown shade that Tatiana associated with pictures of coyotes.

"Is the red in people's fur a North American thing?" Tatiana asked Sacramento as she strolled by, nude, with a bundle of her clothes. It was another question she asked more for the sake of asking than any expectation of useful information coming out of it, but part of her also wondered if she could draw out another laugh like the one Sacramento had given at dinner.

Sacramento did laugh, warm and surprised again. "You know, I'd never noticed that. I suppose it could be, if you don't have it at home. We have red true wolves in the southeast, here. Or we used to. They might be only in zoos now. And the original Roanoke pack landed in what's now North Carolina."

Sacramento glanced at Tatiana as if to check that North Carolina meant something to her in conjunction with south

... from the colonists. Sacramento shrugged, caught her panties trying to escape from her clothing bundle, and lobbed everything underhand into the minivan. She turned away toward the others, but spoke back over her shoulder, showing off her ass at the same time. "If you see any tinge in my fur, we can nose through my ancestors when the hunt's through."

Sacramento wandered off to shift with a bit more privacy, leaving Tatiana alone with Silver, still in human. Tatiana refocused her attention on the alpha with a promise to herself that after she'd found out more about the alphas, she could let her information-gathering carry her back to Sacramento at the end of the night—but only if she didn't allow herself any distraction now.

Tatiana wasted time folding her clothes very precisely, but Silver didn't even make a move to undress. She lounged with her ass against the closed passenger door of the minivan where everyone had been piling their belongings. Did North Americans leave a guard on their belongings, since they ran in such populated areas? But why in the Lady's name would that guard be an alpha?

Silver bent and retrieved a shirt that had fallen short on the van's step, thrown from too great a distance. She tossed it on the seat and folded it over, only using one hand the entire time. She must not be able to run properly with that arm, Tatiana realized. Certainly, one could travel on three legs, but not well, and not as quickly. Some of the stories about Silver said she couldn't shift at all, but Tatiana didn't believe it. No one could be alpha and not shift. It was rare enough to be an alpha and choose not to remove your scars. Tatiana wasn't surprised that such an injury had been exaggerated to being unable to shift.

Tatiana bet Silver thought enigmatically refusing to shift was better than fumbling weakly around on three legs. She wasn't wrong, either. Tatiana carried over her clothes and nodded respectfully to Silver before stepping back far enough for privacy when she shifted.

She might have made the same choice herself, in a similar situation. After all, staying so calmly in human when it was near full and everyone was itching to get into wolf showed a definite strength of character. Not the same as the physical strength of four sound, fleet legs, but better than nothing.

Tatiana surfaced into her wolf form with a gasping sort of relief, similar to that of leaving a room you hadn't even realized was stuffy for a cool breeze outside. Sharper scents, not the same as those at home, but carrying the same association of simple rightness. Hunts in wolf form were simple. Not like her mission hunts for information.

Usually. The last mission she'd finished in wolf form slipped to the surface of Tatiana's mind before she shoved it down again, hard. No human women were being hunted tonight.

A wolf body slammed into her from the side. Tatiana stumbled and caught herself, braced to fight before she real

an for a return strike, because that was clearly what was actually expected of her. They tussled, rolling around in the pine needles.

It was expected of her, but it wasn't exactly a hardship, either. Tatiana hadn't had a chance to play like this very often since she was a young woman. Alexei probably would have indulged her in the name of training, but when new to adulthood, she hadn't wanted to look unprofessional, and then it had become a habit.

She enjoyed it a little too much, in fact, and pulled away after a few moments. She was here for a hunt, not to play. No distractions, she'd promised herself. Everyone in wolf form was gathering around Andrew. Tatiana joined them, hanging to the back, since as an outsider she would not be part of any tactics that the alpha directed. Sacramento slipped into the crowd, but not too far away.

Tatiana tipped her head back and howled. It felt a little lonely, knowing the voices that answered and blended with hers would hold none she recognized, but she was here to learn the North American voices.

Andrew shifted back, fast enough to make the usually

graceful process jerky. "Quiet," he snapped, then panted a few breaths, crouched with one hand on the ground. He straightened after Tatiana fell instantly silent. What had she done wrong? How could they not howl?

"You'll have Fish and Wildlife up here in an instant. They keep track of practically every true wolf in the state." He touched his neck, humor returning now his perceived danger had passed. "I don't know about you, but a radio collar isn't my style." Tatiana dipped her head in acknowledgment. She'd never considered the danger, but she understood it perfectly now. And she was sure Andrew didn't mind showing off his ability to shift twice in succession without too much visible effort, either.

Andrew shifted back and returned to the head of the pack, but he didn't particularly direct anyone. Instead, he loped away and everyone followed, fanning out into the trees in small groups. Tatiana didn't move, trying to figure it out. They must be scouting for prey, and the alpha would direct matters once a quarry of the correct size was located.

Fair enough. Tatiana would scout with them, and watch their behavior, and see what she could find out. Hopefully without stumbling onto any other forbidden things.

As soon as Andrew lost the envoy, he circled back around downwind of the area he'd told the pack to keep to. At the moment, that was conveniently at the vehicles, but Silver knew to meet him elsewhere if it hadn't been.

Silver waited with her ass hitched on the SUV's front

bumper, creating a great line of hip and leg. He nurtured a wish to appreciate it properly to provide motivation to shift when he was tired and rather sore from so many in a short period. At least this time, he could take as long as he wanted, though too long and the process got painful.

She smelled of a reluctance to go back to worries that matched his own.

"Should be, as long as we keep our noses to the wind. We should have plenty of warning if she gets within earshot." Andrew exhaled in amusement. "Plus, I asked Sacramento to distract her." He'd planned to ask Felicia to do it, but with Sacramento's obvious interest, it had seemed like a good use for her.

"Are you sure that's a good idea?" Silver flicked him a sharp sideways glance.

"What?" Andrew matched her glance.

Silver frowned at the ground, mostly covered with hardy weeds rather than grass here in the usual parking area. "Sacramento loses her judgment when she gets romantically attached, and she falls into attraction so easily. I'd worry the envoy might try to manipulate her."

Andrew frowned in the direction Sacramento had run with the others. "She's not stupid. She's certainly a competent alpha, just not when it comes to delegation."

"You weren't around the last time she fell for the wrong woman," Silver countered, though the beat of silence afterward sounded at least thoughtful.

"It's probably too late now, anyway. You saw them after shifting, just now. Do you think warning Sacramento will do any good?" Andrew looked back at Silver.

"A reminder of what she's not supposed to be talking about might not be bad." Silver shrugged on her good side. "I doubt anything will keep her from playing chase if they're both interested."

Andrew looked out at the familiar trees, checking by sight what he already knew by scent. Everyone was still off running, except for—there. His daughter's scent. Good. He'd asked her to circle back a little after him. He wanted to know what had happened in the house. "What do you think of Tatiana?"

Silver hugged her good arm across her chest, her version of crossing her arms. "She's watching far too hard." Her eyes flicked down to an empty patch of ground and she sighed. "And Death compliments me on my grasp of the obvious. So, yes, she watches. That doesn't mean she intends harm with the information she collects." Silver frowned. "I don't dislike her."

Andrew tore his gaze away from at the line of trees. He'd been staring hard enough he'd imagined Death into being again, laughing silently and padding through pools of shadow. He hadn't expected that answer from Silver. "She's got to be up to something. Her whole manner screams that." Didn't it? Or was that his paranoia fooling him?

"She's judging us. But she hasn't made the final determination yet," Silver said, slowly. "And now we have her interest.

Did you see her, when we spoke of cubs? That was important to her. I'd bet her father had other children."

A reddish-black wolf, much more real than Death, loped

by making it too clear I didn't want a Russians teeth anywhere near intimate areas, even if I wasn't with someone. So I refused politely and then grabbed him to be a buffer."

Andrew clenched his teeth on an automatic order for Felicia to get out of the house and go back to roaming immediately. His daughter was an adult, and she'd handled the situation as well as anyone could have. Even if there was something to protect her *from*, she wouldn't thank him for trying. He supposed he'd already been luckier than many parents, in that she was roaming with a boyfriend. He recalled a particular roamer's chase of his own, a few weeks with a guy who'd been fond of starting bar fights with humans when he got bored. What at seventeen had seemed terribly exciting to Andrew now seemed dangerously stupid, but it had been his mistake to make.

Anyway, this invitation to chase, carefully turned down, didn't put his daughter in any more danger than she or any of the pack was already in. With one Russian in a house full of Were, that wasn't much.

Still, he didn't like dangerous Russians inviting his *daughter* to chase.

Silver squeezed his hand, breaking him out of his thoughts.

She looked sympathetic, and Felicia looked slightly amused. "Sorry, Papa," she said. "Nothing much happened other than that. She was actually happy to play with Edmond and his stupid squadron, if that means anything." She shrugged.

Andrew coughed. "I think we can assume her treatment of you is confirmation of what she wants with Sacramento." He pinched the bridge of his nose. "Lady damn it. I wonder if it would be too obvious to send her home now, to keep her safe."

Felicia looked off into the trees, probably in what she imagined was Sacramento's direction. "Do you want me to fetch her for you now? If you want to stop her, you're a little late."

Andrew flicked a glance at Silver, and she nodded, echoing his own feelings. "Yeah, go ahead. We'll talk to her at least. If she can get away without Tatiana noticing," he said.

Felicia ducked her head in acknowledgment, jogging off into the trees in human to save shifting back and forth another time to speak to Sacramento. Since they'd probably have a wait until Sacramento could get away discreetly, Andrew turned to the vehicles and rummaged around in various bags in search of energy bars. All that shifting was making his stomach grumble.

Sacramento arrived after about half an hour, when they'd moved to sit side by side on a log on the other side of the clearing to keep downwind. She shifted under cover of the underbrush and came out with her hands already spread apologetically. "I can guess what you're going to say, and I just want to say one thing first. May I?"

Andrew raised his eyebrows, and let his silence turn interrogative. Her scent and body language were respectful, and he had to admit his curiosity was piqued.

"This is where you specify that while you told me to distract her on the hunt, distraction shouldn't go too far, right?" Sacramento grimaced and looked at her feet. "I know I've made bad decisions about women in the past, and then ɑ____·¹·
Craig todav wɑⁱ ⁱ ᵇ⁻ ¹ ·

_____ answered her, leaving Andrew to watch her face. He was impressed, though he probably shouldn't have been. Sacramento was good with her pack, and that took observational skills. Just because she got carried away and let her own emotions influence her actions too much sometimes didn't mean she couldn't read others'.

"I figured." Sacramento crossed her arms over her stomach. "Here's what I was thinking: she's not going to talk to you guys. Ever. But she might talk to a lover."

"Are you sure?" It wasn't quite as visceral, but Andrew definitely felt an echo of what he'd felt with Felicia earlier. Sacramento was one of his people, and Tatiana presented an unknown amount of danger to someone who got so close to her. On the other hand, she was an adult and could make her own choices. "Really sure, Allison? That's not something we'd even considered asking of anyone."

Sacramento's lips twisted into a smile, starting at self-deprecating, and ending up somewhere sharper. "If I do tend to chase women too quickly, why not own it? I mean, you guys weren't even surprised to see me flirting with her, were you? I doubt many others will be. And I'll be really careful. I won't let anything slip in return. Even if I don't get anything out of her, she'll still be tied up trying to question me rather than anyone else."

Silver took Andrew's hand and squeezed it, so he let her take the lead. She smelled reluctant, but also impressed, and he agreed. "Be careful. Very careful," she said, and paused as Sacramento blew out a breath in triumph. "And see if you can bring up Edmond again. There's something there."

Sacramento bobbed a quick bow, one knee bent, to informally evoke kneeling. "I will."

Andrew wasn't sure how Tatiana's reaction to North American family structure helped them, but he'd trust Silver's instincts. Silver shoved his shoulder until he stood. "You should both get back before she notices. Go find a deer or something big to take down and impress her."

"I don't think she impresses that easily," Andrew said, and shifted to run on four feet back to the hunt, to be judged once more.

7

On their return from the hunt, the pack left the vehicles for the house chaotically, not in precedence order as Tatiana had expected. It took a little maneuvering for her to slip into the house just after the alphas. Now seemed like a good time to speak to them alone, if she could. "I brought some wine from home," she said with a diffident smile. "If you two want to try some."

"I didn't know Russia was particularly known for its wines," Andrew said, tone lightly teasing.

"In the Caucasus region, they make it," Tatiana explained. And then the Were took it and added something of their own, but she wasn't going to mention that to the North Americans. When Andrew nodded, dubious but not particularly suspicious, she tipped her head in the direction of the guesthouse. "I'll go get it."

The walk back through the yards was enlivened by small lanterns set into the sides of the path, like a little road flanked by stars. Tatiana didn't need them to see, but she could appreciate why the pack had added them nonetheless. She rather liked walking among the stars, imagining each humming their snatch of song, shattered pieces of the Lady's first child who liked to sing.

She used the time to review what she knew, and consider what suggestions she should make. She still needed to get the story of Silver's injury out of her. No point appealing to her vanity by referencing the stories about her being Lady-touched. Tatiana didn't know what Silver would think on her own, but Andrew would definitely influence her with his loud scoffing. And maybe Silver would consider it blasphemous if Tatiana implied that anything—like their stepping down, for example—was the Lady's will.

They were both clearly effective alphas, but they did not necessarily look that way. Tatiana suspected they must know that, so perhaps she should foster that insecurity. But all that would depend on what else she found out when she spoke to them alone.

She gathered up two bottles, one under her arm and one in her hand, leaving her other hand for the glasses. Fortunately they were Ceremony glasses, so they stacked within each other.

The walk back with the wine was just long enough for Tatiana's thoughts to turn to worry, instead. She squashed it firmly. Nothing would go wrong because there was nothing *to* go wrong. If the wine and her suggestions didn't work, no one would realize she'd done anything. But there was no reason it shouldn't work. That kind of worrying was useless.

She eyed the back door when she approached it, not eager to juggle everything again, but it opened for her. Andrew ges-

still swathed in the Ceremony cloth. This wasn't a Ceremony, but it padded them nicely, and it felt like a little bit of the Lady's protection to offer them, and herself.

She supposed it looked a little like a wide silk scarf to the North Americans. They had no Ceremony, she knew that, whatever else had taken her by surprise. The dark blue almost vibrated through some optical trick, it was so vivid against the scarred wood. Yellow moon and star patterns twisted in the center, though fortunately the Lady Herself was not pictured.

Andrew set a corkscrew on the table in front of her, then seated himself, and Silver picked up one of the Ceremony glasses to look it over. Its base was as round as possible while still allowing the glass to stand upright, and the Lady's phases were etched around the rim. "Pretty," Silver said, then set it back down for her to pour.

Tatiana sat and splashed wine into three of the set of four glasses she'd brought, set the bottle aside, and waited for the others to choose theirs before she lifted the remaining one. She sipped generously from it immediately, keeping herself relaxed as if she hadn't carefully thought out each step to reassure them.

One source of the wine, so that couldn't be dangerous. She let them dictate which glass she took, so nothing could have been in the glasses. She drank first. "Reminds me of home," she said with a small smile.

Silver sipped next, and Andrew followed soon after. They probably hadn't even needed all that reassurance; it was a rare poison a werewolf couldn't heal. Of course, wolfsbane wasn't a poison, as such. Tatiana wasn't looking to kill them.

Silver grimaced, and though Andrew didn't react visibly, she noticed that his second sip was smaller. The process of adding the wolfsbane concentrated the alcohol, so it probably didn't taste like they thought it should. If they tasted the wolfsbane, they wouldn't know what it was, though she doubted they could. She sipped again, searching for it, and found the tang of acidic sweetness more quickly than she'd expected.

"Interesting," Andrew said dryly. "The Northwest is known for its beers. We'll have to have some kind of exchange."

Tatiana nodded. She'd stalled long enough the suggestibility should be beginning, she hoped. "It's good, yes?" she said, catching both alphas' eyes briefly as she said it. Not long enough to be challenging, but enough to set the suggestion, powered by wolfsbane, into their minds. "A little strong, but that just makes it more fun."

Silver's eyes widened, as if at a sudden realization. "It is good." She lifted her glass and tipped it back. Andrew looked amused at her, but his swallows grew more generous as well.

Tatiana continued to drink, but very carefully. She'd brought the Ceremony glasses because she knew how much of one she could drink safely. The effects of wolfsbane accumulated, and she'd done a Wisdom Ceremony a little over a month ago, just before she left home. A Wisdom meant she'd drunk less wolfsbane wine than for a full Vision Ceremony, but she

Her mind was certainly wandering now, though. Tatiana frowned at her glass. She could safely have a little under one and a half glasses, which was good because Silver and Andrew needed two for the effects she wanted. Refilling their glasses and not her own would look odd.

"I feel like we've been circling around each other in our questions all evening." Tatiana made her smile rueful. "Perhaps we could just answer. I promise to answer yours." She pressed her thumb to her forehead, promising on the Lady.

Silver snorted. Her body language was softening as she drank, probably from the alcohol, and she relaxed back in her chair. "You want to know what happened to me." She set her glass down and used her hand to pull her opposite arm across her lap.

Tatiana tipped her head down. "Among other things. I'd love to hear the story of how you two became alphas." She swirled her wine. They would want something from her first. Pack numbers, maybe. Or the general location of her alpha's home. Her alpha had even given her permission not to lie.

"You have siblings?" Silver smiled when Tatiana's head

jerked up. "Half-siblings? A brother in particular, perhaps? Is that why Edmond bothers you?"

Tatiana bit her lower lip. The alcohol and wolfsbane brought the answer close to the surface. She should be glad that they hadn't asked after anything tactically important, but this was something that belonged to her alone, not her alpha. "I have no idea if I have half-siblings, since I don't know who my real father was. And I want to *know*." She felt the next part bubbling up, but she diverted it into Old Were, because she didn't want to tell them but she couldn't help herself. "*I want to know he wasn't killed because of me.*"

Silver's expression eased into sympathy. Tatiana saw an assumption of a mother's infidelity there, and didn't bother correcting it. It would be too complicated to get the North Americans to understand, if they took parents acknowledging their children so much for granted.

Andrew frowned at her for the rest of her answer. In relaxing, he leaned back, but his hand also strayed unrepentantly to Silver's knee. "What was that language? It sounds familiar, almost."

"Like the children's rhyme." Silver tapped her fingers on the table and recited something. It took a couple repetitions for Tatiana to sort through the horrendous pronunciation. "*Full-half-new-half. New-half, full-half.*"

Tatiana repeated it for her properly. "It's Old Were. The original language all of you have lost." She'd always looked down on the Europeans for not even knowing the language of their people, but now she was starting to wonder what the North Americans had gained instead. "Your turn. What happened to your arm?"

Silver set her glass down and rolled up her sleeve to just above the elbow. White lines of scars showed, beginning at the inside of her elbow and climbing up her arm. "There was a

She looked at Andrew, face tired from old pain, and he picked up the story for her. "Injected them all, like he had been. Silver was the only survivor. I stumbled on her after she escaped, and we killed that monster together." He squeezed her knee.

"Injected them with—" Tatiana stared, trying to wrap her mind around the idea. Humans, she could understand, but one Were doing it to another? How could one of the Lady's children even conceive of such a thing? "But how can you shift?"

Silver laughed, a sharp jolt of sound. "I can't."

Andrew murmured a soothing sound. "She gets seizures if she tries," he said, leaning on the word "seizures" like its scientific tinge would distance Silver from the emotional pain.

Silver smiled like the sharp edges of the expression were aimed to cut herself. She lifted her dead arm with her opposite hand to set it along the tabletop. "But there are some benefits." She reached into her hip pocket and brought out a necklace chain, ordinary enough. She threaded a length among her fingers and dangled the rest over the table, then lowered her hand so it curled into a shiny pool of links. Then she waited.

It took Tatiana several seconds to realize what her nose

was telling her. The chain was silver metal, separate from Silver's own strange scent. An effect of the injection, she supposed. The chain was silver metal, and Silver wasn't burned.

Tatiana drank again to give herself time to think, though her thoughts were already too slippery. Maybe it was the shock. A Were who could touch silver? None of the gossip had mentioned that. But more importantly—a Were who couldn't shift? How could she stand it? Tatiana tried to imagine what it would be like to lack half of herself, and couldn't. Silver didn't seem empty and despairing. Far beyond that, she'd helped her mate win and hold a pack—for years? And not just as an alpha's mate, as an alpha in her own right. "So your name—?"

"It's who I am now," Silver said.

"It used to be Selene," Andrew said, overlapping. Silver punched his shoulder, and he looked instantly contrite, which made Tatiana feel a little better. At least she wasn't alone in blurting out things she knew better than to say.

Tatiana needed to remember the rest of her questions, and not keep getting sidetracked. "And then you two became Roanokes?"

Andrew drained his glass and set it close for Tatiana to refill. Two glasses, wasn't it? She thought so. Two glasses for each of them, but not for her. She filled Andrew's generously. He nodded his thanks and reclaimed it. "After I returned from Spain, I was Roanoke's enforcer for about a decade," he said.

"But you're not Spanish." Tatiana cursed herself mentally. What was she doing, interrupting? You never interrupted a source who was finally talking.

Andrew laughed, a bit too loud. "Thank the Lady for that.

No, my wife was. I joined her pack, but after she died, I got kicked out." He lifted a finger from his glass to gesture emphasis The wine sloshed "You tell that to your alpha. The Butcher

voices back to the Lady. She had met many people, but she did not see the face of someone who would do such a thing in the man before her. It seemed time had changed him . . . but the potential for that kind of violence might remain.

"When he hindered us in hunting the monster that killed my pack, the former Roanoke exposed his growing incompetence." Silver picked up the story, and threw an amused glance at her mate. "If he ever had any competence in the first place without his enforcer to lean on." Andrew laughed and waved that away. "Together, we challenged him. In his fight to retain power, he allied himself with Dare's Spanish enemies and used them to set the packs against each other. In defeating Roanoke, we proved to the other alphas the necessity of standing united, and so we expanded Roanoke territory to the rest of North America."

Silver handed over her empty glass, and Tatiana refilled it too. That was Silver's second. A trickle escaped down the side to puddle on the tabletop, but Tatiana wiped it up with her sleeve after handing the glass back. "So it was Lady's luck, wasn't it? Without your monster, your wife's death, you wouldn't be alphas." Tatiana tried to slow herself down, but with the perfect suggestion so clearly in sight, she couldn't help it. This was what she'd come here to do. "I think being alphas of a whole continent can't possibly be worth it. Especially if it's something you stumbled into by accident. Your positions are the product of bad circumstances."

Tatiana tried to focus on the others to see if the suggestion took, but they spun a little. She frowned at her glass instead. Her first, and it wasn't even quite empty. Something wasn't . . . right. She hadn't felt this out of control since her last Vision Ceremony, but she hadn't drunk enough even for a Wisdom, even with the wolfsbane lingering in her system. Not nearly enough.

"*Stop—*" The word came out in Old Were, which wasn't right. They wouldn't understand that. "Stop . . . drinking." Her heart tried to pound and adrenaline seeped through her blood, but rather than banishing the wolfsbane, it mixed with it, swirling her fear into something surreal. No! She wasn't here to kill them, she wasn't here to strand them in dreams. Too much wolfsbane, and you never woke from the vision again. She'd been so careful with her measurements. They'd both had only what was safe.

But it felt like too much. Far too much.

Silver and Andrew peered at her. Silver did set down her glass, but only so she could pillow her head on her arm on the table. Her eyes began to drift closed. Andrew blinked several times, and frowned at her. "Why?"

But Tatiana's ability to sit straight folded under her and she leaned on the table, too. Just for a moment. Just . . .

8

Selene woke somewhere that didn't smell right. She was surrounded by Were, but not the right Were, in a house that
smelled like half a century or more of fustiness, dirt, and
ground-in human occupation. The Roanoke pack house was
much newer than that.

She pushed herself up, out of the tangle of dozing bodies,
some in wolf, some in human—

With both hands. She pushed herself up with both hands.

Selene took a deep, calming breath. She'd had this dream
before. Plenty of times. Any moment now . . .

"Selene! How in the Lady's name are you still sleeping?
We'll be late." Her brother strode into the room. Ares: warm
blue eyes, hair the same shade of brown hers had been, with
their mother's bones under the strong lines of his face. He'd

actually shaved this morning, it seemed, which made the lines stand out. It hurt so much to see him, even in a dream.

Selene pressed her hands to her face. She didn't want this dream. She didn't want to remember her brother, to have two working arms again. That part of her life was behind her, and she didn't want to relive it. She was going to wake up.

She didn't wake up.

She took her hands away, and her brother was still there, glaring at her, muscles tight in his jaw. "We have to get to the ferry. If the delegation arrives with no one to meet it, who knows what tricks they might try to pull." He grabbed Selene's shoulders, and shoved her at one in a line of trunks along the wall. "You have just enough time to get dressed. You'll have to eat in the car."

She was lucky her brother had given her the shove. The trunks all looked the same to Selene, so aside from eyeballing the sizes of the clothes inside each, she wasn't sure how she would have found the one that belonged to her. As she bent over it, she caught a whiff of her own scent—though of course it wasn't her scent, it was Selene's scent, hers as it had once been, before a silver taint had become forever incorporated into it.

As she sorted through the neatly folded clothes, Selene glanced around her. Down at the other side of the room, along the shorter wall, someone had screwed a closet bar into the old-fashioned cheap wood paneling. The room as a whole looked like a living room, perhaps in an old farmhouse, because space was plentiful, but the construction was utilitarian. But why did her dream have everyone packed into the living

room of a farmhouse? Selene appreciated pack togetherness—
she twisted to count people still dozing together in the nest of
blankets and pillows—but this was a bit much. There must be

She'd expected something of the kind, but facing her re-
flection still made her voice tighten. Brown. Her hair was
brown. She touched the surface and the woman in the mirror
touched back, but that did not make it any less like looking
through a window at someone else.

She checked a brush beside the sink for wolf hair and then
ran it through her hair without looking again in the mirror. If
she wasn't waking up, perhaps she needed to get something
out of this dream. Lady knew what, besides pain at what she
had lost. But clearly she'd find her lesson where Ares wanted
her to go.

Ares was accepting a peck from his wife on the driveway
when Selene picked her way down the steps from the decaying
porch. A young woman, tall and narrow-hipped. Lilianne. The
name came so easily Selene almost stumbled off the last step.
As Silver, she had to fight for each name, fight to hold it so it
didn't escape, and tie it tightly to the right person. But now she
thought of names and they bloomed up, whole packs of names.

"Everything will work out." Lilianne squeezed her husband's hand, then slipped back to the house. "Selene," she mur-

mured, and paused to kiss Selene's cheek as she passed.

Selene could smell her brother's unease as they climbed into the minivan. She wondered if the dream would grow snarled if she asked him what he was worried about. It seemed the Selene of the dream's logic was already well aware of their purpose at the ferry terminal. Would her brother become upset if she was missing memories, and divert them from the path the dream was determined to lead her down before she was allowed to wake? Better to stay silent. Selene wished she knew which ferry, or even where they were.

Her brother driving too fast gave her the first clue. Selene flicked her eyes to the nearest speed limit sign and found a ridiculously high number. Seventy miles an hour on this modest-sized highway? But not a ridiculous number in kilometers. Now she was looking for it, she noticed a stylized maple leaf in a gas station's logo. They must be in Canada.

Slowly, a bridge here and a building there started to look familiar to Selene. When she and her brother had lived in Bellingham, there had been no Canadian pack closer than the Prairies, and they'd crossed the border to visit Vancouver plenty of times. Occasionally, they'd even gone as far as Victoria, taking the ferry out to the island. It was the Vancouver-Victoria ferry they were meeting.

The terminal didn't look quite as Selene remembered it. She frowned out at the sleekly modern buildings, glass and white and blue-painted steel beams against a backdrop of the gray sea and the rocky, tree-covered hillsides beyond. If this was a dream pretending to be real, shouldn't it be exactly as she remembered it? But maybe that was an extrapolation. Public transportation always seemed to be under construction.

Rather than drive up to the ticket booths and join the row after row of cars laid out in the center of the complex, Ares

cases on wheels, and a line of cars waited in the lane in front of the building to pick them up.

Ares's tension ratcheted up even higher as he parked and climbed out of the car. Selene put a hand on his arm automatically. Diverting them from the dream's path or not, she couldn't smell her brother feeling like that and not comfort him. "Why are you so worried?"

"Because I don't know what this delegation wants, and they could seriously hurt us if they try." Ares paused, and looked out over the water visible between the terminal building and the ferry berth next to it. "There aren't enough jobs on the island to support us. We need to return to the mainland. And I know you've been saying there's plenty of empty continent for the Europeans to squabble over if they choose, but I doubt they'll see it that way. They'll grab everything they can. So why talk to us first?"

"Because they want something. Whatever it is, if they're asking rather than taking, we have some power." That was obvious enough she could reassure him automatically as most of her mind struggled with what he'd revealed. Empty continent?

Did that mean all the Were in North America were here on this island? But in the real world, the Roanoke pack had nearly five hundred members. No one could pack that many into one farmhouse. What had happened to all the rest? Selene's instincts told her nothing good.

Her words must have been too abstract for how she used to think, because her brother frowned at her for a beat before striding toward the terminal. "Come on." Ares parted the slowly diminishing stream of people with the strength of his dominance. By the time they reached a waiting area with rows of seats identical to those in dozens of transportation settings, only a few stragglers from this sailing and a few waiting for the next remained. The scents were too confused to spot a Were that way, so Selene started scanning faces, starting with the people standing alone. Before she finished more than a few people, a family grouping caught her eye.

Dare. Dare was here.

He looked wrong in this world too, dark hair unmarked, and wearing thin lines of a goatee. Something about his expression was hard in a way Selene didn't like, but she didn't bother chasing it down. Thank the Lady Dare was here to share this stupid dream world with her. Even though it wouldn't actually be him, the dream's facsimile was better than nothing. Selene pulled away from her brother and strode forward.

And Dare looked at her blankly. No hint of recognition, and when he recognized the direction of her path, he only nodded in polite greeting. He put his hand on the back of the Were woman next to him, affectionate. She had beautiful black waves of hair, and Selene recognized the angle of her cheekbones. She'd seen it in Dare's daughter.

Selene stopped, voice dying in her throat. Cruel, cruel dream indeed.

Ares caught up with her, and she could feel his displeasure

"Andrew Dare, representing Madrid." The two men shook hands. Selene had a sudden impulse to offer hers next, though that wasn't strictly protocol, like Andrew would remember everything if he just touched her. She clenched her hands—both hands—instead.

"My wife, Isabel." Andrew looked over his shoulder, and motioned the others in his party forward. Felicia, Selene knew, though she moved wrong. Like her mother, Selene realized, when Isabel stepped sideways to nudge a boy of perhaps ten years forward. Andrew set his hand on the boy's back. "My children, Felicia and Arturo. May we have permission to enter your territory?"

"You may. This way." Ares held out his arm toward the exit. The adults and Felicia had roller suitcases of carry-on size, though Isabel's was slightly larger, probably because Arturo wore only a small backpack. All three rolled them rather than carrying them, to avoid showing too much casual strength.

In the minivan, Selene watched the middle set of seats with the makeup mirror in her sun visor. She tried not to, lest Andrew catch her gaze in the mirror, but she needed to keep reminding herself. This was not her Dare. No matter how much he smelled like the man she was engaged to, the man she loved. This was some cruel dream creation.

When they reached the farmhouse property, Ares pulled off on a side spur of the driveway before the trees cleared enough to see the house properly. A garden party open-sided tent had been set up a field, white tablecloths on the picnic tables beneath lending it a charming sort of formality. Selene knew better, because she'd seen the house. Nothing could make that old, worn wood look worthy of formal visitors, and besides, where would all the Were inside go, to leave their alpha privacy?

When they'd all climbed out of the car, the boy headed immediately for the trees, head tipped up to track the path of a gray squirrel. Felicia looked just as intrigued, but hid it better. Ares and Andrew strode toward the tables together, and Selene gritted her teeth. From the back, she couldn't find a point of difference to hang on to.

Isabel strode up beside her, but stopped, rather than passing by to follow her husband. Selene twisted to face her in surprise, looking at her properly for the first time. She was gorgeous. Felicia was beautiful too, but this was beauty with maturity and confidence, and intensified for it.

"None of us can control our physical attraction—" Isabel inhaled pointedly, "—but I would appreciate it if you would stop staring at my husband." She smiled, a quick flash of teeth. "Thank you." She followed the men, as calm as if nothing had been said.

Selene felt on her right hand where her ring should have been, and squeezed the finger until it ached. She wanted to shout after the woman—scream after the woman—that Andrew wasn't Isabel's. He was Selene's. Isabel was dead. But in this dream, she was not dead, so of course he was still hers.

Selene whirled. Enough. She might be trapped in this dream, but she'd had enough of playing along. She ran into the trees, away from the dream figment that was not her brother, and the one who was not her Dare, and away from Dare's wife. Away.

9

Andrew woke with his head pounding. It hurt too much to chase the memories of what had caused the state. He scrubbed at his eyes and sat up. The subliminal familiarity of the dusty scents around him snapped into focus. He was in one of the cabins at the ranch the Were rented for the alphas' Convocation. The pine forest had seeped into the smell of wood and stone of the cabin's construction.

But the Convocation was in April. April was . . . not now. Andrew stumbled to his feet. He must have been drinking if his head still hurt this badly. Even Were healing couldn't fix a dehydration headache if he hadn't had any water before collapsing last night.

In the tiny bathroom shared by the cabin's two bedrooms, Andrew turned the cold tap on full force and bent to drink directly from it. When he'd swallowed enough to start feeling bloated, he twisted it off and straightened to look in the mirror. A ghost of a yellow bruise stained his cheekbone and

What kind of fight had he been in, that his healing would have been soaked up before it got to such a simple bruise? He splashed water on his face and then pulled off his shirt. Maybe he'd been concussed, and that was why his memories didn't line up with where he found himself. He needed to go find Silver. She could chew him out for getting into the fight, and fill him in on what had happened.

Someone knocked, and Andrew strode out through the living area. It didn't take more than a few paces: the living area adjoined the kitchen and held only a battered couch and a stone fireplace. He didn't see evidence of any other Were, which was odd. The ranch had a lot of cabins, but not enough for each pack to have more than one. The one used by the Roanoke home pack should have had Silver, John, and some young pack members, along to meet other singles.

Andrew opened the door to bright sunlight and Benjamin. Andrew relaxed. He didn't really feel like dealing with anyone before he found Silver, but his old mentor was another matter. In the light, Benjamin's skin was burnished like warm mahogany, but his expression looked carved, far too neutral.

"Boston?" Andrew asked, cautious enough to use the sub-alpha's title.

Benjamin invited himself inside, moving Andrew out of the way with the controlled dominance of his manner. "You've started cleaning up. Good." Worse than his expression, his tone held disgust. Once the door was shut he faced Andrew and crossed his arms. "You can't go on like this, Dare. In the Lady's name, stop picking fights with Sacramento."

Andrew stared. Picking fights? Sacramento needed to find herself a beta, he remembered that much. But firmly enforcing his order on that matter was hardly picking a fight. Benjamin was an accomplished leader; he of all people should understand that. "Believe me, I don't plan to pick a fight with anyone." He stepped into his bedroom long enough to grab a clean shirt out of his open suitcase, then returned to Benjamin as he pulled it on. "I'm going to find Silver. Do you know where she is?"

Benjamin looked at him, eyes narrowing. "What?"

Andrew winced. "Is she that pissed that she wants to be alone? It happened last night, though, so we might as well get it worked out now." He scrubbed fingers through his hair and let himself out of the cabin. It was always better to give Silver a cool-down period, but a period of an hour or two, not days.

Andrew paused on the gravel drive that divided the two rows of nearly identical cabins. The Roanoke home pack always took the one at the head of one of the rows, but the one he'd stepped out of was one down. Had he collapsed in the wrong cabin by mistake last night? No, his suitcase had been there.

Andrew scanned the familiar surroundings. The gravel road led to the converted barn serving as the ranch's main hall.

Behind the cabins, sparse pines gradually increased in density with distance from the buildings, though without much un-

··· ·· ·· ·· ····-ld ----hs and fences clearly visible. Andrew

couldn't tell with Edmond in the way, but he thought his beta might have lost weight.

Andrew strode over. Clearly, the blow to his head had made him forget quite a number of things. John couldn't have gotten this bad overnight. "John!"

John flinched. Actually flinched. He twisted immediately to put Edmond on the side away from Andrew. "Yes?"

Andrew swallowed his first impulse to snap at the man that he had nothing to fear. That wouldn't help anything. Before he could help John, he needed to get a clear picture of the situation. That was obvious now more than ever. He opened his hands a little, loose by his sides. Nonthreatening. "Have you seen Silver?"

John stared at him in utter confusion for several beats, then shook his head. Andrew pressed his lips together, summoning patience. He had trouble believing *no one* knew where Silver was. It wasn't like she blended into the background, and she was one of their alphas. "When did you see her last, then? Last night?"

"Who?" John's expression darkened with frustration, like

he suspected Andrew was mocking him with incomprehensible questions. At least the emotion was better than a deepening of his earlier fear, but Andrew couldn't understand what was so difficult. Where was Silver?

"Dare!" A younger man Andrew didn't recognize came jogging up from the direction of the hall. Rage suffused his face. "Roanoke may let you run wild, but you're not going to pick fights with my people. Step back." He interposed himself between Andrew and John, and Andrew did step back out of sheer reflex.

"I *am* Roanoke. Who are you?" Andrew growled. He slapped the man's hands away when he reached up to shove Andrew back. He was a few inches shorter than Andrew, but no bulkier, which was unusual. Andrew was lean for a Were. The young man had light brown hair and blue eyes of an oddly familiar shade. Andrew stared at him, chasing the resemblance. Who did he remind Andrew of?

The man burst into a sharp laugh. "I'm sure Rory would be surprised to hear that. Did Sacramento knock you stupid last night? I'm Seattle."

"Ares? What's going on?" A female voice. Andrew turned toward it with a feeling like his heart had paused and was refusing to restart. Ares. Ares was the name of Silver's brother. The one who was dead.

The woman who had spoken was clearly Ares's sister. They had the same eyes, the same grace to their build. But she wasn't Silver. Her hair, caught back in a long braid, was brown, yes, but worse, she held herself as a different woman. Silver walked with the confidence of someone who had been through the fire and survived, someone who knew her own strength. The brown-haired woman before Andrew moved with the confidence of someone who had never been tested, who took her

bled back. What in the Lady's name was going on? Had the past five years never happened? Selene's pack had never been killed? He'd remained enforcer rather than challenging Rory? He wanted to scream and press his hands against his temples until his thoughts were forced straight.

"He was asking about silver," John contributed, hefting Edmond to a more secure position on his hip. He slipped away from the group, head down once more, like some low-ranker who didn't want to get caught in a bigger fight.

But John wasn't low ranked; he was beta of the entire Roanoke pack. Or he was in Andrew's memories, which were . . . wrong? Had it all been a concussion dream, built of the elements around him? Helping Silver, challenging Rory, winning his daughter back from her mother's relatives . . .

Selene frowned at him. "Are you feeling all right?" Her tone held more challenge than concern, but at least she'd asked the question. Her brother looked ready to start throwing punches any minute.

Andrew held up his hands. "I think you may be right. Something about the blow to the head—my memories have gotten fucked up somehow. How long have you been Seattle?"

Selene answered first, while Ares was still looking suspicious. "We joined Bellingham with Seattle five years ago, after John had his thing with the human."

Andrew's memories—false memories?—told him that Ares had been Bellingham, before Stefan had killed him. About five years ago, give or take. So he remembered the past five years wrong? Some kind of dream had overwritten them? Andrew supposed if he was going to dream something, it would be that, a fiancée and daughter, the alphaship of a powerful pack. But what about everything else?

His breath caught with a sudden thought, and Andrew slipped a hand under his shirt to feel the skin in the small of his back. Stefan had broken his back with a silver-plated crowbar, leaving thick scars.

Smooth skin met his fingertips. He tried to think back to looking in the mirror, remember whether he'd had the white locks at his temples that had resulted from the same silver injury. But he'd been too focused on the bruise and blood to notice.

Ares snorted, and Andrew realized he'd been quiet for too long. "You should go eat something," he said, unbending slightly. But not much. "And stay away from my people." He and his sister entered the cabin John had left. Selene glanced back once with idle curiosity.

Andrew stood in the center of the gravel for a while, directionless. What was real? His memories of the past five years seemed real, but didn't dreams sometimes seem like that, when you remembered them? This seemed pretty damn real, too. And exactly the kind of situation it might be nice to escape from into a dream.

And if this was reality . . . he had nothing. No Silver, be-

cause she didn't really exist. No Felicia, because she was presumably still in Spain, happily allowing herself to be warped
by his in-laws. No beta, no pack—he yanked himself out of the

Rory. The former Roanoke Andrew had challenged and beat-
en, then exiled to the wilderness in Canada. Or at least, that's
what he remembered doing.

Rory stopped in front of Andrew and rolled his neck and
shoulders. He was built like a tank, so it was a rather impressive
exercise. An angry tank, too; the scent of his rage rolled off him
in waves, and he was making no effort to control it. "Do you remember what I told you would happen if you got into another
fight at the Convocation?"

"As a matter of fact, I don't." Andrew forced calm into his
voice and tapped his temple. "Lost some memories from the
concussion." Inside, he braced. He remembered something, at
least: when Rory was like this, it was no good trying to talk him
down. The most you could do was remain calm and hope he
shouted himself out before he started in with his fists.

Rory snarled. "You've strained my patience long enough."

"You have patience?" Andrew hadn't meant to say it, but
he *remembered* beating Rory, being alpha. He'd lost that victory, that position, along with Silver, but with the dreamed memories fogging his brain, he couldn't make himself bow his head
to this bullying asshole.

Rory swung for Andrew's jaw, and he knew he should just

take the blow. But he couldn't. He dodged, and kicked at Rory's knee.

Rory avoided the kick like he knew exactly what Andrew would do. He slammed a blow into Andrew's stomach. Andrew folded around it, gasping, and tried to use the angle to return a punch to Rory's solar plexus. Rory dealt him a shattering blow on the chin, and he went flying, gravel grinding into his back as he landed.

Rory laughed. "Come on, Dare. You know this dance better than this. You're off your game."

Andrew scrambled to his feet, still gasping for breath. Sometime in those missing years, Rory had learned his moves. He remembered Rory as soft, too used to relying on his enforcer to deal with anyone who would fight back. This Rory must have fought often. Fought with Andrew often.

Rory swept Andrew's feet out from under him, following the move with a rain of kicks every time Andrew looked like he might make it to even his hands and knees. To his stomach, to his back, to his face. Blood stung his eye, the one that wasn't already swelling shut, and each breath became agony as cracked ribs screamed. He should have healed the injuries easily, but too much of his healing must have gone to the fight last night. Blood seeped steadily as he lay on this stomach, and the pain didn't lessen.

Damned if Andrew was going to let Rory win, though. He shoved his arms straight, and got one knee under him.

"No more fighting," Rory said, and hooked a kick into Andrew's stomach that flipped him onto his back, grinding against the gravel once more. When Andrew didn't try to move, Rory crouched over him, and smiled with too much teeth. "Unless it's with me. Got it?"

"Got it," Andrew slurred through a fat lip, and slammed
his knuckles up into Rory's nose. Rory gasped in pain, and

The beating ended eventually. Andrew's vision cleared in
his open eye, and he watched the searing blue of the sky for a
while. He needed to eat, before he could heal. But he needed
to be able to walk before he could eat. No one seemed to be
running out to help him. Andrew supposed if he was picking
fights with everyone, that was fair enough. He'd have to shift, to
help the healing along a little. It was easier to limp on four legs
rather than two, as well. Not as far to hoist yourself up.

Of course, the Convocation was held in the new, to let the
painful effort needed at that time of the month discourage people from shifting. Andrew loosened his clothes enough to wiggle out of them and reached for the shift before he could think
about how much energy it would take. It couldn't feel worse
than the sea of pain he already floated in. He fell into wolf before he quite realized, far too easy for how it should have been
in the new, but he'd never shifted when so badly hurt before.
Maybe it was a self-preservation reflex.

Andrew flopped onto his side, the more natural position in wolf form, and panted, waiting for the pain to recede, at least a little. Why wasn't he healing?

10

In her vision, Tatiana watched a car burn. Young trees surrounded it, straight and so tall, but very thin. Patches of snow, unmelted, lingered here and there, icing over in the darkness of night. They didn't care about the fire. Few things did, here. Its light was deeply, intensely orange, but it didn't carry, scarcely casting shadows on the surrounding moss and grass.

She was holding a Were baby. Tatiana looked down at her, swathed in a blanket perhaps her human grandmother had knitted, and she screwed up her perfect little face and screamed and screamed. Tatiana bounced her, but she wouldn't stop screaming. The fire pulsed with the screaming, and the baby's human mother reached out of the car window, desperately.

She was perfect too. Skin still healthy pink and even, hair still sturdy brown and silky smooth, fanned over her shoulders. "*Tatiana. Please!*" she said in Old Were, tears in her eyes. "*Please.*" She reached, reached for the baby, flames licking all around her but not touching her yet.

Tatiana turned away from the car, and held the baby close, rocking her. Her cheek stung, and when she put her fingertips up to it, they came away kissed with red from a scratch. She extended her arm, tracing scratch layered on scratch along it with her eyes.

Of course, it was all wrong.

The baby's mother had already been dead when Tatiana had returned her to her car and pushed it off the road. She'd snapped the human woman's neck somewhere in the woods beyond the reach of this fire's light. In the chase, branches had scratched her, but they'd healed immediately. The human woman had been the one with the angry-red crisscrossing of lines. She'd begged in Russian, not Old Were.

But the baby had screamed.

Father slipped from the trees. The Lady's light caught the gray in his fair hair and beard, making those sparse strands glint where usually they blended with the rest. His face was cold, cold as the air freezing over tiny patches of snow that only wanted to escape, to finally change their form to what they were meant to be.

"No more," Tatiana said. She looked back at the fire. This wasn't where this conversation had happened either, but it had a certain rightness. She stroked the baby's soft hair. "I will kill no more for you. You have plenty of other Teeth to do your bidding in those kind of matters."

"If you wish." Father's voice was low and soft, commanding attention. "But be warned: your purpose in my pack will change."

Tatiana remembered what she'd really said: "As long as

and the baby would be hurt. She had only two choices: a child who was hurt, or one who was not. She could not keep the child.

She gave the child over, but she did not stay silent. "Why not?"

Father gave her a very thin smile. "Because you want her too much. You might forget she is the alpha's child, not your own."

Because this was a vision, and not real, Tatiana lunged for the baby. She didn't care. The child deserved better than growing up, wondering about her absent parent, wondering whether her existence as a Were had killed that parent.

Father thrust his hand into Tatiana's throat and pulled at her voice, at her life, holding the baby back against him with his other arm. Tatiana's vision began to fade. No! Tatiana refused to let go, refused to let him win, but she could hardly breathe, and the light from the fire contracted smaller and smaller, leaving her nothing but darkness.

The tiny spark of that fire flared as Father punched her in the chest. It didn't help her breathe, but again and again he punched, until the darkness before her eyes flared with false colors. Again, and again, in odd sort of rhythm—

Tatiana's chest hurt. Her whole body felt drained, heavy, hopeless, but her chest radiated a sharper pain. She thought she should perhaps move—should perhaps want to move, but she couldn't, and didn't. She couldn't even summon the will to move her head, so she lay there, breathing.

A human woman was kneeling over her where she lay on her back on something hard, she presumed the floor. Tatiana wondered for a moment if she was still in the vision, but this woman wasn't the baby's mother from back in Russia, years ago. This was the Roanokes' human. Susan.

"Was that . . . CPR? You know how to do it?" The beta's voice, from outside Tatiana's range of view.

"The bank has us all certified, in case a customer keels over." Susan smoothed Tatiana's hair off the side of her face, and peered carefully into her eyes. The string of letters made no sense to Tatiana, and she couldn't summon the energy to puzzle it out. The beta must have made some expression of confusion out of sight, because Susan expanded. "Since she didn't have a pulse, I figured the principle of restarting the heart was the same, Were or human." She held a single finger in front of Tatiana's eyes, moved it side to side. "Tatiana? Are you with us?"

"*Lady,*" Tatiana whispered in Old Were. She'd meant it to come out in English. She was understanding the English, after all, but everything was a battle at the moment. The pain in her chest was ebbing, but the overwhelming weakness lingered. Her thoughts started to move at something approaching nor-mal speed. Overdose. She'd overdosed on wolfsbane, enough

"Relax," Susan said firmly, exactly like an alpha might have said it. "Stay still for now. I don't know how poison works for Were, but I'd bet your body has a hell of a lot to heal at the moment. Rest, and we'll get you something to eat."

John snorted. "The answer to how poison works is generally that it *doesn't*. You're probably better informed than any of us."

"But what about Papa and Silver? What did she do to them?" Anxiety shaded into anger in Felicia's tone, drawing Tatiana's attention to her where she was leaning over the alphas. Silver dozed apparently peacefully, head on her arm on the table, and Andrew had slumped into his chair, chin on his chest. Tatiana would have liked a closer look, but her position on the floor put her at too awkward an angle. And craning her neck made her head swim. Breathing. She was staying calm and breathing for now.

"They seem to be just asleep for the moment. The poison was in the Russian wine, so I suggest we get the Russian to the point of talking in case she can offer us some information about how to help the Roanokes." Susan tipped her head up to glare at Felicia, then frowned back down at Tatiana.

In the wine. Of course the wolfsbane had been in the wine, but too much. Far, far too much. Tatiana had gotten the wine from Father before she left—no, that wasn't right. The priestesses had brought it. Yes, he'd handed the bottles to her after giving her his final orders, but one of the priestesses had lingered by them the whole time, almost protectively.

But why? The priestesses did not make such earthly decisions as whom to kill; they only advised. Had the Lady spoken to them? Tatiana refused to believe that. But it would make a convenient excuse for an earthly motive.

Or did one or more of the priestesses see themselves as doing the Lady's unspoken will by disposing not only of a false Lady-touched North American, but also a Tooth who'd dared to refuse part of her duties? Tatiana had gathered a few disappointed looks from her fellow Teeth when her request to her alpha had become known, but she hadn't imagined anything like this.

If the priestesses had tried to dispose of her, Tatiana would be delighted to disappoint them. She'd followed Father's orders: she'd suggested the alphas step down, she'd kept her ears turned to everything said. Now she could go home. Leaving the alphas alive, by the Lady. And she'd damn well try to help keep them that way as well.

She cleared her throat, remembering how to use breath for voice as well as living, and everyone's attention snapped to her. "Wolfsbane."

"Is that what you poisoned them with?" Felicia bent and reached out to grip a handful of Tatiana's shirt in the middle of her chest, perhaps intending to shake her.

Tatiana caught Felicia's wrist on the way there, but she could feel in her shaking muscles she didn't have the strength

hadn't been familiar with human first aid, she would be *dead*. You think she's suicidal? If she knew it was poisoned, do you think she would have drunk that much?"

No, Tatiana answered silently in her head. She would not. The pack didn't command her loyalty to that degree. But as long as the human was making her arguments for her, she might as well conserve her strength.

Felicia growled. "And now she knows about you, Susan. Humans who know are supposed to be killed on sight. What if she tries to kill you next?"

"I don't kill," Tatiana said, intensely, while her mind grappled weakly with the rest of that. The human clearly did know about the Were, she hadn't thought about that until now. How could they let her—? But Tatiana had bigger problems. She could think about the human later. "Even if I did, Susan saved my life."

"See?" Susan stood up and offered her hands to Tatiana. "Can you stand?"

The analytic part of Tatiana's mind, the part trained as a Tooth, ground into motion. She needed to think beyond the

North American's next question, to a real strategy. It went
against her instincts, but her best option at the moment might
be to emphasize her vulnerability. Either the North Americans
would read her as too weak to have the will to poison the alphas in the first place, or they'd think her too weak to answer
for her crimes at the moment, too dishonorable a target for
punishment before she healed. Either way, Tatiana's heart beat
a little longer.

She shook her head. "Not yet. I need a little more time."
She planted her palms on the wood floor beside her hips, brac-
ing. She probably could stand, if she had to. Whether she could
walk . . . she'd have to see when she got there. She certainly
couldn't stay here. When she found her moment, she needed
to take it.

Felicia crossed her arms, glowering. "Tell us what in the
Lady's name happened, then, while you're sitting around."

"We were having a drink together, that's all. I did not
know what was in the wine. It was a gift, before I left." Tatiana
twisted to check on the bottle, still on the table with a thin layer
of liquid in the bottom. "Apparently from one of my enemies."

Felicia prowled to her father and checked his pulse, probably not for the first time. She shook his shoulder violently, and
he moved with the motion without resistance or reaction. "So
you say," she muttered. John and Susan ignored her, so Tatiana
did too.

"But they should not be in danger, with the amount they
had. Wolfsbane is commonly used in modest amounts for visions, from the Lady. If their hearts haven't stopped by now,
they will be fine. They'll dream, unwakeable, and rouse on

their own when they are ready. Maybe tomorrow morning."
Or maybe not. If the dose had been large enough to stop her
heart, Lady knew how much stronger the effects on the Roa-

and drag him, too, into visions.

"Not if you pluck and eat a leaf or two, no. You have to dis-
till it." Tatiana gestured a vague sense of a plant. "Eat a whole
stalk, you might get a—" What was the word she'd heard up
in Alaska that had seemed so apt? "Buzz." The more true but
harmless information she could distract them with, the less attention they'd pay to her physical state. She hoped.

"You choose to make and drink something that stops your
heart if you get too much? How does that make sense?" Felicia seemed to be calming a little, at least. She considered Silver's position, then removed her glass from range of getting
knocked over. The silver chain in Silver's fingers gave her pause,
but when she lifted Silver's arm, the chain slipped between her
fingers and remained on the table.

"I'll get it," Susan said and stepped over to scoop up the
abstract swirl of links. She slid it into her pocket.

Felicia nodded in relief and lifted Silver into her arms. Silver's hair was so fine and slippery, the white strands fanned
picturesquely over Felicia's arm. The way Silver's head lolled
was not so poetic.

"Choosing to drink wolfsbane makes as much sense as most of the exciting things in life," Tatiana said dryly. "Get too much . . ." And in reality, the line was not that thin. Had the wine held wolfsbane in the proper proportion, it would have taken a full glass more than she'd had to take Tatiana to the edge of danger. She did not feel like justifying the place of a vision from the Lady in one's personal religious life to a sullen teen, however.

"You Russians need better hobbies, then." Felicia hefted Silver to balance her weight more carefully and looked belatedly over at John. Tatiana supposed she couldn't blame the young woman. She herself had forgotten that she should think of John not as the beta, but as the interim alpha. "I'll take her upstairs to their bedroom, okay? Then we can deal with *her.*" Tatiana, her tone specified.

John grunted agreement, not bothering with calling out disrespectful behavior. Her alpha would never have put up with such an attitude, and Tatiana wouldn't have either, from any of her young siblings. She supposed she could benefit from the North Americans being hampered by a weak leader, but not if he allowed himself to be swayed by voices prone to violence, like Felicia's. She'd have to hope for a voice of balance, such as Susan had unexpectedly been.

"I'll take Roanoke Dare," John said, and stooped over him. The rhythm of Andrew's deep, sleeping breaths hitched suddenly. He started panting. Felicia swung around, but John held up a forestalling hand and felt Andrew's pulse himself. "It's racing," he reported, expression darkening with renewed worry. He rearranged Andrew's head and shoulders so he was sitting more or less upright in the chair.

It created an eerie picture: Andrew's eyes closed, and his body relaxed, but his breaths coming ragged and fast like he

The scent of fresh blood burst into Tatiana's next breath; a droplet seeped from one of Andrew's nostrils and charted a course down his lip. His face remained peaceful. John stared at the drop, and Felicia made a low, keening whine.

Tatiana silently urged them to greater focus on Andrew. With Felicia encumbered by Silver, and John's and Susan's attention on Andrew, maybe she actually had a chance of getting out of here. They just needed to stay close to the alphas, far enough from the doorway out of the room . . .

Susan gave a human-toned growl of frustration. "People get nosebleeds. Stop looking like he's fatally hemorrhaging." She stepped closer, as if to wipe it away with her thumb, pretend it had never been there.

"Humans get nosebleeds, maybe," Felicia snapped. "I'm not buying this 'they're just dreaming' bullshit anymore." She changed her grip on Silver to look down at her face more directly. Silver's breathing remained even and her lip clean.

Andrew jerked and started to slide out of the chair. Everyone started forward to catch him. Susan was too slow and Felicia encumbered, but even John failed because none of Andrew's limbs were the same shape anymore as he twisted awkwardly into wolf form. John hissed a curse under his breath and let Andrew hit the floor so he could help with tearing his clothes where necessary.

Everyone was bunched around Andrew, and no one was looking at Tatiana, or the doorway. Here was her best chance.

Tatiana balanced her weight, and pushed up. Up, and running—or stumbling, rather—out of the room and they were all slow to look over when they'd assumed she couldn't even walk. She wasn't even sure she could. Her motion seemed more like pure luck of momentum and controlled falling.

Out to the hall and to the bowl where she'd seen Tom drop the keys when they'd arrived from the airport. Tatiana grabbed the top two sets and stumbled to the front door, leaning one hand against the frame as she opened it. Angry voices chased her, Felicia's most strident, but John's holding a deeper growl. Were they following yet? They'd have to put Silver down, avoid stumbling over Andrew. Tatiana couldn't afford to let the scuffle of footsteps resolve itself from under the voices.

Through the door and she mashed buttons on both key fobs at random. A silvery car near the end of the curved driveway flashed at her, while other honks came from inside the garage. Tatiana dropped the useless keys on the concrete and stumbled her way to the car. It purred into instant life when she started it, nothing like some of the ancient vehicles they maintained at home.

She peeled out of the driveway, leaving a tire track over one landscaped border. She clenched her hands on the wheel to pretend they were steady. That worked for a few blocks, a few more, but then her vision started to blur.

Tatiana squinted and clenched her hands harder. She wasn't standing. She couldn't fall even if she were feeling dizzy.

ner.

She took the first turn into a parking lot. She needed to park somewhere she couldn't be seen from the road and pull herself together. The lot seemed to go on and on, rectangular sections in front of stores chaining ever outward until she realized that the mall must be built in a rough hollow circle, with some kind of courtyard or park in the center, and lots in a larger circle around it. Tall evergreens around the edges helped to make the mall feel isolated and cloaked it in greater darkness that the streetlights couldn't dispel.

Tatiana picked a spot near an alley between two huge stores, where she hoped no one much would be walking, and pulled in. She was probably straddling two spots, and her training shouted at her to pull out and correct to look less conspicuous, but dizziness made it all she could do to shut off the car by feel as she closed her eyes to hold off the feeling of falling.

She could keep driving after she rested for a little while. Just a little while.

* * *

Susan winced at the clonk Silver's head made when Felicia dumped her on the table to dash after the Russian. She didn't even try to follow. Except for instinctive lunges as with Andrew a minute earlier, she didn't bother pitting her speed or reactions against werewolves'. She could make sure Silver didn't slide off the table, though. She caught her husband's sleeve as he, having at least managed not to step on Andrew, tried to get by. "Were you planning to just leave them here, unconscious?" God knew—Lady knew, as they'd say—they didn't need a whole procession of people chasing one escapee who seemed like she might already have gotten away, if the sound of squealing tires was any indication.

Felicia reappeared from the front hall before John could reply. "She got one of the cars. We have to—"

Susan settled Silver's head at a better angle, titled back slightly like they taught for an open airway in first aid. "We have to take care of the alphas, Felicia." She used the best beta tone she had, quiet but firm.

"She's right." John's voice strengthened with an alpha's authority, following Susan's lead. Good. When Felicia opened her mouth, he glared her down. "What are you going to do, enact some car chase like in the movies? I'll call the doctor, we'll get them comfortable, and then we can see about tracking her."

John got out his phone, and some of Felicia's anger slipped away into anxiety as he spoke calmly. She gathered Silver back up into her arms, with extra tenderness as if to apologize for dropping her earlier.

John gave the doctor no details, just asked her to get there as soon as possible. Susan wasn't really sure what good the Were doctor would do. They were skilled at digging out bullets, rebreaking bones that had healed wrong, and helping women through childbirth, but Susan doubted they knew any

John slipped his phone away and knelt over Andrew, limply sleeping in wolf form, to carefully work the fabric of his torn clothing out from underneath him.

"So he shifted in his dream?" Felicia sounded merely curious for a moment, then she gasped and clutched Silver closer. "Silver *can't* shift. What if she tries? What if she's still whole in the dream and she tries to shift?"

Susan drew breath automatically for a reassurance, but she didn't have one to give. The worst seizures had apparently happened before she knew Silver, but she'd seen Silver walk the edge of pretty bad ones when she forgot and got too close to shifting during the full moon. "She always stops them by ceasing to try to shift," she said, and wished she hadn't said it out loud. If Silver didn't know to stop in the dream . . .

John nodded, expression bleak. He had been absently smoothing the fur along Andrew's flank, and he stopped abruptly. "He's burning up."

Susan felt in the fur of Andrew's ruff, then drew her hand back as he shifted again. In human form, his skin's flush was clear. She found his pulse. It pounded, but slowing now, faltering. Like watching marathon runners on TV, still yards from the finish line as their legs gave out beneath them.

"She said he was fighting . . ." Susan held up a preemptory hand when it sounded like Felicia would break in and disrupt her train of thought while it was still fragile. "Assume she wasn't lying. He can't think he's dead or something, or his heart would have stopped like hers. If he's not dead, maybe he's *dying*, only you guys would be healing—" Susan looked up, letting the logic connect itself almost on its own. "What if he's healing in the dream, only there's nothing to heal in reality, so it becomes a fever?"

"If he was healing, he'd need food, so if he's spending all that energy in a fever . . ." Felicia's eyes widened.

Susan bolted for the kitchen. The others might normally have been faster, but she was closest. "The nutrition shakes are in the cupboard over the fridge, aren't they?" she called, but she'd already found them there. She gathered up four bottles, clutched between two hands, and hurried back.

John supported Andrew upright, and Susan tilted his head back and poured the protein drink. He swallowed automatically, even dreaming. Felicia came to watch, Silver still unnoticed in her arms, as if she could urge her father to health by sheer strength of will.

Susan counted, without quite being sure what she was counting. Breaths, perhaps? She couldn't take his pulse and pour at the same time. More than anything, she supposed she was counting seconds that Andrew didn't get any worse. Slowly, his flush faded. When the last bottle was empty, Susan sat back while John took his pulse. When his expression turned to relief, she let out a breath she'd been holding.

Someone gasped in the doorway and Susan turned quickly. "I'm sorry. I think I left my phone over here— What

"Poison," John said, short, as he picked up Andrew. "Sacramento, this needs to stay quiet. Swear on the Lady that you will tell absolutely no one."

Sacramento growled softly, as if in automatic reaction to being asked to promise explicitly, but she cut off the sound quickly. "I swear." Her tone sounded worried, not insulted. She pressed her thumb to her forehead. "Can I help?"

John tipped his head toward the hall. "We can talk upstairs," he said. He and Felicia carried the alphas up to the master bedroom, Susan and Sacramento trailing along behind. Susan didn't know about Sacramento, but she felt pretty frustrated and useless herself, with no one to carry. She used the time to fill Sacramento in on what they knew, which only served to highlight how little that was. Susan wished they'd had more time to question Tatiana.

John and Felicia both set their burdens down on their bed carefully, but Felicia fussed with getting the covers over them and then lingered to brush a couple errant stands of hair out of Silver's face. John straightened and turned to face Sacramento, and Susan could see the pressure of needing to arrange too many things at once crowding into his expression. Much as she really did love him, his strength lay in organizing things once the steps of a plan were already laid out.

"Someone needs to go after the envoy," Susan said, taking a deep breath and channeling Silver's tone. "But I think John's right that we want as few people as possible to know what's going on."

"I'll go." The rage Susan had hoped might be easing off went from zero to sixty in half a second in Felicia's tone. She put her head down and strode for the door.

Sacramento stepped to block her way. "And by 'go after,' you mean 'bring down with your teeth in her neck'? How's that going to play with the Russians? 'Oh, sorry, we killed your alpha's daughter.'"

"After she poisoned our alphas!" Felicia spat the words in Sacramento's face, but the older woman didn't flinch.

"We should bring her back alive," Sacramento said, and they both turned simultaneously to look at John. Out of sight, Susan allowed herself to bite her lip. Dammit, he was the beta, now interim alpha, and she couldn't help him with his decision in front of the others.

A muscle jumped in John's jaw, then he gestured to the door. "Both of you, go. If we can't get everyone on it, better to have two trackers rather than one."

Susan swallowed a noise of wordless frustration. Deciding not to decide. Nice one, John. She didn't know what he'd intended, but the implication she read was that whoever got there first could kill or capture the envoy according to her individual preference.

Felicia was gone instantly, running downstairs and out, but Susan managed to catch Sacramento's arm before she made it out of the bedroom. "She's going to track by scent, I presume?

flicked a look at the ceiling for a second as she mentally rifled through the house's various junk drawers. "The lap drawer in the desk in the office. It has all the spare keys and fobs. I don't think their range is great, but even if her scent's shut in the car, you can make it honk. Retrace the route they used to bring her home from the airport." She twisted to look at John, who described the route without argument.

That seemed to engage John's brain as well, as he nodded decisively. "I'll get Pierce to go straight to the airport by another route and stake it out. Won't have to tell him what the envoy's done, just that we don't want her getting away."

Sacramento flashed Susan a wan smile, then pulled free and took off at near Felicia's speed, downstairs to get the key. John thumped down the stairs a moment later, off to find Pierce.

Susan went to the end of the bed. The alphas looked like they were sleeping peacefully, though Silver being fully clothed under the blankets sounded a false note. Relaxing before sitting up and getting back to the stressful business of running a pack, perhaps. The room had always felt calm to Susan, without the clutter of the one she shared with John. Without much in the way of furnishings, really. Their large headboard stood out, carved in smooth lines, along with a series of black and white photos of stars over a backwoods lake in different seasons on the wall across from the French doors. They were what dominated the feeling of the room, especially when it was sunny—light flooded through them and the surrounding windows, inviting one out onto the balcony.

But it was night now, and the alphas were not-sleeping. To wake in the morning, if Tatiana was to be believed. John's footsteps approached behind her, and Susan stepped away when he would have pulled her against his chest. "The time to pull Felicia up short is when she first starts her temper tantrum, not later when she's turned it into a personal mission. You know that. What happens if we kill the daughter of another alpha? War?"

"Susan." John drew the name out, coaxing. "She won't kill the envoy, when it comes down to it."

"We'll have to hope so." Susan turned away from the bed and allowed him to embrace her this time. "She can't have gotten far. She was awfully weak."

"And the alphas might be awake by the time she's found, so they can deal with her." John's voice rumbled against her shoulder. She wasn't a Were to smell his mood, but using human intuition, she doubted he quite believed that either.

11

Selene ran until her legs ached, until her chest ached, until she could hardly breathe, but she didn't wake up. The dream world stayed as it was. Her arms worked, and she saw all the things of this world, and none of her own. No wild selves, no Death, only old barbed wire and crumpled beer cans.

When she had no choice but to rest, she found a seat at the base of a red cedar, back against the long lines of bark. If physical exertion could not break her from the dream, it might be that the path out lay in her own mind. As her breathing slowed, Selene sought a different set of sensations, a connection with her sleeping self. Wind slipped through the cedar's needles and her hair, scents of this place twisting with it, and her ass went numb. She found nothing beneath what surrounded her.

Eventually, she stood and followed her trail back. To hide

from this dream world longer would be juvenile self-indulgence.

As she approached the farmhouse, she smelled and heard a girl among the trees. The smell was familiar somehow, but Selene couldn't place it. She detoured slightly and found a large ring formed of branches. Ginnie sat on a fallen tree beside the ring, gnarled bark and moss cleared away down to wood to give her a smooth seat. Selene recognized her scent now. Rory's daughter, whose mother had taken her to be with her exiled father, the former Roanoke, in the real world. Selene supposed with all the upheaval in this dream, it would make sense for Ginnie to be here with the rest of the remaining Were.

The girl was stripping twigs from a large branch, then snapping it into lengths small enough to follow the curve when laid out. Her brown hair was long and lank, hanging around her face, obscuring her delicate features. Like everything in this dream world, she was wrong somehow, but beyond the neglect of her hair, Selene couldn't see how with her face hidden that way. "Ginnie?"

The girl's head snapped up. She should be about fourteen, but she looked simultaneously older and younger. The tight way she sat made her body look smaller, more like she was twelve or thirteen, but her eyes were ancient. She looked Selene over, seemed to dismiss her, and went back to her branch snapping.

"What are you making?" Selene bent and nudged a twig into a more circular alignment. The look Ginnie gave her this time was withering, and she remained silent.

Something was seriously wrong here. Selene didn't know

what, but she knew her protective instincts were screaming at her. She could at least take Ginnie back to the house and get her something to eat. She looked far too thin. "Are you hun-

onus. She hadn't felt were-speed healing for so long, she registered the unfamiliar rush of departing pain almost as euphoria. "I won't touch you, I swear on the Lady. But will you come with me and have something to eat?"

Ginnie assessed her with that old gaze for several moments, then nodded. She waited for Selene to go first and get a good distance ahead down the bumpy dirt of the trail before she followed. Selene would have guided her to the farmhouse, but the smell of food drifted from where the tent was set up out of sight and earshot of the house. Wouldn't want the delegates to see the real dingy living conditions. Probably wouldn't want them to see Ginnie in her current state either, but Selene cared less about that than she did about Ginnie not having to deal with the strangers. In the end, Selene didn't want the girl to feel forced in any direction, so she paused and followed when Ginnie turned off toward the food smells.

Ginnie got hung up on the edge of the trees surrounding the field where the tent was set up. Selene continued and Ares strode to meet her, anger written clearly on his face. When he spotted Ginnie, he unbent a little. "Oh, good, you found her. I

guess you were right that she'd be back when she got hungry."
He raised his voice to address Ginnie directly. "Help yourself,
puppy." He held an arm open to indicate the table where Andrew and his wife were already seated. Selene avoided looking
at any of Madrid party directly.

Ginnie eyed both her and Ares suspiciously, then jogged
for the table. She picked things off of platters with her fingers
and stuffed them into her mouth. Selene wondered how long
she'd been out in the woods alone. A day? More? In the world
of the dream, it seemed everyone—even her—expected that,
which was quietly horrifying in its own way.

Ares followed not far behind, and coughed apologetically.
"Forgive her manners. Ginnie runs off so often, we need to feed
her when we can."

Ginnie snorted, grabbed a last bread roll, and danced back
to eat it out of reach of anyone around the table. Andrew's eyebrows rose. "What happened to her?"

Selene watched Ginnie eat, trying to make sure she didn't
look like she was listening too hard. She wanted that information desperately herself.

"It's part of what brought us here today." Ares paced a couple steps, then returned exactly to his original position, awkwardness showing through in the fidgeting. "You know how
the pack wars began in the Eastern packs that had once been
united as Roanoke? Well, she belonged to the pack that began
it all, the only one we know for sure died by silver at the hands
of the Tainted One."

Andrew raised his eyebrows. "The only one? I thought the
Tainted One was responsible for the deaths of a dozen packs."

Ares rocked onto his toes with another aborted round of pacing. "We don't know. He was undoubtedly responsible for any number of deaths hidden among the rest, but with every-

much more than that. If Roanoke had been divided, individual packs once more, she could all too easily see how lack of communication could lead to paranoia, given the right push. And Stefan would have given it that push. Say to the pack in the north, the southern Were killed them, they'll kill you next. Say to the pack in the south, the northern Were killed them, and now they're coming for you. Say to both packs, strike first. And in the chaos, he'd have every victim he ever wanted for himself and all the time he wanted with them.

Andrew looked grim. "I think I remember now. Rory had a daughter named Virginia, didn't he?"

Ares dipped his head in a reluctant nod, as if denying the connection could deny the whole chain of events. "As far as we can tell, the Tainted One saved her when he killed the rest and treated her as if she was his own daughter. Took her with him as he traveled, had her watch him work—"

Selene knew what Stefan had done to her and her pack, but in this dream, she could not find the memories. She remembered having them, and she remembered what was in them, but she could not find the emotions, the feeling of being there. Perhaps that was a kindness. Even the abstract knowledge burned, knowledge of how Stefan had bound them with silver, injected them with silver, and tortured them with silver as they died. He tortured them because he was so angry, because the injection didn't work. It didn't cleanse them of their wolf form; it only killed them.

Except for Stefan. And for Silver.

"We found her hiding under the bed in the hotel room where we finally tracked down the Tainted One and executed him. She won't speak, won't let anyone touch her. And she won't shift. She's past her Lady Ceremony, you can smell it on her that she's mature enough to shift, but she won't. She just suffers through every full. At this point, she won't even stay in the house. We have to tempt her in every so often for clean clothes and food."

Selene retched. Her muscles contracted so violently she braced herself with a hand on the corner of the picnic table as Andrew and his family stared at her. "Poor thing," Isabel said, and Andrew murmured agreement, but Selene could tell they didn't understand. Not like she did. She'd known Stefan, when he was charming his way into her pack, heard his ranting when he stood over the bodies of Ares and the others as the silver burned in her blood.

"Why did he save her?" Andrew asked, politely ignoring Selene's reaction.

Ares frowned, probably wondering why Selene was reacting this way now, when she had to have already known about Ginnie, but Andrew's question pulled his attention away. "We don't know. She's the only one who could tell us."

"He was lonely." Selene couldn't stop the words. She wanted to force the others to share the understanding that twisted up her stomach. She wanted the understanding to steal their voices too. "That's why he kept trying. He didn't want to kill anyone really, he wanted someone to survive the cure. When someone survived—" She swallowed acid, caught herself. "If

the only way to stay safe was to be still a child, still unable to shift. Because then he'd keep putting it off, let them continue as they were."

Ares pulled her away from the table, turned her toward him, fingers tight on her upper arms. He leaned close and lowered his voice, scent sliding from shock to frustration with her. "Selene, what are you doing? Don't talk like that in front of her."

Selene looked past him, to Ginnie. She had tipped her chin up, so her hair fell back from her face a little. She stared at Selene with wide, startled eyes. Ares followed Selene's gaze just in time to see Ginnie nod, once.

Selene jerked away from her brother and picked up another roll. She didn't offer Ginnie platitudes, just the bread in an outstretched hand. Ginnie's eyes darted from the bread to her face, and then she stepped forward.

When she took the bread, her fingers touched Selene's. Then she ran, back into the trees once more. Selene gritted her teeth against any more rebellion from her stomach. This dream Ginnie wasn't real, but oh, Selene bled inside to see her.

Andrew made it back to human a final time, and energy rushed back into him. He was wary of it, given how he'd been feeling just a moment before, but he made it to his knees and collected his clothes. He pressed them against his chest as he got careful-ly to his feet. Time to eat something. Past time.

Benjamin strode up as Andrew approached his cabin and opened the door for him in dangerous silence. Andrew tried not to think about how he didn't remember seeing Benjamin this angry before in his life. It wasn't the strength of the anger that worried him; it was the fact that it was banked so deep in his mentor's expression, suggesting it had had a long time to grow.

"Let me eat first, please." Andrew dropped his clothes on the rickety kitchen table and jerked the fridge open. Not much food there, unfortunately, since meals at the Convocations were catered for everyone at the main hall. He found a package of hot dogs, though, and devoured all of them cold.

Benjamin watched him, arms folded, for a while, then lift-ed Andrew's shirt from the table and checked it for stretched or popped seams. It must have passed muster, because when An-drew dumped the empty package in the trash, Benjamin held the shirt out to him.

Andrew considered dawdling over pulling on his clothes, but he did it quickly in the end. No point putting off the chew-ing out he was in for. He did hesitate once, on pulling up his jeans. The skin across the small of his back was still smooth. "Look, Boston. I suspect you're going to say that I know better than to handle Rory that way, but I *don't*. I'm missing mem-

up is your life when a concussion makes you imagine yourself alpha of the world?" He forced a laugh. And how fucked up was *he* when he missed someone in that dream so much it hurt? "That's all I've got."

"You truly don't remember the last five years?" Benjamin bent over him and ran gentle but firm fingers over the back of his head. Nothing hurt, and Benjamin grimaced like he hadn't felt anything either. "To state the obvious, that's not good."

"Maybe things will come back, with time. But right now, frankly, I don't see how I didn't consider this situation untenable. Someone needs to get Rory out of power immediately, if this is the low he's sunk to." Andrew spoke without thinking, but as he said it, his thoughts finally dropped into alignment. Maybe that was what his unconscious had been trying to tell him with the dreams: he needed to do something about Rory. The glimpse of a goal, a *direction,* cracked some of the congealed pain from around Andrew's voice.

He pushed to his feet and started pacing. The cabin didn't offer much scope for it, but at least it had a path across the kitchen and living area to the fireplace and back. He ignored Benjamin, too caught up in following his own train of logic. "That someone challenging him can't be me, though. I never could match Rory in pure strength. I could gather support, like I did last time—like I dreamed—but all the support in the world won't help in a fight when he knows my moves as well as he clearly does."

Andrew frowned in the direction of the other cabins, though the window ahead of him showed only a scrap of gravel road and some bushes. Alphas might have changed since five years ago, but not that much. What about Rory's beta? In Andrew's last real memories, that had been Laurence. "I wonder if—no, I doubt Laurence could best him on pure strength either, even if he did have the personality for it."

Benjamin rested a hand on the back of one of the kitchen chairs, expression growing more unreadable by the second. Andrew drew a deep breath and found surprise in his scent. "Laurence left for the Alaska pack three years ago."

Andrew barked a laugh. "No wonder Rory's beating me up, then. Got no one else to take it out on. Can't say I blame Laurence, if Rory was acting like that." Andrew started running through his sub-alphas in his mind. Maybe he wasn't actually Roanoke, but the habit of organizing his thoughts that way wouldn't die so easily. Several would jump at the opportunity to gain that kind of power, but they were precisely the ones he didn't want within howling distance of it.

He snapped his fingers. "John. He's close enough to Rory physically it might work, and since he's not Seattle anymore, he might welcome the opportunity to regain authority. He's a better beta than alpha long-term, but getting Rory out is what matters at the moment. We can deal with long-term when it arrives."

tion. Who are you, and what have you done with Dale?

"I don't know who I am anymore." Andrew ran his fingers through his hair—all dark? He still needed to check that in the mirror—and growled. "And maybe it sounds crazy, but I'm not going to just sit back and take Rory's bullshit." If nothing else made sense, at least this was something to *do,* some forward momentum.

Benjamin embraced him, and Andrew staggered a little, caught completely off-guard by the gesture. "I'll tell you who you are," Benjamin said, intensely. "You seem to be climbing back to being a man I once knew, before that man let himself be changed by grief into someone else entirely." Benjamin pulled back and caught Andrew's eyes, pulling them both into a measuring of dominance.

Again, the Roanoke in him bubbled up before Andrew could stop it. Benjamin was a powerful old man, and due great respect for it, but Andrew was the one who held the authority. Maybe it had only been in a dream, but Andrew and his mate had united all of North American and *held* it. That mate, that world, didn't exist, but the confidence and dominance it had created in him lingered.

Benjamin dropped his eyes first, and his scent filled with satisfaction as he stepped back to consider Andrew more broadly. "John isn't the man he was five years ago, but until this morning, you weren't either. If anyone can call that man out of him, maybe it would be you."

Andrew nodded, and purpose settled into him, lending him energy. The plan would have to change as he found out more of the situation, but that was the nature of plans. He strode to the cabin door and opened it before the relief at finally having a direction gave way to logic. He should find out about how people expected him to act before he ran into more trouble like he had with Ares.

He turned around in the doorway, resting the side of his fist against the frame. "What have I been like, the past five years?"

Benjamin's lips curved in a thin, sad smile. "You've been Roanoke's enforcer. And essentially his beta, once Laurence left. You've been lonely and angry, lately just angry, like you hate your situation so much you'd like to destroy it. You've been working quite hard at destroying it, in various ways." His eyes searched Andrew's face. "What did you dream?"

Andrew summoned Silver to his mind's eye—her white hair; her tantalizing body; her gaze, simultaneously sharp and vague as she looked past the world to what was really important. "I dreamed someone who made me want to *change* my situation."

And now she was gone. Worse. Never had been.

Andrew shoved the thoughts of Silver away, nodded a

farewell to Benjamin, and pushed off the doorframe and out of the cabin. Forward, he was moving forward, not getting caught in his dreams.

with a reminder of what he'd dreamed. He fed it and cupped it close, letting the resentment strengthen him. He didn't want Selene because she was a taunt, a trick. He'd conduct his business with her and nothing more.

She must have seen his glance behind her into the living room, because she snorted. "Seattle's not in. What do you want?"

"To talk to John." Andrew stepped back from the cabin, an invitation to what was essentially neutral territory. The formality helped him keep his mind on track. A little. Selene looked him over with narrowed eyes for a few seconds, then joined him, closing the door with a precise click behind her.

She crossed her arms. "Why?"

Andrew held his hands wide while his mind scrambled, trying to read Selene. He knew exactly how he'd try to convince Silver of something, but Selene wasn't Silver. Would the same strategies work? He supposed as long as he didn't have a better idea, he might as well appeal to her protectiveness of her pack members, and see what happened. "I could use his help with something. Unless he's totally happy as he is in your pack now, showing his belly where once he was alpha. Forgive my memory problems, but what rank is he now, anyway?"

Selene's lips thinned. "My cousin chose to stay in the pack. There is no resentment." After a beat where it seemed like that might be all Andrew would get, she let her arms drop. "He's not happy. We stretched a point to bring him here as a single so that he wouldn't be left alone." She shrugged—with both shoulders, which looked wrong to Andrew after knowing Silver for so long. "Something to do would be good for him, but how do I know that you're not looking to bully him into it?"

"You're welcome to chaperone." Andrew tried to match the nonchalance of her shrug, though he was nowhere near that sanguine. She was welcome to listen in if she didn't go running to Rory to tattle about his plans. There was no love lost between the Western packs and Roanoke as Andrew remembered it, but each person who knew still added risk. He moved closer to Selene, lowering his voice. "If you'll give me your word to keep what I say in confidence."

She laughed, scent gaining a note of surprise. Andrew suspected he'd be smelling that a lot for a while. "You're getting twisty, Enforcer. What's happened?"

"I—" Andrew didn't get a chance to explain, because he heard Rory's voice as he left the Roanoke cabin. He stepped quickly back from Selene, but of course that only made him look guiltier.

Rory's mood didn't seem to have particularly improved, either. He jogged over to them, snarl already curling his lips. "Plotting, Dare?"

"Just talking to Selene," Andrew said. A crazy idea occurred to him, crazy and sure to tear his voice into shreds with
pain, but he didn't have time to find anything better, dam-

⋯⋯ ⋯⋯ ⋯⋯ ⋯⋯ ⋯⋯ ⋯⋯ ⋯⋯ ⋯⋯ been
right to stop himself.

Selene remained mostly unresponsive from shock, but she
didn't remember to push him away for several beats. When she
did, her growl held laughter.

That made it all worse. Andrew could see the trail stretching out in front of him. She was attracted. He could flirt with
her, nurture that attraction, court her until he'd tied himself
to her and the thoughts of Silver she evoked so tightly they
formed a weight and he set himself to drown, held under by it.

No. Andrew couldn't bear those thoughts. It was just too
damn painful. Every moment would stab him with a reminder
of what he'd thought he had. No Selene, no other woman. He'd
concentrate on deposing Rory. After that, he could reach out to
his daughter again. At least she was real.

Rory's laugh now was louder and more mocking than Selene's had been. "If you're sniffing down that trail, watch out for
the brother, Dare," he said, and clapped him on the shoulder.
"Hurry up, or you'll miss the morning session." He headed off
for the main hall where the Convocation sessions were held.

Selene crossed her arms again, whatever laughter Andrew had imagined fading, and waited until Rory was out of earshot. "Never mind Ares; *I* will beat you."

Andrew smiled thinly at the ground. "I know. But not as hard as him." He tipped his head to his alpha. He'd meant the comment to sound like a joke, but it just came out sounding tired. He had a hard trail ahead of him. But it was true—he'd rather Selene's rage than Rory's any day.

Selene stared at him for several long moments. "You're serious."

"As a rifle shot." Andrew lifted his head. "*Someone* needs to do something about Rory. I think John can help me do it." He gestured widely after Rory. "And if you want to tell him I'm plotting, go and get it over with now."

Selene shook her head, hesitated, then sighed. "Tonight. I'll bring John by." She held up a forestalling hand. "But only if he agrees to it. I'm not going to order him to come. It'll be his decision."

"That's fair." Andrew bowed to her, which made her smile. The smile almost reminded him of something, but he pushed away the memory rather than letting it reach his conscious mind. Selene seemed happy in the real world. Maybe happier than Silver, in some ways. She was whole in body, untroubled in mind, and definitely better off without Andrew sniffing around her. Yet another reason to leave her alone—not for himself, but for *her*, and her life without getting dragged into all his fights and mess.

Andrew strode off for the hall. He'd best go and pay sharp attention at the Convocation session to try desperately to catch up on more of the things he didn't remember.

12

The honk from her own car startled Tatiana so badly that her hand spasmed where she'd left it on the keys in the ignition. The keys rattled and dropped free, down somewhere under the seat. Tatiana groped after them, fingertips encountering only the fuzz of carpet and metal of the seat's tracks. What had set off the horn? She hadn't been anywhere near it, even if she probably had passed out or nodded off or whatever had caused the fog in her head.

The horn honked again and the lights strobed the concrete wall of the store ahead. It was acting like someone had pressed the wrong button on its fob, but the fob was under the seat with nothing to push it—

Tatiana checked the rearview mirror. Headlights swept purposefully over the parking lot toward her. The North Americans must have a spare fob. And they were using it to find her. She scrabbled under the seat again, but she still couldn't feel the keys. She had to drive away, drive quickly, or they'd catch her—Lady damn those keys!

Tatiana jerked the door open. The North Americans weren't here yet; she could still run, cut through the wooded dip probably hiding a stream behind the store. Her legs wavered, tried to tip her down. Maybe she should have stayed in the car—but with the spare key, the North Americans could have unlocked it before she had time to find the keys.

Tatiana made it as far as the curb where the parking lot ended at the trees before the car slammed to a stop beside her stolen one. Only one person got out. Blond, lean, and angular. Sacramento. Tatiana mentally kicked herself back into motion again. It didn't matter who was chasing her. She couldn't stop to gawk.

She should have been using that time to look over the terrain, as it turned out. Tatiana got two steps before her foot punched precipitously down through the blackberry leaves instead of stopping on level ground beneath. She slid on her ass down into the brambles, only a few feet, but her legs got well tangled. Thorns, foiled by the denim of her jeans, quested for blood around her ankles and at the small of her back where her shirt had been pushed up.

Tatiana thrashed free, back onto level ground beside the pavement, just in time to stand nose to nose with Sacramento. She kicked to take the other's woman's legs out from under her automatically, but her muscles moved with excruciatingly slowness, and Sacramento dodged easily.

"No one's going to execute you," Sacramento said, hands spread calmingly. "We just need you to come back to the pack house. You don't look exactly healthy yourself. You need to ....."

.... Tatiana felt Sacramento's approach a split second before the woman slammed into her, carrying her to the ground. Heart thudding each beat of her desperation, Tatiana told her body to squirm, to roll to get Sacramento down into the dirt under her . . .

Tatiana straightened from sitting on the edge of her mother's bed and smoothed the quilt where she'd creased it. The tiny space, hardly big enough for the dresser, bed, and chair, smelled musty like the occupant had been absent for a few weeks. But this was more her memory of the place than anything, Tatiana decided. She'd spent as many nights here with her mother as she had in the nursery, growing up. She touched the nose of her stuffed puppy flopped over the top corner of the dresser, then traced the carvings. Circle around that full moon, run down that curled vine, end at the bottom drawer. Pull it out, reach under her mother's formal dresses, not often used, and touch the smooth slippery slide of the long, coiled braid, cut off when she left the priesthood. She didn't lift the fabric enough to see it, but she knew it was the same golden shade as her own. Her mother would have laughed at her, threatened again to burn it as other former priestesses did, but Tatiana had always felt it would grant her luck.

"When you were a child, I thought you might join the priesthood someday." Tatiana's mother came up behind her and threaded a hand under her hair to expertly ease a tight knot in the muscles along one shoulder. "You were so very serious."

"So I joined the Jaw instead," Tatiana said lightly. She'd never known what her mother thought of the Jaw, but she'd never questioned her daughter's choice.

"But they were *too* serious for you." Her mother kissed the top of her head. "You may have gone too far, puppy. I'd help you if I could." She'd never been so explicit before, but Tatiana had heard the offer dozens of times, hidden inside "Come by and visit, after your next mission" and "At least stay for the meal, I cooked too much to eat alone."

Unease shivered along Tatiana's spine. She shut the drawer quickly. By the time she straightened and turned around, she was alone in the room. This was a vision. That's why her mother was saying things she'd never said out loud before.

The priestesses always advised you not to try too hard to remember what had happened immediately before you entered a vision, but Tatiana knew from the way her muscles tingled from tightness that didn't exist here that something was wrong. She strode for the door. "Mother?"

A human stepped into the doorway. Skinny, points of bone at wrist and shoulder and cheek standing out so sharp.

She clutched a bundle, knitted stitches of the baby blanket pulling wide where her fingers stretched it too much. She held it carefully like it covered something, but the bundle was too

— — — .... you. ....,
and tossed the blanket aside. Swathed inside was a knife, and she took a firm grip like an experienced fighter. "That's not true, you know." She advanced on Tatiana, and Tatiana's mind crowded with all the moves to knock the weapon from the young woman's hand, take her down.

But Tatiana couldn't move. Did she deserve this? The human came closer, backed her against the bed, laid her flat with a bony hand against her shoulder, and straddled her hips.

"You just—" The human set the tip of her knife against the underside of Tatiana's jaw, urging her head back, back. It pierced. Tatiana felt just a drop of blood roll over her skin. "Have to know how it's *done.*" The human laughed, a shrill and glittering sound, and leaned her weight on her free hand, pressing down on Tatiana's chest. Her heart labored, slower—

"*No!*" Tatiana's eyes snapped open. Blackberry vines. She was lying on her stomach, looking at the underbrush at the mall. Her heartbeat wasn't slow; it was fast. Too fast. Too fearful.

Sacramento's knee was on her back, but lightly, and it lifted when she spoke. Tatiana knew she should use this opportunity to run again, but all the strength had left her for the moment. Lady. She'd had a vision without wolfsbane. Visions without wolfsbane didn't happen to anyone except the priestesses who'd been having regular visions for a *century* or more. She couldn't be having them.

But why couldn't she? She'd never heard of another Were who'd been brought back from the edge of death from wolfsbane. What if her death had simply been delayed? What if she continued to have visions until her heart stopped without the human there to start it again? Tatiana curled up on her side, muscles almost seizing with the visceral denial and fear of it. No!

"I swear I felt your heart slowing," Sacramento said, sounding pretty worried herself. Tatiana exhaled on a dark laugh. Worried about not having a prize to return with.

That thought got her out of her own head, though. With each succeeding breath, a little calm and sense seeped back into Tatiana. She was having aftereffects, yes. But aftereffects of an injury grew weaker as one healed. She didn't know if wolfsbane worked that way, but Lady, she was going to *believe* it did with every tone of her voice. Once she got away, she'd rest and the visions would fade.

Sacramento reached out for her again, and Tatiana got her hands under her. She wouldn't lie here and wait to be dragged back, even if it did provoke another vision.

Sacramento settled back hurriedly. "No, wait. I'm not going to take you back if chasing you makes you kill yourself try-

ing to get away." Silence stretched between them, and Tatiana
started to believe maybe she was telling the truth. She doubted the woman was going to let her just get up and walk away,

or her pulse behind her eyes. Sacra-
mento seemed to be telling the truth, still smelling of that worry about her prize, rather than the smug notes of deception.

"All right," she agreed. She'd be a fool not to accept—a hotel room with Sacramento wasn't freedom, but escaping from a
room under a single person's watch was much easier than from
a cage in a pack house full of North Americans.

She accepted Sacramento's tug to her feet, allowed an arm
around her waist, like they were drunk humans on their way
home. Sacramento guided her to the back seat of the car she'd
arrived in, and beeped the other locked a final time. Tatiana
thought about how she should probably run for it as Sacramento climbed into the driver's seat. She didn't move. That was
something that could wait for tomorrow morning.

Sacramento fussed with buttons on the door and then
pulled out her phone. Tatiana listened to half the conversation
with less than half of her attention. She heard the female voice
on the other end, but the poor quality of the sound transmitted
through the phone was too much for her English skills. "Susan? I've got her, she's secure, but I don't think she'll make it

back to the house. She nearly killed herself trying to get away. Literally. How are you supposed to treat a human after CPR?"

A pause, a low embarrassed laugh. "But you're *good* at explaining things to your husband. My word on the Lady, she's not going anywhere. We'll crash at a hotel and be there in the morning."

Sacramento ended the call too quickly, clearly avoiding pointed questions, and started the car in silence. For all her nonchalance in the call, she forgot to turn on the headlights until they were at the turn out of the parking lot and the trickle of other lights slid past them. Easy enough to do as a Were, when you could see fine without, but Sacramento struck Tatiana as someone who usually moved comfortably within the necessary set of human habits.

"So wolfsbane really is poisonous to us?" she said at length, looking straight ahead at the road.

"Not poisonous." Tatiana was tired enough that the word she wanted eluded her, and she didn't bother groping for it for very long. "It . . . has effects. We use it in our ceremonies." She supposed she didn't have such a pressing need to earn sympathy with information now, but she could see no reason to withhold it either. If—when—she escaped, Sacramento would hopefully take the information back to her packmates and reassure them a little.

"Wolfsbane—" Tatiana gestured near her temple. "Frees the mind. Takes you closer to the Lady. In small doses, it gives inspiration. The Wisdom Ceremony. In larger doses, it allows the Lady to give you visions."

"And if you overdose, it kills you?" Sacramento flicked a

glance to her in the rearview mirror, probably thinking of her faltering heart.

"Apparently." Tatiana couldn't stop her voice from getting

~~/   ~~~/ ~~~~~ ~~~~. ~~~y ~~ ~~~~~~g ~~~~~~~, ~~~~~ ~~~~~y clear."

Sacramento turned off the straight line of road that unfolded the lights before them, presumably getting close to the hotel she'd chosen now. "How long do visions last?"

Tatiana shrugged. "A few hours, usually. It depends less on the dose, and more on how much the vision needs to convey."

Sacramento snorted like she was suppressing a comment on how helpful that wasn't. "Can you kind of . . . wake yourself from it? Or do you even know it's a vision?"

"Sometimes it feels completely real; sometimes things seem a little off . . ." Tatiana let her words fade away as a realization seized her. Whether anyone at home knew consciously that they were having a vision when in the midst of it, they went in expecting to have one, expecting it to end. What about the Roanokes? They'd just been drinking wine.

"What do you think they're dreaming about?" Sacramento's voice broke into her thoughts.

The unexpectedness of the question threw Tatiana off balance, and then the silence was stretching uncomfortably, so she didn't have time to make up something pretty. "We were talking about the past when we were drinking. Wolfsbane often likes to dig up ancient history, like you didn't learn from it properly the first time." She shrugged.

"They do have plenty of past to choose from," Sacramento said, with a huff of dry laughter. They'd reached a building and she pulled under the arch over the doors into hotel reception. It was a nice enough place, not a roadside motel, but Tatiana didn't bother squinting at what chain-related color of window trim and roof tile it embellished its beige stucco with.

Sacramento glanced back at Tatiana, who did her best to return a bored gaze, and then climbed out and strode quickly in. A breath, two, and Tatiana finally remembered that she should be trying to escape. Her door wouldn't open, however, even when she shoved at the locking mechanism. She scooted painfully across the seat and discovered the one on the other side was the same. She set her forehead on the shoulder of the seat in front of her and thought about climbing up to the front. Sacramento had obviously gotten out, after all. By the time she got as far as that thought, Sacramento was back, tucking her bill clip back into her pocket. She got in and pulled the car around the back of the building.

Sacramento gave her a dry smile as she opened the door for Tatiana and helped her up and toward the hotel back door. "We can rematch in the morning, promise."

Tatiana huffed a laugh despite herself. In the morning, definitely.

Susan wished she'd thought to memorize the alphas' positions before she left them last night. This morning, they looked identical, eerily so, but she couldn't be absolutely sure. Sunlight from the French doors sliced right across their faces, and they

John entered, scent of bacon preceding him, strong enough even for Susan's nose. "Nothing?" He grimaced at her, then placed the tray with two plates heaped high with breakfast on a flat spot between the sleepers' feet at the end of the bed. Sound, touch, and now smell failed to make any difference to the alphas' states.

John mirrored Susan's place beside Silver with Andrew and dipped his nose over the side of Andrew's neck. "It's hard to be precise with scent, but I think he's just as deep under as last night."

"We need to start thinking of long-term arrangements, then." It wasn't like she hadn't been thinking that, but saying it out loud made it real. Susan smoothed her hair out of her face. It fell immediately back, so she growled and tugged out an elastic to fasten it messily into a ponytail. She was going to call in sick today anyway. "Humans in a coma are usually in the hospital, but I think you can get life support equipment for the home for hospice care. I don't know that it would fit in here. We might have to set the beds up in the basement or something."

John's lips thinned for several moments, then he sighed.

"They could still wake up today." He sounded resigned, however, allowing himself one last protest before he buckled down to her plan.

"And then we'll all be very happy." Susan stepped back around the bed to take John's hands. She could afford to be a bit more diplomatic about this than she had been last night. "Not to tell you your job as interim alpha—"

John barked a brief sardonic laugh. "You mean rest of the pack, don't you? I'm thinking the Roanokes should be out of contact to deal with the Russians for the foreseeable future. I can manage daily business for a while in their names. It'll be much smoother than the alternative."

"And I'll take the logistics of caring for them," Susan said. She was relieved he agreed, though this wasn't the tough part. "Do you think we should keep everyone out of the basement? We'll have to swear this pack to secrecy—I'd think they'd be used enough to that by now, being the Roanoke home pack— but it might worry them if they can't see what's going on." She freed a hand to gesture to the bed. "They don't *look* bad."

"Discourage tramping through for incomprehensible medical reasons," John said, after a few moments of thought. He smiled weakly and kissed Susan's forehead. "You bullshit those well. As long as we don't outright forbid it, I think people should stay calm for a while."

"Good point." Susan took a deep breath. Now the hard part. "Have you heard from Felicia? She's not still out searching, is she?"

"She got back early this morning for a couple hours of sleep, I gather. She wasn't answering her phone for me to call her back when we heard from Sacramento. If Sacramento doesn't show up this morning, though, I'll send Felicia back out to help her." John seemed to take Susan's question for noth-

...straightforward find enemy, lock her up' kind of equation."

"I also know they wouldn't sacrifice anyone's well-being to the 'political situation.' " John crossed his arms.

"You just don't want to have deal with the scene when you tell her no." That slipped out in a burst of frustration before Susan could stop it. So much for diplomacy. "I can't say I'd be excited about the idea either, but you're one of the only ones awake at the moment with a hope in hell of making her listen. Andrew might treat her like the equivalent of an alpha elect, but she's only nineteen, for God's sake."

"You have no idea what you're talking about." John gestured broadly to Andrew, volume rising. The inappropriately humorous corner of Susan's mind pointed out the worse their fight got, the more chance it might wake the alphas. "That's her father—and your alpha—that Russian cat poisoned. I'm not going to tell her to just sit around scratching her flank."

"Fine. *Control* her, then." Susan strode over and captured the wrist of John's pointing hand to press it to his chest to illustrate. "However you do it. Make her swear not to kill the

Russian, send her to reinforce Sacramento only with someone else—not Tom, he might not have enough time to talk her around in that kind of situation like he usually does—I don't care."

John was silent for several moments, and Susan didn't need a Were's nose to smell his frustration. "I'll talk to her," he said finally. Susan wanted to keep at him, demand that he tell her *how* he planned to talk to Felicia, so she could see if it would be likely to succeed, but that wasn't fair. John had agreed, so she let the topic go.

Reluctantly.

15

Selene and her brother avoided speaking of business over dinner, until they'd finished eating and Andrew had sent the children away. Selene was surprised Felicia left so willingly. The Felicia she knew would have dragged her feet, desperate to hear what was discussed, but perhaps this one, with family more stable around her, had not internalized a need to keep tabs on her situation at all times. Or perhaps she was willing to accept that her brother needed supervision, and she was not being shuffled off like a child herself.

The four of them, including Isabel, went outside and settled on benches on the porch of the guesthouse where the Dares would be staying. Once an outbuilding of some kind, it retained the weathered siding, but the interior had been completely renovated. It was another nicely calculated stroke to make the Vancouver Island pack's position seem more comfortable and secure. Selene wondered if it had been her or Ares's idea. Lilianne's, perhaps. Certainly, she detected her brother's wife's direction in the quality of the craftsmanship in the renovation.

The late-summer sun set through the trees, colors bleeding through the dark branches of evergreens at the horizon before falling fully behind, leaving the adults in steadily chilling twilight. Ares was the first to break the silence as they watched. He let his open beer rest on his knee, and didn't drink. "Silver," he muttered, low. "So much changed, when we forgot about its evil."

Selene looked up too fast, and then glared at the ground between her feet when her brother's next words made it clear he wasn't speaking to her. Of course he wasn't. No one in this dream knew that name. And if she was going to get out of this dream, she needed to stop fighting it, dwelling on how it differed from reality. Clearly she had something she needed to do here before she woke, and she'd only find out what by playing by the dream's rules.

"It's not the weapon; it's the wielder," Andrew said, but without heat behind it. Selene supposed even one used to the European view of silver as sometimes necessary couldn't argue abstracts in the face of what Stefan had done. "Apart from anything else, I'm glad of the chance to speak with you about that, Vancouver Island. Our information was quite garbled. You said the Tainted One killed at least one pack—Ginnie's, correct? And you truly have no idea which of the other deaths were his kills?"

"Only guesses." Ares's lips thinned as he glared into the trees. "That's why we're on the island. We've got the Graveyard of the Pacific protecting us to the west, and limited airport and

~~and they and were able to hit him in force.~~

"A single man started a war that spanned a continent." Andrew switched his beer to his other hand so he could lace his fingers with his wife's on her knee. "How is that possible?"

Ares swallowed with difficulty, then sipped his beer as if wetting his mouth would help him speak. "I've especially never understood that. It's like everyone took leave of their senses. Yes, a pack mysteriously dead and tortured with silver is terrifying, but why jump immediately to blaming another pack for such an atrocity?"

"He posed as a survivor." The words slipped out before Selene could stop herself. It might not count as playing along with the dream, but she couldn't sit silent and listen to the others pool their ignorance when she could offer something to help them understand. "He did to his victims what had been done to him, after all. After he killed the first pack, he must have traveled from pack to pack, spinning a story of being attacked by whoever he wanted to set them against. Why wouldn't they believe him? He had the silver scars to prove it, and he knew the intimate details of the deaths—because he'd been there." It was only a logical extension of what he'd done to her pack, in the real world. He'd come to them an injured and weak Were, needing to be protected.

Ares stared at Selene for a long moment, then reached out and squeezed her hand. Selene supposed he meant it to be comforting, but she felt patronized. Poor, soft-hearted Selene, working herself up over imagined theories about the tragedy. If only they knew. Both Andrew and Isabel looked shaken, but hiding it, unwilling to lose an advantage in the coming negotiation. Isabel's expression returned to pleasant neutrality more quickly.

"But you can see how moving to the island was only a temporary measure." Ares straightened. "We'll be moving back to the mainland soon. Washington State, probably."

Andrew's scent sharpened as if he were readying himself for something, but his body language remained relaxed. Selene wished she could see his wild self, and judge its behavior instead. People couldn't hide their emotions on the self that no one could see—though of course now Selene couldn't see it either. "Perhaps we could help each other, on that front," he said.

Ares stiffened, but only jerked a nod for Andrew to continue. Selene could read that her brother guessed they'd come to the reason for this delegation. She agreed. She took a deep breath to make sure her heart didn't speed with anticipation. The dream had begun with the delegation, so clearly its true purpose was important.

"I mean no disrespect, but you've let it go too long. The territory is open. It belongs to anyone who wants to claim it now." Andrew pulled his hand free from his wife's and sat forward on the bench, the better to gesture.

Ares's lip lifted with an unvoiced snarl. "Too long—what, a few months after we finally killed the Tainted One, when Europeans jockeying for territory when the East was unoccupied because so many were dead, and so many more were still dying." Ares jabbed the air with a forefinger. "We got rid of the Tainted One for you. We ended the war for you."

Andrew held up his hands, wide and apologetic. "Don't lump the Madrid pack in with the rest. We're here, aren't we? Talking to you, not claiming territory. The bravery of you and your people is to be commended. We certainly appreciate the service you did all Were by disposing of that man. But the fact remains that Were territory is won and held, not claimed by right. That's why we can help you."

Ares growled. "Help—!"

"Yes, help." Andrew paused for any more outbursts, then continued unhurriedly. "With Madrid's strength, we can help you reclaim the territory you need. You need it desperately, don't you?" He sounded sympathetic. He even smelled sympathetic, though Selene did not quite trust it.

Ares might not have trusted it either, but he seemed to decide that didn't change the truth. He nodded, once. "Too few of us have citizenship or the expertise to make IDs to get jobs in Canada. There are pack houses that need to be cleaned properly, so the humans don't find them with blood still on the walls, and sold. We need to report pack members dead and get their resources out of probate." He looked in the direction of the farmhouse, filled with displaced Were, and squared his shoulders. "We have no need of Madrid's strength. We have the numbers to claim our own territory."

"Numbers, yes. Fighters, no. Those are not the same."

Ares opened his mouth to refute that, then shut it again. Selene had to fill in the rest herself, tracing the logic of this dream world. If it had been pack war, this collection of survivors must have a much higher proportion of nonfighters, protected at home, until none of their protectors remained. Nonfighters would have been more likely to listen when Ares urged them to retreat, regroup. "And what does this gain your alpha? He could send his fighters to gain territory without bothering with us," Ares finally said.

"He avoids the need to pit his fighters against your numbers, which benefits neither of our packs, Vancouver Island. Better a truce and no other lives lost, don't you think?"

It sounded so reasonable. Selene could smell that Ares wanted to believe it was reasonable. She supposed she couldn't blame him. In his place, having lived through this dream world, not just having stepped into it at the end, she would be very tired. Ready to take an offer, and willfully ignore what might lie below the surface.

But she wasn't tired, and she didn't believe she would be trapped in a dream simply to drift along with the easiest path. She crossed her arms. If she couldn't see wild selves, she could at least use both arms. At the moment, she didn't see it as a fair trade. "Why you?"

Andrew's and Isabel's heads both snapped to her. She

~~Andrew frowned. What?~~

Selene shrugged. "You're not the only hunt in town. Why should *we* help *you*? You make it sound like we get the better half of this deal. You'll help us win back territory, help us defend it, and all we have to do is share it with you."

Andrew's lips thinned. "It *is* a good deal—"

"Selene, what—?" Ares spoke on top of Andrew. His scent made him seem truly angry, not just acting, but Selene was committed to her bared-teeth manner now. She couldn't switch to coaxing, nor did she want to.

She jerked a gesture to cut them both off, then leaned forward, smiling again. It paid to know your opponent. "It's not a good deal. How long until sharing turns into control? The truth is, you need us more than we need you. You need legitimacy. It's open season out there. How many European packs have sent people out already? How many territory squabbles are already starting? How do you divide an entire continent among viciously competitive packs, when anyone can land in any airport? But you, you meet with the remnants of the old owners. You convince them that they have no claim to their own territory, that they'd never regain it without you. Then you can turn around and tell all the other Europeans that you have a *right*." Selene paused, watching shock on Andrew's face and dawning anger on Isabel's. "We'll assert our own right, thank you. If we do need fighters, why don't I call Barcelona and ask him what terms he'll give us?"

Isabel shot to her feet, accent thickening. "How dare you? We come here in good faith . . ."

Ares leaned close to Selene, expression of anger crumbling into confusion. "What—?"

Selene supposed he would have no reason to know the particular divisions of Spanish packs. She wouldn't have, except for her Dare's hard-won expertise. "They're Madrid. Barcelona are their bitterest competitors for territory." She pushed herself standing too, but more controlled. Andrew remained sitting, a false, teeth-gritted sort of neutrality pasted across his face.

"We have many other choices," Selene said slowly, precisely, rubbing it in. "Your only particular value is in that one of you used to be North American." She nodded to Andrew. "But given how he seems to have abandoned his values . . ."

Andrew rose in a movement as smooth and steady as his growl. "Careful."

Selene sensed her rhetoric getting away from her, the careful calculation to her tactlessness slipping through her fingers, but this Andrew was wrong, fundamentally wrong, and she didn't understand how he couldn't see that. "What do you call it, then? That you would defend the use of silver, defend the violence of pointless territory squabbles. There is a whole continent for the Were to spread across. It was divided among dozens of packs, and yet you cannot allow the survivors a single state unmolested. Why? Not for the good of Were, not for

One, I'll have you know," he said.

"And how do you honor their voices? Cast them to the wind as you run by, so focused on your prize?" Selene paced a step closer to Andrew. "Territory is fought for, perhaps, but it is held with honor, and family. Otherwise it would never pass from one generation to another, and the fighting would never cease. You know we have a right to return to the mainland."

"We have no wish to overstay our welcome. If you do not wish us here, we will leave your territory." Andrew gave the last word snarled, mocking overtones. Clearly, Selene had gotten to him. She could only hope that uncomfortable thoughts about how European he was acting would spur him into some kind of positive action.

Of course, they couldn't precisely stomp off, when the Vancouver Island pack had been their transportation from the ferry terminal. Andrew chose instead to vanish into the guesthouse, Isabel following closely. Selene assumed they at least meant to spend the night, as they didn't call the children back first.

Ares remained seated until the door had closed, then

pushed to his feet. Selene could read his deep frustration, but he didn't voice it. He tipped his head to where a road of two wheel tracks, baked to hard clay for the summer, but probably a muddy mess in the winter, led down over a hill. Selene followed him down. He took one rut and she took the other.

A barn hulked black against the dimming horizon as they approached. Here and there a knothole or slight gap in the planks showed elusive light from inside, but it seemed basically sound. Old, but repaired. Wouldn't keep the drafts out, but at least the roof wouldn't leak.

"What was that?" Ares didn't look at her as they walked. Even with the short pause of their walk down here, the worst of the anger had faded from his tone.

"A better strategy than allowing them to devalue what we have to bargain with." Selene ducked her head apologetically as she reviewed the words. She'd told herself she'd been trying to tap into their old strategy, but was that really true? She wasn't Roanoke in this dream. She'd had an idea, yes, and she still thought it could work if they saw it through, but she had to work through Ares, not around him.

"And so you made them angry instead. Come on, wake up, Sister. You know better than that." Ares unlocked the padlock on the barn door, which slid sideways along a track rather than pivoting. Inside, the dim light became recognizable as candlelight, dancing in the drafts. Ahead of them, propped against a thick post that vanished from sight to hold up the ceiling above, sat an outdoor announcement board. Perhaps it had once belonged to a church or a community center, but now the little roof was weathered and mossy, and the glass over the board surface was scuffed. Sandwiched beneath its protection were pictures. Hundreds of snapshots, some older photos, some clearly printed from a computer. A single tall candle

disappeared. White circles giving soft light, floating in a sky of water, as the Lady in the full. Selene knelt too, to look at the photos. People. So many people she *knew*. Even now she could easily remember names, she couldn't find all of them, but she remembered the faces. She and Dare had traveled often throughout Roanoke, stayed with each of the sub-packs for a little while.

She touched the glass atop faces, here and there, tracing patterns within the chaos, even as her voice longed to sob. Alphas' faces, anchoring clumps of their people, even in death. There was Rory. Though she had never liked him, he did not deserve this, even in a dream. There was Benjamin. And—

John. Her cousin. His photo looked more serious than most, stolen from something official and human, perhaps. And it suited him the least. She longed to see him smile, cowlick in his hair making it perpetually untidy.

Selene stumbled back up to her feet. Because she could not allow herself to see the faces anymore, to imagine what had happened to each person—she *knew* what Stefan did, she'd watched it—she looked at the memorial as a whole. It was a very human sort of shrine. The small candles evoked the Lady, yes, but Were worship did not use candles.

But what would a proper Were memorial be? Songs sung and stories told, to fix the voice of the dead in everyone's memories. But when had the Were ever had to mourn on such a scale? There were too many dead here, too many voices to remember properly. Faces would have to do.

The atmosphere seemed to have quieted Ares's mood, though not precisely soothed it. He broke the silence at length. "You always told me if you could no longer take being beta, you'd tell me. We'd work something out. What's wrong, Selene?" He turned back to face her suddenly. "Why now, when it's so important? Why can't you just back me up for another few days?"

"I'm trying to help." Trying to solve the dream. Selene took a deep breath, and closed her eyes against the flickering light for a few moments. She had been acting as an alpha, when she wasn't. But how could she not? For four years, she had never *not* been an alpha. The habit of holding tightly to control did not disappear so easily. "I love you, Ares." Perhaps that's what she needed to do with this dream—say a few of the things that could no longer be said.

"Now I know something's wrong, if you think you have to say that out loud." Humor tinted Ares's voice, and he came to hold her.

"You're not real." Selene kept her eyes closed, which made it easier to say. Should she be concentrating on that instead? What did it matter if dream figments of shattered packs could not reclaim their territory? What did it matter if a dream figment of a girl wouldn't speak or shift? The only real thing here was her, so perhaps she should be focusing less on what she needed to do in the dream, and more on what she needed to

..., but there he didn't . . . things fell into place in Selene's mind with a jolt that felt almost physical. "Because Dare's wife never died. He never had to flee home, he never became Roanoke's enforcer. He never held the Roanoke pack together, and that united pack never made the Tainted One seek easier pickings in the West." She pulled out of her brother's grip and paced to where rotten stairs had once led up to the hayloft. "One life saved, and the whole world tips out of alignment."

Selene glared up at the ceiling, shadowed and cobwebbed far above. If this was her own mind, no one was listening, but she shouted it defiantly anyway. "Am I truly so selfish, deep inside? If Dare's happiness is with another, not with me, the whole world bleeds? I did not ask for this!" She screamed that last, both hands clenched. "Or worse, do the lives of hundreds of Were count for nothing against a perfectly natural wish that my brother had not died? I would not make that choice. I would not make any of these choices, so why do you show them to me?"

"Selene!" Ares caught her, crushed her to him, and stroked her hair. "It's all right, Selene. You need to rest. We've none of us had time to mourn properly. I can get someone else to help me with the negotiations." His voice grew soft and soothing, as if she were as mad as Ginnie.

And perhaps she was. Perhaps all this was real, her mind had broken somewhere along the way, and she'd imagined all of it. She didn't think so, but how would she prove otherwise? So Selene let her brother coax her out of the barn, and back to the house, to rest. As if resting would help any of the problems, real or imagined, currently surrounding her.

After dinner, Andrew went walking, though it didn't do much to clear his head. He mostly spent the time longing for Silver to talk out his strategy with, or wishing he could shift and chase the rabbits he smelled. He'd already broken the Convocation prohibition against shifting once, though. No one had mentioned it, given the extenuating circumstances, but once more and he suspected he'd get kicked out. Still, he wanted to hunt and kill something. The sharp pine smell and the crunch of needles and dirt under his feet reminded him of other Convocations, ones he remembered leading.

He circled back around to the cabins before sunset, aware of his appointment. Even so, three figures were already waiting behind his cabin. Edmond rolled over an old, collapsed fence post, probably to look for insects beneath, while Selene and John watched. John kept twitching toward his son like he wanted to save him from some danger, but Andrew couldn't imagine what. Splinters?

Selene noticed him first. "Andrew." She lifted her fingertips in a small wave, and even smiled slightly. Andrew looked past her, so she stayed slightly out of focus. John looked up and frowned, much more suspicious. He shoved his hands into his

constructed explanation. John growled, scooped up Edmond and turned to go.

Edmond squirmed. "Daddy! There was a lizard! I was going to catch the lizard!"

Selene blocked John's way and held out her hands for Edmond. "I know where lots of lizards are. Want to come with Aunt Selene?" Edmond immediately jerked his weight toward her, and John nearly lost hold.

"Selene," John growled, though when she took Edmond from him, he didn't fight her. "I'm not cut out for leading. You know that."

"Maybe you should try again and see, you coward." Selene made the last word into a joke, but Andrew suspected it wasn't, quite. She hitched Edmond onto her hip, and headed off into the trees, away from the cabins.

John glowered at the ground. "What in the Lady's name did you say to her?"

Andrew shrugged. "I guess she doesn't like Rory." He hoped Selene's help wasn't due to his personal charisma. He didn't want anything from her on those terms, so he pushed the idea out of his mind. He was going to depose Rory, how-ever he did it, so he wouldn't ignore an abandoned fresh kill if that got him there faster. "Look. I've been where you are, okay? You make mistakes, but sometimes you're a better leader for having learned from them. You don't know if you don't try."

"You have it in for Rory, why don't you take him down yourself?" John finally looked up long enough to search An-drew's face.

"He knows my moves." Andrew pinched the bridge of his nose. "Let's pretend for a second I wasn't intimately familiar with the scandals of the Western packs, even before my mem-ories got scrambled. What did you fuck up so badly, anyway? Was it something to do with Susan?"

John shoved him, fast enough Andrew stumbled back. He caught himself and redistributed his weight quickly enough. He'd take that as a yes. John opened his mouth for some kind of angry retort—and stopped. "How in the Lady's name do you know her name?"

"I must have heard it." Andrew assumed that sometime in his missing years, someone had talked to him about Su-san, if she'd been enough to cost John the Seattle alphaship. "What happened with her?" He assumed John had been forced to break things off with her in an ugly way. Given how much they'd loved each other in his false memories, he wouldn't be surprised if the stress had made John retreat from his duties as alpha.

"Even Selene can barely remember her name. I don't think Ares ever knew it." John examined Andrew tightly. Andrew waited patiently, and finally John sighed. Old pain stretched across his shoulder muscles. "I got her killed. I revealed what I was, and . . ." His voice failed and tears came to his eyes. "They had to kill her."

~~light your own damn challenge right.~~ He strode for the trees.

Andrew watched his best chance to defeat Rory walk away, but all he could think of was Susan. "How could they—did they even bother to *talk* to her first?"

John slowed, stopped. "Come on, wake up. You'd have killed her if she was in the Roanoke pack."

Andrew growled at the very idea. "I'd have *talked* to her. Figured out if she was intelligent enough to keep her mouth shut for the sake of her son. Which she was—would have been . . . I mean, she could well have been. Now we'll never know."

John looked up at the sky for a few moments. Andrew glanced up too, automatically, but he saw no birds or anything else to catch the attention. He supposed John was using the intense blue, orange-tinged now with the approaching sunset, to organize his thoughts. With no clouds and the new moon tonight, Andrew supposed the stars would be beautiful.

"It's a very pretty speech." John looked down again. "I wouldn't have thought you were the pretty speech type. But Susan is gone, and you don't have to do much to prove it, do you? I'm not going to fight your challenge fight for you. You want Roanoke, get it yourself."

He strode off once more, and this time Andrew didn't try to stop him. Damn it all. What now?

14

Tatiana took stock with her eyes closed when she woke, by habit. The smell of a hotel room was unmistakable. So many small brushes of different humans that, like a huge murmuring crowd that moved past individual words, it merged into a featureless scent that her mind linked with the species as a whole. She was surrounded by *human*.

And Sacramento. Her scent and a thin trickle of fresh air came from the same direction, so Tatiana assumed she'd been smart enough to sleep in front of the door. In wolf, the scent clarified as she drew another breath. Tatiana let her eyes slit open, and she found the gray curve of a flank where she expected, striped diagonally down the center by sunlight from where the drapes didn't meet in the middle. She opened her eyes fully, but there was nothing else particularly of note in the room: bland walls, blue carpet, art based on leaf patterns. A hotel room.

Sacramento lifted her muzzle from her paws, less like she'd somehow smelled Tatiana's eyes opening, and more like she'd only been dozing and checking on her prisoner every few minutes. She stood and stretched, bowed over her front legs, then turned her back for at least the illusion of privacy while she shifted. Tatiana rolled over to look away. There was no value in embarrassing her captor.

She heard the shuffle of cloth as Sacramento dressed, but Tatiana didn't roll back yet. Now she knew her situation, she needed to figure out what she was going to do next. Last night, she'd thought only about getting away, but this morning she remembered all too keenly that her passport was sitting in her suitcase back at the pack house. And her phone. And her money. How was she supposed to make it home with none of those things, swim in wolf?

"You could come back with me voluntarily," Sacramento said, voice coming closer. Tatiana sat up and turned to her. The way the comment followed from her thoughts was eerie, but of course Sacramento was taking stock for the morning as well. She had a stubborn prisoner she needed to transport.

"Why would I do that?" Tatiana eased herself against the headboard and put a hand to her temple like the movement had made her head swim. She felt stronger—if rather desperately hungry—this morning, but better Sacramento underestimate her.

Sacramento started dragging her blond hair back into a tail, getting tighter and tighter with each pass before she fastened it off. "Because you're not going to get anywhere, trying to run. The Roanokes aren't stupid; they're not going to execute you for something that wasn't your fault. You don't have anything to fear."

ιαςς ѕιιυννςμ ιιιαι ιιις ѕςιςςιι was just as blank of good news as it had been all night. She slid it away again. "But you still won't get too far."

"No," Tatiana admitted, pushing with her hands on the mattress to sit up straighter, then slumping as if the effort had been too much. She must have made the word sound too weak, because Sacramento's expression sharpened.

"Not with the whole pack looking for you on our home territory, I meant. You don't have to do the 'poor weak little mid-ranker' thing again."

Tatiana couldn't think of any protest that would help her, so she settled on silent confusion instead, even as she swore in her head. Had she moved too quickly, too easily since she'd woken up? But she'd hardly moved at all. Sacramento had to be just guessing.

Sacramento smiled thinly at her expression of confusion. "You're the alpha's daughter, for the Lady's sake. And I'm not in the Roanokes' league as far as intelligence, but I can spot when someone's playing a role because I know a little something about playing one myself."

She sat down on the second hotel bed, facing Tatiana,

knees wide. She rolled her neck, then released her hair. She shook it out and combed the front locks up over the crown of her head so they fell back just so. She leaned back on her palms, lounging, body language becoming so relaxed as to be uncaring.

"My former alpha, Nate, he was kind of an asshole, and his son was a little prick, but what a pack needs is authority, you know? And he was authoritative. Man knew how to chase." The pitch of Sacramento's voice hadn't changed, but her tone made it seem like it had, light and quick, almost giggly. "I did help him out a little, with the small details, you know? Nothing important. That was his job. Mostly, I just listened."

Sacramento sat straighter and pulled her hair back, even more tightly this time. "Ugh. Listening and agreeing all the time is useful occasionally, but I'm glad not to have to do it with that cat anymore."

No wonder Sacramento seemed uptight if she was over-compensating for having to act that way. Tatiana nodded in respect for her skill, then caught herself. What was she doing? Sacramento had all but accused her of trying to manipulate everyone. Where did that leave them? Did Sacramento mistrust her, or was she trying to forge sympathy by pointing out similarities?

Either way, Tatiana clearly needed to do much more than pretend weakness. Sacramento wasn't going to turn her back on her, no matter how much she flopped against the pillows. What she needed was another Lady-damned vision, a real one, now when it would be useful.

"I won't go back with you." Tatiana shoved to her feet and

threw a punch right at Sacramento's jaw. She had no idea if it would have done any damage had it connected, but that wasn't the point. Sacramento's automatic reaction was everything

Alexei finished out the game of Round the Round with a flurry of jumps in the circle drawn in the dirt—feet to sides, to center, to top and bottom, to center. He was a big man, far too big to be playing a children's game, but he moved with his habitual grace. "Did you catch that, Tania?"

Tatiana sketched her own round in the dirt with her toe. She nodded. Alexei had always asked that after his fighting demonstrations when he was in human. In wolf, he'd looked at her with his head slightly tilted. If she hadn't caught it, he'd show her again, as many times as she needed. If she lied and said she had, he'd knock her on her ass when she failed to reproduce the move. Then show her again.

Tatiana took a couple practice jumps in the center of the round, compacting a leaf into the dirt. She was far too old for this game as well, but Alexei was showing her. He was the one who'd made her feel like she really could be a Tooth, when she'd joined up as a gangly teen, longing for a direction in her life. He'd never taught her anything lightly, so this must be important. First center, then edge, edge—she counted each step in her head, and gave him a little bow when she finished.

Alexei didn't say anything in praise, but he smiled. It lit up his whole face, usually flat like a plane of rock, his jaw was so square and his dark blond hair buzzed so short. Tatiana stepped over, and he clapped her on the shoulder. "At least I can do something right, yes?" she teased.

"Except follow orders," Alexei said. The light of his smile drained away into solemnity and a flicker of pain. Orders were very important to Alexei. Thinking for herself, Tatiana had had to learn on her own.

"Father's orders." Her hair wisped soft against her cheeks, disturbed by her jumping, and she scraped it back. "The North Americans say 'alpha's daughter' like it's important. An honor, not a fact of life."

Alexei hunched his shoulders and looked away. "I wish you wouldn't do this."

Seeing the hurt in that hunch, Tatiana didn't want to, but she couldn't stop herself either. "Do you know who my father was? My *real* father?" Alexei was older than her. She didn't know by how much, but he might have been old enough to know if her mother had a lover at the right time. Or if she'd been chasing among the humans.

"I wish . . ." Alexei loosened his muscles and touched one of her shoulders, turned her to face him, caught the other. "That I could teach you to be content, Tania. You always nip at the heels of whoever's trying to lead the pack. Knowing a fact won't make you stop that. If I'm not your *real* brother, does that make me love you any less? It doesn't matter who your father is."

Surprise held Tatiana still as Alexei enfolded her into an

embrace. That was like him, that hug, love in every point of touch. He didn't say the word. Tatiana couldn't remember ever hearing him say it, to anyone. "I love you too, Alexei."

"That's it, breathe." Sacramento's voice. Sacramento's arm, across the back of her neck, supporting her head. Tatiana opened her eyes and blinked until the far wall of the hotel room didn't swim. Now all she had to do was recover faster than Sacramento expected her to. Lady. Easier said than done. Air still clotted on the way into her throat like it was heavier than it should have been.

She slid her arm over Sacramento's back to cling there, fingers bunching the fabric of her shirt. She struggled to sit up, her arm slipped, and in the general confusion of Sacramento helping her, she got her fingertips on the bill clip in Sacramento's pocket. She collapsed on the bed with the clip in her hand, a hard lump against her back. She tucked in under her waistband. Sacramento didn't seem to have noticed anything, though Mikhail, who'd taught Tatiana basic pickpocketing skills, would have disowned her on the spot for awkwardness.

Tatiana pulled her hand free but otherwise lay flat and offered Sacramento a thin smile like she couldn't manage anything more strenuous. "Can I get some water?" Her accent came out stronger because of the remnants of the dream, which probably helped her case.

"Just a sec." Sacramento hurried into the bathroom. Tatiana waited until she was through the doorway before pushing up and grabbing the car keys from the cabinet and stumbling to yank open the front door. She paused to slam a fist down on the inside handle. With a screech of stressed metal, it snapped, and she pounded into the hall and pulled the door shut behind her. She dropped the handle to *thunk* on the hall carpet as she ran for the staircase. Hopefully that should slow Sacramento down a little. Kicking doors down took time, and attracted attention. Sacramento might well waste more time hesitating over bringing humans running than she would actually opening the door.

In the stairwell, Tatiana wanted to stop and pant, but the sudden concrete after the carpet echoed her steps and her harsh breaths back to her. She used the feeling of being surrounded by noise to push herself on. She tucked the bill clip more securely into her own pocket and ran. Down. Down and outside. Running down stairs was a little like controlled falling, wasn't it?

She could manage falling for now.

15

Tatiana checked the windows and the car's rearview mirror regularly as she punched through the endless menus to get the phone she'd bought activated. All the vehicles on the rural highway flashed by, paying no attention to the car pulled over with two tires in the weeds. She'd debated getting lost as one car among many in a more densely inhabited area, but meanwhile she'd been driving as far and fast as she could in a random direction. That direction had brought her to this two-lane highway, fields on either side with trees between. So she'd gone with the protection of being lost somewhere in too large an area to properly search. She kept the windows firmly shut to hold in her scent.

When her hands started shaking again, she twisted to pull another sub sandwich from the overstuffed bag she'd dumped on the passenger seat and ate it one-handed while she punched in Sacramento's credit card number. She hoped—truly hoped—that the woman's pack would reimburse her, because the international calling charges were going to bite a hunk out of her bank account.

Finally the phone announced itself happily connected to both the outside world and a revenue stream. Tatiana checked all around for any sign of pursuit again. A squirrel bounded across the road and up someone's mailbox on the other side. Whom should she call? Her alpha didn't have his own cell phone, and he might be out running anyway, this late in the evening over there. And if she called one of the house phones, who knew if the priestesses would even transmit her messages. It would have to be one of her fellow Teeth.

She dialed Alexei's number without further consideration. He'd help her out of this, no questions about how she'd gotten into it asked. The wolfsbane had left her weak in ways not even sleep and food could touch—if the visions hadn't told her that already—because just hearing his confused greeting in Old Were brought tears to her eyes.

"It's me. The mission went all wrong. There was too much wolfsbane in the wine. The alphas won't wake, and I nearly died. I need to get out of here, but I escaped without my passport . . ."

Silence for a beat, Alexei taking it all in before he reacted. "Where are you? Are you safe for the moment?"

Tatiana gave him her best guess of her location based on the names she'd seen on street signs coming up here. He probably only wondered if she was still in Washington State, but more information never hurt. The second question brought up more than she could easily fit into the kind of concise answer she was trying to give. For the short term, maybe, but what about the visions? And more important, what about the priest-

____ ___ _____ _____ *having visions without wolfsbane? How dangerous is it?"*

Alexei huffed in surprise, the fact that it was audible a measure of the strength of the emotion. *"I will."* Voices in the background, too far for the phone's cheap mic to pick up. *"Father is here, you should speak to him."*

There was a pause as the phone was handed over, but not nearly long enough of one for Tatiana to push her thoughts into better order before her alpha's voice came over the line. *"Tatiana?"*

She laid out the events without emotion as best she could, and at least managed to be concise enough that she detected no impatience in Father's listening silence. At the end, she chanced a venture into speculation. *"The priestesses prepared the wine, did they not? If they had some reason to sabotage—"*

A venture too far, apparently. Her alpha cut her off roughly. *"I will look into it. In the meantime, we must deal with the current situation with the North American alpha. It would be best if you could finish him off, while he is weak."*

Tatiana was too shocked at first to even try to correct his

selective memory about what she'd just told him of the balance of power between the two Roanokes. "*Father—my heart stopped. And I barely made it out of their pack house alive. You expect me to return there? They'll kill me before I get within snapping distance of him.*"

Father blew out a breath. "*If it is impossible, it is impossible. You said you lost your passport? That will make it difficult to return home.*"

Tatiana gritted her teeth, then transferred the pressure of her frustration to a white-knuckled grip on the steering wheel when her jaw muscle screamed a protest. No, she was such a scared bunny that she could get a plane this minute, but she had called home in a panic anyway. Of *course* returning home was difficult at the moment. That was why she needed support from the rest of the Lady's Teeth. Had he forgotten the part where she was nearly forty, and therefore not a *child*? "*Do we have any contacts in Alaska who could get me ID? I think there's a ferry that can get me there without crossing a border.*"

"*I'll make some calls. Check in again once you reach Alaska. Lady light your trail, Tania.*" With the familiar blessing, he closed the call.

Tatiana made herself set the phone aside and calmly chew through half a sandwich before she let herself think about her next move. She knew as well as anyone how Father thought of the big picture to the exclusion of everything—and everyone—else. It wasn't like he'd abandon her here unless she threw herself into the suicide mission to kill Andrew. And she'd told him she wouldn't kill for him any longer, yes, but these were rather extraordinary circumstances. He had reason to ask again.

She precisely wiped each of her fingers on the napkin and picked up the phone again to research the details of her next move. The ferry to Alaska left from a place called Bellingham about an hour and a half

, never moved, so there wasn't even a wrinkle in the blankets. They'd set up in the basement, two beds placed with a wide aisle between them, against the empty wall of the room intended for the projector screen. The beds had an unavoidable hospital flavor, with shiny metal frames and white plastic panels as head- and footboards, but the blankets and sheets were warmly colored and mismatched, at least.

She wished that they didn't have to be on their backs, another thing that made her think uncomfortably of hospitals and coma patients. She knew plenty of people slept on their backs—John did, when deeply asleep, but he always had some note of flung arm or slightly open mouth that softened it.

She gave in to a sudden, desperate impulse to break their stillness however she had to, and stepped forward to shake both of their shoulders. "Andrew? Silver? We *need* you back here."

License tags clinked on the stairs behind Susan, and the cat padded up in otherwise perfect silence. Morsel sniffed Susan's pant leg, endured a stroke with pointed forbearance, then launched herself onto Silver's bed with a single arc of a leap. After some comprehensive sniffing, she settled herself tilted downward with her butt at Silver's chin, and her forepaws on her belly. It didn't look like it could possibly be comfortable, but Morsel tucked in her paws to form a meatloaf and purred.

"God, cats," Susan said, huffing more of a laugh than the situation deserved. Well, she'd have some smoothing of blankets to do later if the cat walked all over them, she supposed.

Someone bellowed from upstairs. "Susan?" Sacramento, Susan figured out after a moment. Were could call each other at normal volume over ridiculously long distances, so of course they overcompensated for her. She'd beaten it out of everyone who actually lived in the house long-term.

"Down here." She kept her voice pointedly low, but she did walk to the bottom of the basement stairs. Sacramento appeared a beat later, and closed the door behind her before thumping down the stairs. Susan assumed she wanted privacy. Should she tell Sacramento to hold up and go get John? It had to be something official about Tatiana, but where was the Russian? Locked in the car?

Susan supposed it would be all right to listen to what Sacramento wanted to tell her as long as she didn't make any actual decisions, which would be a slap in John's face she didn't want, no matter how frustrating he was being. She hoped Sacramento hadn't lost the envoy. Then they'd have to clamp down on Felicia all over again.

"Where is she?" Susan prompted when it seemed like Sacramento was going to glare around the room without really seeing it indefinitely.

"The fucking cat broke the door handle off—" Sacramento started near her earlier bellow with frustration, but quickly moderated her tone with a wince and a glance at the alphas.

"If you wake them, everyone will be quite grateful. I'm

...it struck Susan—as beside the point as the realization was at the moment—that that was an aspect of high rank she'd never appreciated until now. She'd seen Silver exhausted or in pain plenty of times. Andrew too, for that matter, though to a lesser degree. Not that he felt less keenly than his mate, but he didn't show it around her.

Sacramento took a deep breath. "Anyway. I lost her. She had another vision this morning, and I underestimated how weak that would leave her. She ran for it and stole my fucking keys and wallet. Had a hell of a time getting back here."

"You could have called for a ride—" Susan cut herself off. Of course Sacramento wouldn't want to compound her humiliation in losing her prey by asking for help. To cover her slip, she hurried into her next thought. Which, to be fair, Sacramento wasn't going to like either, but this time she deserved it. "I suppose you were distracted, too, because she flirted with you?" She'd talked John around to the idea of Sacramento bringing the Russian alpha's daughter in gently, back when the alternative had been Felicia, but if Sacramento was going to think with her hormones, she regretted that.

Sacramento drew a deep breath, suitable for an angry

retort, and then held it instead. When she released the air, it seemed to allow some calm in. "I convinced the alphas that I can think straight, but I suppose you only have my word for that."

She flexed her hands beside her hips. "Look. Yes, I'm attracted, even if you can't smell it. I've been attracted to plenty of women in my time, so I can tell you with confidence, this time it's different. I'd rather . . . *understand* her. She has this impenetrable act, but I can sense the thoughts going on behind it. Sharp thoughts." Sacramento waved her hand in front of her face as if to illustrate something flickering behind the eyeholes of a mask. "I'd love to be able to find out what they are. But that's a side trail. What matters is that we need to make sure she's not killed because—"

Susan cut her off with a gesture. The logical political reasons for keeping Tatiana alive were familiar ground that they didn't need to retread. Maybe Sacramento was kidding herself about her emotions toward the Russian, but at least she'd bothered to try to think them through. Rather than assigning blame, it was time for damage control. "You said she stole your wallet. Have you canceled your cards yet?"

Sacramento looked blank. "No?"

"Good." Susan nodded to the ground as she mapped things out in her mind. "That means you can get online and see where she's spending money. If she's smart, she'll make a big cash withdrawal in one place, but you never know with Were and human record-keeping . . ."

"You mean you can check some secret bank thing, because of your job?" Sacramento said slowly.

"No, *you* can. You know your online statement?" Susan didn't take anything for granted, but she was relieved when Sacramento nodded. Were had blind spots, but they weren't

...was already tapping through menus. Susan went to look around her shoulder without apology. "You'll have to look at the pending charges, things take a day or two to go through. When did she get your card?"

"A couple hours ago." Sacramento muttered it, clearly embarrassed and probably now reevaluating her weighing of humiliation versus lost time from calling for a ride. "Here. Food ... An electronics store? Oh, and then the phone company. She must have bought a phone and activated it." Her words sped with excitement. "Look, more food and gas, in different places. We *can* tell the direction she's going in."

"She's heading north—" Susan imagined a map in her mind. "She's not going to the airport, clearly. Or at least not Sea-Tac. The only commercial airport up there is Bellingham, and that's only international because it hops to Canada . . ." Everything realigned with a snap. "But she doesn't have her passport, that's still here. And Bellingham has a ferry to Alaska, which gets her at least closer to home if she can't get a plane . . ."

"Perfect!" Sacramento pressed a kiss to the side of Susan's forehead with typical Were lack of personal space, and bounded up the stairs. "Bellingham," she repeated to herself, as if cementing the name in her mind. Susan assumed that, being from California, she wasn't familiar with the city.

Susan followed her up the stairs more slowly, only to see Sacramento push past John without even stopping. Dammit! This was just what she'd planned not to do, let Sacramento take action without consulting John. But she hadn't given any orders; Sacramento was doing what she wanted.

She jogged up the last few steps anyway. "John, I didn't—"

John drew in a breath deep enough to visibly expand his chest before he let it out. "I know. Bellingham, she said? Did she lose the Russian, then?"

Susan rubbed a hand on his back, trying to channel Were calming strategies. "She got hold of Sacramento's credit card when she escaped, so we looked up the online statement."

John nodded. "I'll send Felicia after her."

Susan pressed her lips together on her first automatic comment. "To *capture* Tatiana, right? Are you sure you need both of them to do that?"

"Sacramento failed once." John's expression hardened, and Susan could see this was no time to argue with him. She also noticed that he hadn't answered about Felicia and the kill or capture issue. She presumed if he'd raised it with Felicia, she'd just avoided it, so now he was compounding it with willful blindness.

The conflicting impulses felt almost like they were squirming inside Susan's chest, but she nodded. And didn't mention anything about where in Bellingham Tatiana would be. It wasn't like she was helping the Russian get away, just giving the relatively level-headed approach a head start.

16

Selene did not sleep well. She didn't see how anyone could, crammed together in a room-filling mound of pillows and Were. In the full, she'd slept together with the pack, certainly, but that was one night every so often, by choice. Here, she had no choice. Ares and his wife and children had a room together and perhaps she could have asked to join them, but she preferred to avoid Ares and his searching looks for the moment. As if her true mental state would be written on her forehead.

When dawn light started squeezing in around curtains and blinds, Selene gave up. She got up, washed and dressed, and went poking around the house's few corners empty of sleeping Were, upstairs and down, trying to better understand the dream. If it was a dream. She found plenty of impeccably cleaned threadbare carpet, curling linoleum, poorly sealed window frames, and spiders, but nothing that shed new light on the blended pack's situation. With all the Were around with nothing to do, she was surprised that efforts hadn't continued from cleaning into refurbishing, but perhaps any money for materials had gone first into the guesthouse. Only so much repair could be done with strength and nothing else.

Time-wasting possibilities of the house exhausted, Selene paused with her hand on the front doorknob. Should she go try to speak to Andrew privately, perhaps? Or to Isabel? If she apologized profusely, would it help their situation?

Someone came out onto the upstairs landing. Ares's wife raised her voice slightly. "Selene?" Lilianne continued to the head of the stairs. "Ares said you talked Ginnie into coming back to eat yesterday?"

Selene dropped her hand from the door and turned properly. "I don't know how much I was persuasive, and how much she was hungry, but yes. I did."

"Do you think you could do it again? The forecast is for some showers tomorrow, and I've had a coat set aside for her for a week." Lilianne came to the foot of the stairs, and gave Selene a wan smile. "If you think of anything else to promise her on the spur of the moment that might keep her here for more than a few minutes, I'll do my best to deliver."

"I'll try." Selene nodded to Lilianne and let herself out quietly. Yesterday, she thought she'd felt the fragile beginning of a connection with Ginnie. If this was not a dream, all the more reason someone should check up on her. Having found a course of action that would be the same, dream or no dream, calmed Selene and let her avoid thinking over that impossible question.

She made it down to where the track into the woods di-
verged from the main driveway before the relieved feeling of
purpose wore off and she realized how well she'd just has
managed. She should

..........cu with Andrew or his
wife, or even Felicia, it would be offering herself for even more
of the dream's cruel tricks while she wondered if she was putting herself through it for nothing. If this was not a dream, there
was no lesson to learn, no awakening that could be earned by
accepting the punishment.

No, she'd find Ginnie and see if she could do the girl any
good. After all, she was the only living Were in this dream who
had any idea what the girl had seen. Perhaps healing could begin with that.

She kept her steps heavy through the trees, crunching off
the path into the undergrowth occasionally, as if to chart the
path of a squirrel. The air was pleasantly cool, but any dew was
long gone.

If Ginnie thought someone was trying to sneak up on her,
she'd never be found. Selene paused every so often to listen, to
see if the girl would be similarly noisy to invite Selene to her
location. A raven *quorked* at her cheekily, but she heard nothing else of interest.

The forest's scents reminded her of home, home when
Ares really was still alive. She supposed this place shared many
of the same plants with the forests she and Dare hunted togeth-

er, but she saw this with different eyes. Even among the trees, aspects of the modern world stood out, things she would never have seen as Silver. There, old boards set into a slope to form rough stairs, there, half a car, slipping away to rust over half a century or more since it was abandoned.

Ahead, a female voice called out in Spanish. Felicia, Selene recognized after a moment of consideration. Not only did the language confuse matters, but her tone was different in a way Selene could not quite put her finger on. More constrained, perhaps.

The tone was at least amused, however, and Selene picked out the name Arturo in the liquid flow of sounds. Selene took the next branch of the path in that direction, then left it altogether, picking her way through sword ferns and blackberry.

"What are you doing?" A boy's voice, in careful English this time. Before Selene could speculate for very long about who he'd have found out here to use English with, she pushed through a last tangle of undergrowth and saw them. Ginnie had found some twine somewhere, and seemed to be putting together some kind of snare. Arturo watched, his black hair standing up like he'd been crawling through the blackberries instead of detouring around them.

Ginnie lifted the snare, and illustrated how it would pull taut by slipping it over Arturo's wrist. The boy laughed, and Ginnie even cracked a smile. Selene froze where she was, lest she break the moment. She looked quickly around for Felicia and found her a few yards away, watching. Silver strode over to the young woman to prevent her from interrupting the children either.

Felicia crossed her arms, looking very much a big sister in the exasperation of her expression. She probably hoped she looked maternally protective, but Selene could spot the residu-

versation appear more casual. So you're stuck with babysitting for this trip, huh? What do you think of the reason your parents are here?"

Selene caught Felicia's frown out of the corner of her eye. "What do I think?"

"Do you want to move to the States?" Selene kept her tone light. If Felicia didn't bite on that one, she didn't see how to get at what she wanted to know without being stupidly blatant. How far did Andrew and Isabel plan to go? How desperately did they want the territory? The idea of a Felicia who wouldn't lose her grip on her discretion and offer her opinion on anything at all with a little careful prodding seemed so strange.

As different as her father was, Selene supposed. Selene simply hadn't had the time to plumb the depths of it yet. She and Felicia had been getting closer only lately in the real world, feeling out the relationship between stepmother and stepdaughter. She rubbed where her engagement ring wasn't, stopped when she caught herself doing it.

Felicia looked up and around her. "It's pretty. And less crowded, yes?"

Selene snorted. Anywhere would be less crowded than Europe, with too many packs always fighting over too little territory.

Arturo succeeded in wresting the snare away, and he triumphantly dashed into the bushes—straight through the blackberries. Ginnie sighed, grinned, and ran after him, though she had the advantage of the trail he'd blazed—or crashed—through the prickles first. Felicia frowned and hurried after them, but Selene touched her shoulder and pointed to a mostly parallel deer track. No particular point getting scratched when they could chart the kids' progress perfectly well by all the noise they made.

"Mother said the girl knew the Tainted One," Felicia said at length as they walked along. "I thought there weren't any survivors."

"She survived his care, not his silver." Selene pressed her lips together, using the pressure to keep her mind from once more painting a picture of what it had been like. She could imagine it all too well, but she didn't need to. "It is undoubtedly the crueler fate."

Felicia shook her head, not understanding. Selene sorted hurriedly through different amounts of honesty. When implication failed, how much would Isabel blame her for opening her daughter's eyes to the darker parts of the world around them?

"He took her with him, cared for her while he did terrible things to other Were. Years, she was raised by him, if you can call it raising." Better Felicia understand a few things about the world, now she was all but an adult. In the real world, her

Felicia hadn't had any choice in having her understanding expanded.

This Felicia stuttered to a stop. "He—?"

~~shocked, he seemed to~~ have forgotten he held her. The snare lay snarled on the ground between them, forgotten.

"Let her go!" Selene shouted, at the same moment Felicia shouted something in Spanish. Their words overlapped and Arturo only looked more confused.

Ginnie used his grip to throw him to the ground. Finally he let go, but she sat on his chest instead of letting him up. She snatched up a stick from the ground beside her and snapped it. Selene darted forward as Ginnie discarded one half and held the other, sharp point down, like an arrow. She grabbed his wrist and pinned it, inner arm upward, and aimed the point at the inside of his elbow.

Selene caught her wrist before it descended. Felicia hardly seemed to realize what was happening yet. Selene made sure the grip was firm and tight. If Ginnie didn't like being held, that would certainly get her attention.

"Do not be Stefan," she said.

Ginnie's fingers instantly went limp, and the stick fell. She stared at Selene, wide-eyed, then the sobs began, and she shook her head wildly. Selene tugged her standing, and Arturo made good his escape, crying himself, to cling to his sister's side.

"They come when you're angry, don't they? Those things he did, as pictures in your head. And the anger comes when you're scared, because you were scared for too long, and if you're scared for too long, you either get angry or you give up and throw your voice to Death. And you just want to get rid of the anger." Selene didn't quite know where the words were coming from, but she knew deep in the fundamental tone of her voice that they were true. Just because they were true didn't mean they were the right ones for Ginnie at this moment, but some instinct told her that no one else had been willing to give Ginnie any truth lately.

Ginnie's sobs turned to silence, intensity of emotion suppressed down to a steady stream of tears that could be hidden at need. Selene suspected there had been need. Her eyes stayed tight on Selene's face. "Those pictures aren't *real*. Not for you. Not unless you make them real. And you don't need to make them real. They're a part of you, but you are not only your parts. *You* decide who you are." Selene felt like she was running down a hill now. She had to keep going until the end, or she would fall and things would be worse than before.

"You are not what he made you. You are what you make yourself. Remember that. *Always* remember that."

"What doesn't kill you makes you stronger?" Felicia offered hesitantly.

Selene had forgotten the young woman was there, and she clenched her teeth at her words. Good, that Felicia was trying to talk Ginnie down, not attack her for her behavior, but that was not the kind of talking down Ginnie needed. "I think to see where he'd come from? But after so long not knowing his real name, why change now, for a dead man?" All a lie, but then again this whole world was probably a lie or a dream, so

Ginnie shook her head once, a small movement he didn't seem to notice, but Selene did, as had probably been the girl's intention. She didn't buy Selene's story. But somewhere in her face dawned a kind of hope, or fellow-feeling. Perhaps the idea of someone sharing painful secrets reassured her.

But not enough to stay. Ginnie turned away into the woods, but she walked this time, instead of running. "I'll bring some food out later," Selene called after her. Ginnie didn't turn around to acknowledge the promise.

"What's wrong with her?" Arturo whined into the silence. "She hurt me and didn't get in trouble." Felicia gathered him close to her, frowning and protective.

"Because she's been hurt herself. She has to learn not to hurt others because of that. It's a long trail." Selene blew out a breath. Felicia glowered at her, not seeming to understand, and ushered her brother roughly out of the trees.

Selene followed them back toward the guesthouse at a distance large enough Felicia hopefully shouldn't object. No need to stay out here when Ginnie wanted to be alone. She could at least go tell Lilianne that she'd laid the groundwork for later healing for the girl.

most who say that should be almost killed to test t
she said, keeping her tone teasing, but pointed. Caref
This needed finesse, not platitudes.

"You do not choose what has been made a part of
lene swiped some of the built-up salt from Ginnie's ch
her thumb. "And it is not stronger, or better, but it is n
either. It's what we all must build ourselves from."

Ginnie's tears slowed, gradually, and Selene relea
wrist. Ginnie didn't run, but she did back up a step. H
moved in a word, and it took Selene several repetitions t
it. "Stefan." She said it out loud, to make sure she was righ
Ginnie nodded emphatically.

Selene shook her head in response. They'd been ta
about Stefan for this whole conversation, but she didn
what Ginnie's final point was.

"Who's that?" Felicia asked, eyes narrowing with suc
suspicion at Selene. She petted her brother's hair.

Only then did she get it. No survivors, no one save
mute girl knew the name of the one they'd finally killed, kil
before he could say anything. Selene had no reason to know
name, but Ginnie had just confirmed it.

Selene pressed her thumb to her forehead. "His voice
in the void now. The others do not say his name, but I do n
think anything can call him back from the depth the Lady ha
cast him to."

Felicia also touched her forehead automatically, but didn
look convinced that only religious superstition had kept others
from mentioning his name before.

Selene tried again. "You think we didn't check his pockets,

most who say that should be almost killed to test the theory," she said, keeping her tone teasing but pointed. Careful, Felicia

wrist. Ginnie didn't run, but she did back up a step. Her lips moved in a word, and it took Selene several repetitions to catch it. "Stefan." She said it out loud, to make sure she was right, and Ginnie nodded emphatically.

Selene shook her head in response. They'd been talking about Stefan for this whole conversation, but she didn't see what Ginnie's final point was.

"Who's that?" Felicia asked, eyes narrowing with sudden suspicion at Selene. She petted her brother's hair.

Only then did she get it. No survivors, no one save one mute girl knew the name of the one they'd finally killed, killed before he could say anything. Selene had no reason to know his name, but Ginnie had just confirmed it.

Selene pressed her thumb to her forehead. "His voice is in the void now. The others do not say his name, but I do not think anything can call him back from the depth the Lady has cast him to."

Felicia also touched her forehead automatically, but didn't look convinced that only religious superstition had kept others from mentioning his name before.

Selene tried again. "You think we didn't check his pockets,

to see where he'd come from? But after so long not knowing his real name, why change now, for a dead man?" All a lie, but then again this whole world was probably a lie or a dream, so who was to say that it wasn't true, she just couldn't remember? Maybe this world was real and they'd checked his pockets, and that's where her broken mind had gotten the name. Selene hardly knew anymore, and her hands shook from walking so close to the edge with her words to Ginnie. She wanted to stop and breathe, and finally think straight for a while.

Ginnie shook her head once, a small movement. Felicia didn't seem to notice, but Selene did, as had probably been the girl's intention. She didn't buy Selene's story. But somewhere in her face dawned a kind of hope, or fellow-feeling. Perhaps the idea of someone sharing painful secrets reassured her.

But not enough to stay. Ginnie turned away into the woods, but she walked this time, instead of running. "I'll bring some food out later," Selene called after her. Ginnie didn't turn around to acknowledge the promise.

"What's wrong with her?" Arturo whined into the silence. "She hurt me and didn't get in trouble." Felicia gathered him close to her, frowning and protective.

"Because she's been hurt herself. She has to learn not to hurt others because of that. It's a long trail." Selene blew out a breath. Felicia glowered at her, not seeming to understand, and ushered her brother roughly out of the trees.

Selene followed them back toward the guesthouse at a distance large enough Felicia hopefully shouldn't object. No need to stay out here when Ginnie wanted to be alone. She could at least go tell Lilianne that she'd laid the groundwork for later healing for the girl.

Ares met her before she could turn aside to the farmhouse. The wind was in the wrong direction for her to smell his mood,

whatever careful phrasing he'd created in his head. "Lady damn it, we need you back here." He scrubbed a hand over his eyes. "I don't know how you did it, but at least you hit him where it hurts. He talks and talks, so smooth, and doesn't show any reaction to anything I try."

Selene licked her lips. Did she want to get drawn into this again? Get drawn into dealing with Andrew? Every time she stepped away, the dream seemed to herd her back. "Andrew Dare's strength has always been in his words—and his understanding of people. Understand someone deeply enough, and you know which words will flush them in one direction or another." And that was a good thing, when it was on her side.

Ares flicked her a sideways glance, but started striding for the guesthouse again. "Sounds like you understand him right back."

"I don't know. Maybe just enough to dig myself a deeper hole." Selene followed her brother before she'd even admitted her decision to herself. Dream or not, these were her people her brother was fighting for. She couldn't turn her back on that fight.

* * *

Edmond offered Andrew a brief rest from the frustrated circling of his thoughts the next morning. As Andrew paced from
the main hall back to his cabin, a last slice of toast in his hand,
the little boy pounded by, stuffed puppy clutched in his arms.
He had the worried look of a child running from punishment
and knowing he wouldn't escape it for long.

Sure enough, a few seconds later, John jogged up. Edmond stumbled and lost his puppy. It flopped bonelessly on
the gravel. He started to cry. "Papa, please." He pointed down
the road. "I want to go hunt lizards again." Some trick of his
tear-congested voice made his "papa" sound very like Felicia's
for a moment. Andrew winced. Letting things remind him of
his daughter was a trail that led deep into the swamp, going
nowhere fast.

"No, you have to stay safe." John gathered his son into his
arms. Edmond immediately began to scream, because his puppy was still down below.

Andrew ambled up to the pair, stooped to pick up the
toy, and carefully brushed it off. "Why can't he hunt lizards?"
He handed the puppy over. Edmond grabbed it, then started
struggling to get down again.

"It's not safe." John clutched his son closer, which brought
on a renewed spate of tears.

Andrew set his teeth. Far be it for him to tell another man
how to raise his son, but— "Let him use his own two feet, at
least. Lady, man. He has to learn to protect himself eventually."

A muscle jumped in John's jaw, and he turned away, still
pointedly holding his son. Andrew noticed that about a doz-
en paces down the road, he put Edmond down to walk on his

own, though.

Andrew started walking again in the opposite direction, though not fast, because he had no particular destination in

to nap in, even if the sunlight felt nice.

Finally her open neckline and the way she was sitting, palms on the wood back behind her hips to expose her cleavage to the sun as well, gave Andrew the clue he needed: she was tanning. It must be for the vapid act she used to influence Nate, the current Sacramento.

Then it hit Andrew: what he needed to do was set Nate and Rory against each other. He'd bet Allison would be quite happy to help him with that.

He crunched extra hard over the gravel to stand in front of her, eating his toast as he waited for her to acknowledge him. It took several more seconds for her tan to settle into a warm glow, and only then did she open her eyes.

She sat up straighter the moment she recognized him, however. She must not have known his scent well enough to identify him from that. "Does Roanoke want to talk to Sacramento about something? He's not here right now." She gave a little grimace like she couldn't possibly understand that kind of important business.

Andrew dusted toast crumbs off his fingers, and flopped onto the step beside her. She eyed him with surprise, and scooted pointedly away from him. "Actually, I wanted to talk to you about something, Allison."

"Oh, call me Allie." She laughed, shaking her head at the full version.

Andrew eyed her. In his false memories she'd put on a vapid act to be the power behind the alpha, something he must have culled from observation in his missing years, but he hadn't realized it would be this bad. Any minute now she'd giggle. "For the love of the Lady, Allison. Give it a rest for a minute."

"Give what a rest?" Her eyes narrowed at him, at least.

Andrew pressed his thumb to his forehead, swearing on the Lady. "I won't tell Nate. I know you have a hand in steering him, and I need your help."

Allison leaned forward, arms resting on her knees, body language growing tighter. "Just because Nate and I are playing chase doesn't mean I have any influence on him."

Andrew dipped a head in a nod. "You're right, it doesn't necessarily. But you do."

Allison was silent for a while, then she scraped her hair away from her face, and twisted it at the back of her neck. It didn't stay, but at least it kept it behind her shoulders. "You're supposed to be the brute enforcer who picks a fight at the slightest provocation. How are *you* the one who sees through it?"

"Because the brute was covering something else." Andrew illustrated by layering his hands. He turned to face Allison directly, and offered his hand out to shake. "Hi. I'm Andrew. I think only purse dogs pick fights for no reason, and I thi

ɪɪaun t naα time to think the idea through yet. But it should work. "What would Nate do if he found out that Rory was thinking of using his territory to get a foothold in the west? If Nate heard that Rory came to you, for example, and offered you the position of Sacramento sub-alpha in Roanoke if you'd help him get rid of Nate."

Allison's eyes sparked with anticipation. "He would explode. Almost literally. I'd have to time it carefully so Rory was in easy reach so Nate wasn't tempted to take a swing at anyone else, but . . ." She trailed off, apparently picturing it in her mind's eye, then clapped her hands. "Lady!" She grinned at Andrew. "If we can get them to beat each other down so far they're softened up for whoever wants to take them out—that's two birds with one snap of the teeth. It's brilliant."

"If it works." Andrew frowned at the gravel. Here was the hard part. "I know it's risky for you—and for me, but I'm used to it. But you're sure Nate would go snapping after Rory's throat if we set it up that way? It's no good if he strolls up to Rory and asks to discuss it like reasonable men."

"Oh, he would." Allison snapped her fingers. "He'd attack Rory just like that." She grinned. "I know just when and how to let it slip, too. Like I'm so staunchly loyal, I'm almost embarrassed to mention that someone had tried it on me."

"Perfect." Andrew clapped Allison on the shoulder. "Thank you," he said, low-voiced. He knew it would be easier for her to continue as she was, and it was such a relief to find someone who also had the emotional leeway to take risks to accomplish something important. "And now I'd better go before Rory sees us talking, and I have to kiss you too." He winked at her. "Though you could always close your eyes and imagine Selene."

Allison laughed, but she stared after him, looking rather bemused. "How did you know—?"

Andrew waved that away, and headed for his own cabin. Things were finally looking up. He'd have to watch matters carefully, in case Nate exploded too much, or Rory got angry enough to start beating up innocent bystanders as well, but he was finally cautiously optimistic. And once Rory was taken care of, he could get in contact with his daughter.

His heart sped as the door opened under his hand, but it was Benjamin who stood there, not Rory. Andrew grinned at him. "Don't you have your own cabin?"

"It's rather boring in comparison at the moment. You look like something's going right for once," Benjamin said with a ghost of humor as he shut the door behind them.

"I don't plan to go nose over tail by lifting my head so high I can't see the ground, but there's been progress, at least." Andrew glanced around the tiny cabin. With a meal just finished, and not much food in the cabin anyway, there wasn't much he could do to be hospitable. He sat in one of the chairs, letting

Benjamin take the slightly more comfortable couch, at least. "How much would you like to know, and how much do you

Andrew trailed off, waiting for Benjamin to voice whatever thought he was chewing on.

"I know you're tempted to project your enthusiasm onto others, but . . ." Benjamin sighed, and rubbed his hand along his hair. "We need you back here. Don't disappear into the rosy land of the best-case scenario." He rose to his feet and clapped Andrew on the shoulder. "Allison is in a different situation than you. I'm not saying she'll let you down, but don't rely too completely on her when you can't remember the past few years, and didn't know her well in the first place. All right?"

Andrew dipped his head in acknowledgment, because what Benjamin said was sensible. Andrew didn't necessarily agree, but he could see the logic. Sometimes you had to jump and trust your instincts about people.

Only time would tell whether he or Benjamin was right in this case.

17

Despite the continuing drag of exhaustion, Tatiana slept badly in the car that night. She'd parked in a small city lot between trendy little shops and restaurants near the water, in a neighborhood the highway exit had called "Historic Fairhaven." Sailings to Alaska didn't leave every day, so she was only lucky to find when she arrived that one left the next day. She'd considered a hotel room, but if the North Americans had managed to find her, then she would have been cut off from the car and the only reasonable chance of escape. The idea had been that she'd see them coming, but after a night of jumping at shadows and getting a crick in her neck, Tatiana was cursing her paranoia.

After all, how would the North Americans even know she was up here? There was no sub-pack closer to Bellingham than the Roanoke home pack; she'd made sure she got the locations

of all of them from the Alaskans before coming down here.
Tiny rain drops pittered on the windshield intermittently

.... glanced around her as she crossed the street to
the restaurant, allowing herself to notice history now as well
as possible approaches for the North Americans. This historic district didn't look *that* old, though some of the multisto-
ry brick stores definitely had a century on the others, despite
similarities of material and construction. She liked the lived-in
feeling, and touched the keystone in the arch above the door as
she entered the restaurant.

The text arrived when she was seated, rearranging the salt
and pepper shakers as she stared at the door and anyone coming in, waiting on her order of the largest combination of eggs
and meat and pile of pancakes available on the menu. Tatiana
set her phone flat on the table, frowning a little as she paged
through the unfamiliar menus.

I talked to your mother, the message said in Cyrillic characters, with Alexei's typical lack of preamble.

Tatiana wasted some time trying to get Cyrillic characters
out of the phone—clearly they were hidden in its tiny electron-
ic brain *somewhere*—before giving in and using English rather
than trying to transcribe Old Were. Alexei had enough to get
by. *Yes?*

A long pause, before an answer beeped. Tatiana assumed he was typing a lot, but she wasn't sure if that was good or bad. *She never knew anyone personally who had visions without wolfsbane. They tell young priestesses to avoid it at all costs. Very dangerous because you have no control over the strength of visions and other effects.*

By the time she finished reading that, another text had come in. *On track to make it out?*

Tatiana could imagine the words hanging in the air between the two texts: Why? Why do you ask? Her mother would have voiced the question, but Alexei wouldn't. He would have drawn his own conclusions. She didn't feel up to verifying them at the moment. *So far. Ferry*—she looked at it, then deleted it to take pity on Alexei's English. *Boat leaves for Alaska around dinner, local time,* she sent.

"Have you eaten yet?" Sacramento stood on the other side of her table, calm. She stayed that way, even when Tatiana stumbled to her feet. The phone skittered from her hand and clattered to the floor. Lady set her drifting in the void, she couldn't blame a mistake this elementary on the wolfsbane. She should have kept watching the door. Sacramento was so close now that she could grab Tatiana long before she reached any of the exits.

Sacramento slipped her fingertips into her hip pockets in a relaxed stance like she was waiting for Tatiana to make exactly that calculation. "You look like you could use the meal, so we could just talk until you're done."

Tatiana collapsed more than sat in her chair, and felt for the phone without taking her eyes off Sacramento. The other woman delicately took the other chair at the quaint little table beside the quaintly unpainted historic brick wall.

T... ... ...g up, anyway? As a sub-al-pha, shouldn't you be back leading your pack in the city of Sacramento?" Tatiana said.

Sacramento's scent sharpened briefly with discomfort and her lips thinned, then she seemed to decide to let it go and laughed. "The Roanokes invited me to stay until I choose a beta. And by invited, I mean *invited.*"

Tatiana smiled thinly as well. She could imagine that, the same as an *invitation* from her own alpha. She considered her possible misconceptions about how the North Americans dealt with betas from several angles before she tried to formulate a follow-up question to keep Sacramento talking. Her pack ran on betas' strength, and her alpha promoted someone to the position only after careful consideration. But her pack had so many that if one part of the pack was showing discipline problems, he could shuffle them around, rather than create a new one without due thought. "What happened with your last one?"

Sacramento pressed her palms together and tucked them between her knees. She was silent for several beats, and Tatiana got the feeling she was being assessed. She couldn't read

Sacramento well enough to guess with confidence, but she knew what she'd be assessing in Sacramento's place. Personal information often had little tactical value, but great emotional leverage and an equivalent value in fostered trust. Maybe Sacramento was actually delusional enough to still think she could talk Tatiana into coming back voluntarily. That made more sense than anything else as her play.

Tatiana's breakfast arrived and Sacramento waved off the waitress offering to take her own order as Tatiana dug in. At length, Sacramento laughed and picked up the thread of the conversation. "My last beta . . . which one? When I first came to power, I had Jen, but that went . . ." She sighed. "Very sour. She was so emotionally all over the place—that's what attracted me to her, that passion—but then she'd freak out because as an alpha I had to make reasonable, practical decisions she didn't like. And her father, the former alpha, was a cat's bastard and she couldn't see it, so it used to enrage her that I wouldn't pretend I was sorry he was dead."

Tatiana frowned, and mentally picked her way through the web of relationships. "So you took on the former alpha's daughter as your beta?"

Sacramento flicked a glance up, self-deprecating humor in her quirked lips. "Well, I was playing chase with her as well. Made it seem like a good idea at the time, to smooth the transition by keeping someone related to the old order in power." She broke into a helpless bark of laughter. "Lady, I think you have more in common with the Roanokes than any of you realize. That's *exactly* the expression they had when they talked to me about the chasing."

Tatiana tried to analyze her own expression from inside. Pained, presumably. Things were complicated enough in ne

..g-, ...-..., -u. 1 ieei iike 1 started my hunt far behind because of how bad my first beta was. I've had a couple different people since then, but it never quite . . . worked. We'd end up arguing too much. And I'm kind of used to doing it on my own at this point. My pack's small."

"You could go home and do what you like now," Tatiana said, dry. Even if the alphas woke up this minute, they'd still have too much to do, dealing with Tatiana, to bother with one sub-alpha's long-term leadership problems. Sacramento didn't have to involve herself, she could just walk away and let Tatiana get home.

"Nah, I think I'll stick around." Sacramento resettled her hands on the tabletop and winced when her phone purred a brief burst of vibration. "I think you'd rather have me at your flank for what's coming."

Something about Sacramento's sudden tension made Tatiana set down her fork without eating that bite and check the area again. The restaurant was calm, the few other humans talking quietly, but then the door opened. Felicia stepped inside, chin up in full-on avenging warrior mode, Tom-the-boyfriend only slightly behind her. Her rage was a palpable force, almost greater than scent alone could explain. "All I'm saying is, we had to track *her* to the prey, not the prey itself, which says nothing good about her loyalty," she said to Tom, too soft for most of the humans to notice, but plenty loud enough for Tatiana to pick up.

Felicia must be speaking about Sacramento and hadn't yet realized the sub-alpha and her "prey" were still in the building, because she paused before scanning the room. Sacramento had turned to look at Felicia, and maybe that wasn't much of an opportunity, but Tatiana was going to take it, by the Lady.

She bolted. Out, through the kitchen, moving fast enough that none of the kitchen staff gathered themselves to stop her. There were knives in a block on the counter along her path and she grabbed one as she wove through the obstacles, picking by handle size. Something substantial, but not too big. Whatever she had, she didn't look at it, just slammed out the door into the alley and down through the lot with the employee vehicles and delivery space.

It was drizzling only enough to dampen her hair and chill her skin, though there was plenty of mist out over the water. Tatiana looked around wildly, trying to orient herself. There was the ocean, the kitchen door must not have been directly opposite the front door, so to get to her car—

Felicia appeared around the side of the building at a run, coiling a whip into looser loops, presumably ready for use. Tom and Sacramento followed her, with another two Were. One was the teen that had been babysitting—her name escaped Tatiana—and the other was an older man, impeccably groomed and more collected than all of the others, with the air of someone exasperatedly following hot-headed orders to the letter. "Pierce, Tracy, get in wolf, cut her off," Felicia snapped

Tom ...

, ...g latiana in with the possibility of humans who might see. Homes with windows placed for the view on one side, and on the other a steep drop-off to maritime industrial warehouses on the shore. Tatiana kept to the gravel, but sooner or later, Felicia would win if it came to speed, or they'd both lose if someone spotted their weapons.

The slope seemed like it was becoming more gradual, at least what she could see of it under the dense blanket of blackberry and saplings, so when she saw a space without warehouses, she twisted to skid down it toward the water.

It wasn't any more gradual.

Tatiana tumbled, clothes and skin catching on branches and blackberry brambles with little pinpricks of pain underneath the bruising. She lost the knife but got a good grip on a sapling, held on until her feet dangled and she could skid the rest of the way on her ass. She gathered a few more minor bruises hanging up on sapling trunks, but at least she made it down.

She pushed to her feet not in the water or on the beach, as she'd expected, but on an artificially level strip of gravel that formed a railroad grade. On the other side of the tracks, the land dropped straight down about five feet to the water, with no sign of a beach. She had enough room to stand beside the tracks, which was good because she hardly had time to spot her knife and snatch it up before crashing noises rolled toward her and the blackberries spat Felicia out onto the gravel too.

They both looked warily at each other, and down the tracks for possible trains. Even if they weren't directly on the tracks, it couldn't be healthy to be three feet away when a train went by. But Tatiana remembered hearing trains only a few times a day yesterday, so they should be reasonably safe. Both from getting flattened, and from being observed by humans while they fought.

Felicia had kept her whip during the fall, and she shook it out now. Tatiana settled her grip more securely on the chef's knife, but she didn't know how to overcome the basic difference in reaches. She'd never had to fight a Spaniard before. If—when—she got home, she should suggest to the Teeth they add it to their training.

Always better to talk than fight in any situation, however. "You grew up in Spain? Not just born there?"

Felicia snarled, a deep, rolling sound, and flicked the whip out. Tatiana managed to dance back far enough the tip whistled past her chest. "How in the Lady's name could you know that?"

"You're using a Spanish weapon," Tatiana said, trying for a calm tone. Talking wasn't any use unless it distracted Felicia enough not to attack. Tatiana didn't want to add to her rage. "Your father mentioned his time in Spain."

Felicia lunged forward enough to bring her next stroke

into range. Tatiana slashed at the whip as she would have a knife stroke, with the vague hope of cutting the whip ~~ ˙˙ rupting the stroke, but ˢʰ~ ~ ˙

~ ~ʰᵃᵈ too far to cross. ... .ᴄᴋᴇᴜ ᴛne whip quickly, such a simple movement, and it bit deep into Tatiana's chest.

"Or you drank too much by mistake." Felicia raised her hand for the next stroke, calculating angles for something, though Tatiana couldn't tell what. "If too much is dangerous, but a little bit is fine . . ." Even when Tatiana staggered back, the whip lofted and smacked across her wrist with astonishing precision, hard enough for it to go numb. She dropped the knife.

Fine. Enough talking. Maybe losing the knife was a good thing. Tatiana rushed Felicia, absorbing another blow across her belly and upper arm, but then she was inside the weapon's reach. Felicia tried to reverse the handle, bring up the weighted end for a blow, but Tatiana smashed into her and bore her to the gravel. She sat over her hips and ripped the whip away, tossing it as far as she could.

Felicia snarled and bucked, but Tatiana was back on solid ground now. She knew instinctively the feel of the hold, and a satisfying change it was, too, to be the one with the heavier mass, the better muscle. Too often she'd been pinned under burly fellow Teeth.

She landed blow after blow on Felicia's face, going for blood as the young woman bucked. Someone this young, more intense pain, more blood, regardless of the real damage, was more frightening. Ended things sooner.

"Stop!" Hands wrenched at Tatiana's arm and Tom-the-boyfriend jerked her off and to her feet. All the fear of pain and blood was writ large across his face instead. Tatiana let her next blow carry into his stomach but he folded with it and didn't let go.

Now she was up and no longer focused on Felicia, she saw that the two others had made it down the slope as well, probably more gingerly on four feet. Even with too much blood in the air to identify them by scents, Tracy's exaggerated snarling and baring of teeth marked her. Pierce waited, and watched.

Tom hooked her leg, surprised her with the sophistication of the move, and got her down. The back of her head smashed into the gravel, centimeters from the unyielding line of a rail.

This time, she was the one outmassed. She tried to pin him, but he shoved, they rolled. Tatiana lost track of anyone else in the struggle as they grappled. Dammit, he was strong. If she could only get him lined up—

She rolled them a last time and Tom's head clonked resoundingly onto the metal rail and he went limp.

And someone twisted her arms behind her back and the tight, hard line of a zip tie settled around her wrists. "Enough, cubs," Pierce said. Tatiana jerked away from him automatically, but he pulled her off Tom and shoved her down with his knee in her back and let her writhe all she wanted. The brief glance she'd gotten suggested he was nude, and Tatiana couldn't imagine where he'd gotten the zip tie until she saw the spill of them from Felicia's pocket where she lay groaning farther down the railroad grade

_____ her muscles until con-trol started to slip away from her again.

Everyone was gathered in the grove, like for a holy day. But it wasn't everyone, Tatiana realized. Just all of the Teeth. Strange, because they were never all home at the same time. They should be scattered out on missions, or visiting mothers at outlying settlements. Still, they were all here, clustered out of reach of the tree's shadows, so they wore the pooled sunlight like a cloak edged with a ragged hem in a ring around the outside of the clearing. Noon, with the Lady not in the sky: another strangeness, a strange time to hold a ceremony.

She stood with a blanket clutched to her chest, hand-knitted and very soft against her fingers. Just right for a baby. She realized when this must be. She'd just told Father that she would kill no more for him. Small movements to duck a head and speak into an ear filled the group with whispers, like a breeze slipping through long grass.

"Thinks she's the favorite daughter, doesn't she, picking and choosing her missions?"

Tatiana couldn't pinpoint the speaker, but everyone's faces were indistinct anyway. It didn't matter who was saying it. She was sure they were all thinking it.

"There's enough of us. Why shouldn't we specialize? She can talk at our enemies until they surrender." The speaker laughed, too loud. Tatiana kept her chin high, and kept walking toward the center of the grove. She'd gotten the mocking looks, the suspicious looks, the angry looks, from her fellow Teeth when she'd really returned. She'd actually encountered them over time, here and there across the settlement as she ran into people, but she knew the looks ended. She would not apologize.

Alexei was in the crowd, and he nodded to her solemnly as she passed. The silent support steadied her, and she sped her steps. The Teeth had been pressed close, making it hard to get to the center, but with her growing confidence, they edged aside.

Mikhail stepped up to block her path, arms crossed. His dark hair was pulled back into a tail, and he moved even more gracefully than she remembered, like this vision was nothing but one long dance for him.

As if in response to her thought, he extended a hand to her. She took it, and he drew her close, turning them gently so she was facing away from the center of the grove. "Killing is what we do, Tatiana. Plenty of people who aren't Teeth don't kill, but you're a Tooth." He curled his arms around her so his fingertips brushed her Mark at the top of her back. The fabric of her shirt caught briefly on the roughness of the scar tissue, then slid free. "Are you going to refuse to shift, next? Plenty of humans live without shifting, but we're not humans, are we?"

"You're welcome to my kills." Tatiana leaned into him rather than t͟͟͟

... ...c caught her face between his hands. "Did she make you warm, ready to chase?"

He kissed her. Too hard, too demanding, nothing like her association with his lips, of a gentle enough teacher, her first time with a man. She'd been young then, only a year older than her first time playing chase with a woman.

She wasn't young now.

She shoved him violently away, and he went, smiling. "If you're going to die in a vision, don't you want to die dancing, die chasing, Tania?"

"I'm not dying!" Tatiana shouted it to Mikhail, to the Teeth, to the sunlight.

Mikhail gathered her to him once more, resting his cheekbone against her hair. "You will." The knife she hadn't seen went up, from beneath her ribs, to her heart. Wet, sharp slithery feeling, no pain. Her heart slowed as it leaked slowly away, over her belly and Mikhail's hand.

Tatiana tried to press her hand to slow the flow of blood, but her wrists were bound and there was no wound. She was in a car, the smooth movement deceptively lulling. She might have been placed in the backseat upright, but she'd slumped and now lay over two seats. She thought about righting herself to see out the windows, but it didn't really matter where they were. They were going back to the pack house.

A hand settled on her shoulder—in comfort? Apology?—and withdrew again. Sacramento's scent surrounded Tatiana, and her voice confirmed who had touched her a moment later. "We're not going to kill you," she promised, low-voiced.

Tatiana didn't answer. The wolfsbane visions certainly seemed to be trying to do it, if the North Americans couldn't finish the job. Lady damn it.

And yet. In this vision, her voice had been farther along the path to Death's throat than in all but the first, and she was still breathing. Her heart had continued without external assistance. It almost seemed worthy of Mikhail's teaching style, to show her safety by frightening her so badly first. Though if the dream had any teaching style, it would be her own.

And she wasn't dead yet. Maybe she needed to start paying attention to the visions for other lessons she'd need farther down the trail soon, now she was captured.

18

Selene and Ares walked into an intense conversation in Spanish in front of the guesthouse. Felicia was gesturing wildly and pointing to where her brother had tucked himself against his mother's side. Andrew stood tall in front of the house's door and listened impassively. With the late-morning sunlight touching the eaves and the needles of the trees leaning over the roof, it looked quite a picturesque setting for such a dramatic retelling.

Felicia whirled when they arrived. "Not just crazy. Dangerous!" she said, words in English for their benefit, though her accent was extra thick.

"Oh, the beta's back." Andrew gave her an insincere smile, and Selene braced herself. He was planning something. She knew it instinctively. "I hear your broken child is a danger to others."

Ares growled low in his throat, so Selene hurried to fore-stall him. "She fights when restrained, yes." She let sarcasm saturate her voice. "Which is *such* a shocking thing for her to do, considering the dozens—or more—of Were she witnessed being killed after being restrained, don't you think?"

Andrew's smile widened, growing sharper. "Your beta speaks with the skill of a true verbal fencer, Vancouver Island. Where did she learn it?" Selene doubted any of the adults missed the implication that she couldn't possibly have gotten it from Ares.

Selene desperately wanted to tell Andrew, "From you." But in her Dare it had been turned to protect, not defeat. "My question is why it's necessary. Weren't you ready to storm away, just last night?"

Andrew shrugged. "Sometimes emotions run high. Then cooler heads prevail." His message to Selene was clear enough: she would not find that spot tender any longer. He'd undoubt-edly spent the night building up his emotional armor around it and anything connected to it. He smiled at Ares. "But you're still letting your beta speak for you. Don't you have anything to say yourself?"

Ares snarled at Andrew's patronizing tone, and even rocked his weight forward like he was thinking of lunging at him. Selene stared, and then tried to hide the fact that she was staring. What had she missed, out with Ginnie this morning? That had been a mild enough insult, even coming after the earlier implications, and Ares's temper was not generally this quick.

"What would you have done?" Ares snapped. Selene put

her hand on his arm, and he ignored her. "When Were were dying?"

"A strategic retreat to deal with a threat doesn't constitute abandonment of territory—" Selene spoke as quickly as she could, but this time, it was Andrew who cut her off.

"Your beta can dress it up as prettily as she wants, but—"

Ares did lunge toward Andrew this time, stopping just sort of shoving the other man. "I led the pack that killed the Tainted One. How dare you forget that! If not for me, he would have started on the European packs next, count on it."

"An animal that allows itself to be cornered can sometimes accomplish amazing feats." Andrew's tone was at his most reasonable, his most soft-spoken.

Selene's voice disappeared for a moment out of sheer shock. Had Andrew truly just said that? What was he trying to do, provoke Ares into a challenge?

"That insult is too low for my alpha to bother answering." Selene shoved between her brother and Andrew, moving Ares back to do it. She hardly knew what she was saying before she said it, but she had to do something before Ares challenged. He would lose. Loyalty to her brother be damned, she knew with unfailing certainty that Andrew would be too much for him. Andrew looked lean, but he was crafty, and she'd never be able to warn her brother of that in a way he'd believe. Andrew had the kind of clever calculation you didn't realize until after he was the victor, when you analyzed what had gone by too fast for you to understand.

"If you were Madrid, I would challenge your beta. How about her instead? She's like your second." Selene pointed to Isabel. The Spanish woman arched her eyebrows with graceful incredulity, but she nudged her son over to Felicia and walked forward to stand tall, straight and unencumbered. Since it was for an insult, not hierarchy or dominance, Selene could have challenged Andrew himself, but even if the idea of fighting him didn't make her flinch inside, they were too unevenly matched. She would bet that this Andrew had plenty of experience fighting in both wolf and human, where she hadn't had a wolf form, or two working arms, for five years.

She also knew that sometimes the best way to fight a physical battle was to find the way to make it something other than a straight physical battle, but it appeared she didn't have a choice this time.

Andrew glanced back at his wife, then settled into dangerous stillness. "If I am the one who gave insult, why not challenge me, beta?"

Selene's heart pounded, hard. What had she gotten herself into? She was too distracted to use her words as weapons this time. "Because I'm not *stupid*."

Strangely, Andrew laughed, a sharp bark of a sound. "You aren't, are you?" He stepped back out of the way, leaving Selene to face Isabel, with her clueless brother still standing at her back, glowering. "Isabel?" Andrew checked.

"If she wishes." Isabel stepped out of her shoes as she came forward, though she didn't undress further yet. "Take Arturo inside, Felicia." Sh̲e̲ ̲.̲.̲.̲ ̲.̲.̲.̲.̲ ̲.̲ ̲.̲ ̲.̲ ̲.̲.̲ ̲.̲ ̲.̲ ̲.̲ ̲.̲

ɡ̲.̲.̲.̲.̲.̲.̲.̲.̲.̲.̲ ̲.̲.̲.̲ ̲ ̲ ̲ ̲ ̲w̲ı̲t̲ı̲ı̲
many reluctant glances behind her. While she was watching them, Ares grabbed Selene's arm. "What are you doing?" he whispered harshly in her ear.

Selene paused a beat, knowing it would be nearly impossible to speak softly enough to keep Andrew from overhearing. But what did it matter if he heard his own plans, anyway? She whispered, to at least tell Andrew it was supposed to be private. "He was trying to provoke you into challenging. And Lady love me, I can't explain to you how I know, but you *will* lose, Ares. If you fight him. Let this stay a fight between a beta and a mid-ranker over an insult, all right?"

Isabel stepped neatly out of her pants and began shrugging out of her shirt. Selene would have liked to stall about her clothing but she didn't dare in case it looked like fear. It wasn't Isabel she was suddenly worried about. She hadn't considered it when she issued the challenge, but now a single question dug its teeth into her voice.

Did she have a wolf form?

If she was dreaming, she didn't, back in her real body. But in dreams one could fly, or walk through walls, or do any number of impossible things that had nothing to do with one's real body. And if this wasn't a dream, if her "memories" had sprung up from a crack in her mind, shouldn't she be perfectly capable of shifting?

Even before she finished pulling off her underwear, Selene reached for the feel of her wolf form. Was it truly hard to find, or had she become too unaccustomed to the feeling of touching it, pulling it up and through herself?

Selene ignored Isabel and stood nude, gritting her teeth. She could shift. There was no reason for her not to be able to shift. Anything else was the fear talking. She reached desperately for the shift, putting her whole metaphorical voice and every muscle into the effort.

Pain. Wrenching pain, twisting through her whole body. Selene stopped and collapsed to her hands and knees. For a moment, her left arm buckled, not holding her weight, and her vision blurred. Everything hurt so much, she hardly knew which way was up. Her heart labored, slow, too slow. Too much pain, too much pressure, and she was failing. Selene fought, and it did no good.

When they arrived at the pack house, they dragged Tatiana down to the basement for no reason she could understand at first. The alphas were there, laid out in a pair of beds, but their condition looked unchanged. The beta and a stranger, high-ranked by his body language, had gathered there, so Tatiana presumed her interrogation had been added to the agenda of an existing meeting. Oddly, the human woman was also present.

Before she could do more than make that brief survey of

the situation, a low whine caught her attention, like someone
wanted to moan but didn't have enough air.

On one bed, Silver's body jerked

anyone specifically mention sounds seeping through, but in
a Wisdom Ceremony, one could hear everything. The Vision
Ceremony was in some ways just an intense Wisdom. "Silver!"
she shouted, ignoring her captors. "No! You can't!"

The arch didn't ease. Muscles tight, too tight, so tight they
looked like they should be tearing, and still Silver didn't relax.

"No! You can't!" For a moment, Selene imagined that a woman
had said that. She let the fight go and the pain receded. The
world firmed, and she lifted her head. Isabel stood silent and
confused, lips closed. Ares had been the one who'd spoken. The
pain lingered in a wearing wash, but Selene got to her feet and
pulled herself together. She'd already made the challenge, so
she'd have to, whatever Ares said.

"In human, perhaps," Selene said, and smiled thinly at Isabel. The other woman was still in human as well, perhaps distracted from her own shift by Selene's troubles. Selene stooped
to pick up her clothes and start pulling them back on. Better
to wear them when fighting in human to add some protection,
however minor.

"If you can't win the challenge properly—" Finally Andrew sounded less than cool and calm, but only so far as mild frustration and impatience. Selene supposed he saw her as a delay.

Isabel began pulling her clothes back on, too. "Oh, let her use what advantage she can get. She will need it." Smugness threaded through her words. Selene could guess her thoughts: she could have claimed victory by default, but what satisfaction was there in that? Selene would be easy enough to beat.

Selene would indeed need every advantage, but she didn't plan to make beating her *easy*. She considered leaving off her shoes, but those could be useful to kick with. Isabel noticed her pulling them on and did likewise.

Then there was nothing more to stall with. They faced each other, circled, getting scent from different angles. Isabel smelled confident, but Selene thought she had been right before. Isabel hadn't been in a fight in years, and that made her at least pause, if not precisely worry.

Isabel lunged first, punching right for Selene's face. When Selene dodged, Isabel grabbed a handful of her hair, clearly meaning to sling her to the ground. Selene clamped her hand down on top of Isabel's to avoid the pain of pulled hair and kicked at her, again and again, neglecting aim for power.

When she did connect, slamming hard into Isabel's shin, they both stumbled. Isabel jerked Selene along with her as her balance wavered. Selene lost her control over Isabel's grip, and the other woman yanked her head to the side so hard her eyes watered from the pain. Selene kicked and raked her nails at Isabel's face.

Isabel flinched back as Selene neared her eyes, and Selene

seized her advantage. She slammed into Isabel, carrying the other woman to the ground. She got in one punch to Isabel's nose before she needed both her hand~ ~~ ~ ~ ~ ~ ~ ~

ᴣɪɪᴀɪɪᴇᴜ, ana Selene realized how silent the fight had been until that moment, only punctuated by their panted breaths and grunts. Both of them knew better than to bother with taunts. She twisted in turn, punched again at Isabel, and even scored a few hits before Isabel pinned one of her arms. Her right arm, her good arm. Selene tried not to think herself into trouble, but her left grew less and less coordinated as she concentrated on it. She had to move it by instinct, or her mind tried to remember that it wouldn't move at all.

Isabel got another good grip on Selene's hair at the side, lifted her head, and smashed the back into the ground. Gray fuzzed out her vision, and Selene wrenched her hips up for one last effort to dislodge Isabel. Isabel slammed her head down again, even harder this time.

Darkness.

During lunch, the whispers spread across the room almost faster than did Nate's and Rory's voices. The morning Convocation session had been normal enough—arguments over the proper punishment for kids who'd trespassed made a change from wrangling over territory lines, Andrew supposed—but now everyone in the hall suddenly knew something was happening over at the back near the door to the kitchen.

The Convocation hall was a converted barn, weathered wood bones soaring two stories up, except for a balcony made from the old hayloft at the back. Underneath the balcony, two push doors led to the kitchen. People were trying to get a good view without looking like they were watching, so the area around Nate and Rory actually cleared out a little as Andrew watched from the other side of the room.

For a moment, Andrew considered ignoring them and their shouting match, but if he hadn't had anything to do with the fight, wouldn't he go and bask in the schadenfreude? He figured he probably would. He set his plate down on one of the rented banquet tables set in an open square around the room, and sauntered over to gawk openly. At the moment, Nate was the one speaking, biting off words with icy intensity. His black hair was cropped short, not long enough to be gelled as it had been the last time Andrew false-remembered seeing him. It made the cutting sharpness of his features even more pronounced.

Even arriving at the middle of his rant, Andrew recognized it: the usual Western pack rhetoric about how Rory would never catch them sleeping and manage to take over a pack with his power-grubbing ways.

Andrew tuned it out and watched his alpha instead. Would Rory lose his temper enough to attack? He looked annoyed, certainly, standing with his arms crossed and jaw clenched. But

if Andrew was tuning out the Western pack rhetoric, he'd bet
Rory was doing it doubly so.

"If you think you can turn my people ~~~~~~ ~

knows you can hardly even hold Roanoke, without leaning on
your pet berserker. I wonder how many people in other Western packs you've tried to suborn so you can lean on them too."

Rory snarled. "I did no such thing." He rocked his weight
forward on his toes, and Andrew silently urged him on. Lunge,
attack. It wouldn't matter if he won or lost, the effort would
bring him down to a level Andrew could hope to touch.

Rory settled back again. "Bring him forward, then. Let
everyone smell him lying." Just like Rory, to assume that an
influential player must be a man.

Andrew clenched his hands in his pockets. What if Allison did smell like a lie? He had to think that playing the part
she did, she'd have practice at all the Were tricks for avoiding
it—like concentrating on something else that evoked a strong
emotion, or examining all the reasons you didn't care whether
what you said was true or not.

Sacramento turned, but Allison was already striding forward, chin high, before he beckoned. Andrew didn't try to
catch her eye, but he mentally sent her support. He respected
her for brazening it out, even as things seemed to be falling

apart. Maybe they could pull this off yet. It didn't matter what Rory thought, only that Nate continued to believe Allison long enough to attack him.

Rory saw Allison and laughed. "Her?" He grinned, even when he stopped laughing to speak. "Why would I try to suborn *her*?"

Andrew could read the thought plain as day on Nate's face. When he thought about it, he agreed with Rory. None of them knew Allison like Andrew did, so they couldn't understand why anyone would trust her with anything.

Andrew strode forward even as he saw the thought. Lady damn it, he should have thought of that. But he was too slow, and Nate seized Allison's wrist. "Lying cat!"

"Better that than spend one more day under your pathetic leadership, holding myself back so you can catch me in your pathetic version of playing chase!" Rage flashed across Allison's face, and even with her hair down and a ridiculous tan, Andrew saw the Allison he remembered. Passionate, fighting for what she wanted. "If he really had come to me, maybe I'd have said yes, taken the pack, and told him where he could bury the 'sub' alpha nonsense."

She jerked her wrist away from him, but Nate caught it again, and then the other. Andrew reached them and wrenched apart at least one hold, a hand on each person's arm.

Rory stepped up behind him, dropped an arm around his throat, and tightened. "You stay out of this, Dare. Leave the man to his sovereign pack."

Fighting against the gray taking over his vision, Andrew had no choice but to drop their hands, even if he'd been able to avoid the instinctive scrabble of his fingers at Rory's hold.

Rory loosened his arm, dragged him back, and let him go. Andrew knew better than to move forward again, ~~~~~ ~~ ~~~

just that way when he had Silver in his hands, certain that he would have all the time in world to hurt her.

Nate swung Allison by her wrist, throwing her off-balance, then with a hand on the back of her head, slammed her face into one of the tables. She didn't straighten immediately, clearly woozy, and he slammed her down again.

And again. Blood scent went from a seep into the air to a cascade, splashing from the smashed mess of her nose, and pooling up in two black eyes that healed only to be renewed again on the next smash.

Allison keened from the pain, and the room held its collective breath, but no one stepped forward. Andrew grunted under his breath with the effort of holding himself still. He couldn't just watch this. Maybe he'd make it worse, maybe Nate would be done in another moment, but he couldn't— He rocked forward, and Rory touched his back. Damn him! Andrew couldn't help if he was unconscious, either.

"I think she's learned her lesson, Nate." Maybe he could at least distract the man with words.

"Don't know. Shall we see?" Nate smiled a sick sort of

smile, and let Allison rest bent over the tabletop, bleeding quietly. He twisted one arm up behind her back to hold her there, and started snapping her fingers.

Snapping them and holding them there as they healed.

Andrew remembered that trick. He strode forward at the same time Rory shouted, "Enough!" and didn't stop Andrew.

Andrew jerked Nate aside, threw him into the nearest wall. He didn't follow to beat him, just put all of his rage and his shaking disgust into the impact. The boards splintered, and Nate leaned against them, stunned. "If she'd killed you—if a human hunter blasted you in the head with a gun this moment—only your daughter would mourn you. Do you know that, Nate? Not your pack, not your lover. Only your daughter would, because you've had your chance to raise her blind. Your son was a kindred spirit, but he was executed for his crimes. Your time will come."

Andrew put his hand flat on Allison's back, gently. "Can you take it if I fix your fingers now?" he asked, leaning in close to give their conversation at least the illusion of privacy.

"Quick," Allison said, managing a breathy, wretched little laugh. Andrew obliged, and she keened once more.

Nate's footsteps approached with a bit of a stagger, but then stopped when Rory moved. "That's enough, Sacramento." Andrew didn't look up from his task, but he imagined Rory crossing his arms and looking his most tanklike. That's one thing you could say about Rory; he was an ineffective leader because he let his anger get the better of him, and he took it out on his subordinates, but only on strong subordinates. Never the weak. And it was a clean beating, no joy at particularly inventive or slow methods of inflicting pain.

"All right, puppy. Let's do your nose quick too, okay?" Andrew helped her straighten, then turned her and boosted her to sit on the table. She leaned against his shoulder for ---

---, voice, I'm sorry, he said on a low breath. If he hadn't talked her into this—

"Shut up," Allison said with ragged humor. "At least I'm shot of that cat now. Had to happen sometime. Hey!" She protested with a little more volume as Andrew picked her up. The strength of her voice suggested her healing was making it through the worst of the pain. Good. "I don't walk with my face, dumbass."

Andrew surveyed the room as he turned around with her. He saw support, and some remaining shock. It seemed Nate had taken everyone by surprise, and they were happy someone was making some kind of amends for it. A knot of several alphas was converging on Nate, to have words with him, Andrew hoped. Too much to hope that they'd inflict the kind of pain he'd been dishing out as well.

"You deserve to be pampered a bit," Andrew said, and didn't let her down. She subsided against him fairly quickly, humoring him, Andrew suspected. He didn't mind if she humored him, as long as it allowed him to do something constructive.

She fell silent until they were outside and properly alone,

crunching along the gravel to the cabins, sunlight fierce on them, away from the shade of the building. "If it was my idea, Rory has no reason to do anything to you. You'll be in a position for another try."

Andrew stopped short. He'd made his mistakes, and no way anyone else was going to suffer for them. "Allison, don't—"

"No, after that display, there's going to be a shakeup in my pack, count on it. Gets Nate out of power, and that's what I wanted. I've got my win; you should get another shot at yours." Allison patted his chest.

Andrew snorted. "If that's what you count as a win . . ." He trailed off, trying to decide how hard to argue. If that's what she really wanted, it was her right to declare herself satisfied with what had happened. He couldn't escape the guilt over having caused her pain while standing by unharmed, though.

"I'm sure you'll get chewed up several more times before this is all over. I plan to keep my head down and heal in peace." Allison twisted in his grip as he approached the Sacramento cabin. "I can . . . snag a free bed over on the Roanoke side, maybe? I don't want to be there when Nate gets home."

"Of course. I'll get your stuff once you're settled." Andrew detoured to his own cabin. Allison let her head relax. Andrew could feel in her muscles that the posthealing exhaustion had hit.

He had to pause for a few moments at the door, juggling her weight to get his hand on the knob. "How'd you know I have a crush on Selene?" Allison murmured, then laughed, clearly a bit punchy with the exhaustion.

Andrew exhaled in amusement, and humored her in turn.

"Well, you like women, and she's attractive. It seemed like a reasonable guess." Very attractive, was Selene. If only she wasn't so strangely wrong when compared to his false memories.

, in any case, Allison found her way immediately to the empty bedroom. The springs creaked like she'd flopped onto the bed from a mostly standing position. She wasn't asleep quite yet, though. Her voice floated into the kitchen where Andrew was getting himself a drink of water. "Seriously, though. How in the Lady's name do you know I prefer women?"

"Lucky guess." Andrew sipped the water, and frowned out the window at the rocky soil dividing the cabin from the trees. How had he known?

How were his dreamed memories so accurate?

19

Felicia had been strutting proudly before "her" captive on the way down into the basement, but when Silver started seizing, she left Tatiana for Silver's side instantly. "Come on, come on," she whispered under her breath, and tried to ease Silver's body down, massage the muscles back into a more relaxed position.

Tatiana remained tethered by Pierce's firm grip on her arm, her wrists still secured behind her back. He tugged her aside to let Tom out from behind them. Sacramento seemed to have disappeared sometime on the journey through the house. Undoubtedly a sound tactical decision, to avoid people asking questions about why Felicia had succeeded where Sacramento had failed in the capture.

Tom went to hover over Felicia and Silver for a beat, seemed to realize he couldn't help, and went to check on Andrew, who was sleeping on, oblivious. John and the stranger remained where they could keep an eye on both alphas simultaneously, though it seemed more of an effort on John's part to

, ... around to Iom. "You should go get one of the shakes. She feels a little hot. She's probably got to heal it, like Papa." Tom jogged up the stairs, as ordered.

With Silver out of danger for the moment, Tatiana turned her attention to the newcomer. He had richly brown skin and an air of grace to how he stood. When he caught her examining him, he tipped his head in greeting and examined her in turn.

He reminded her of her alpha, Tatiana realized with a shock. He had the air of a very old Were, someone who had experienced more than she'd lived in her entire life, someone who could predict what she would do simply because he'd seen so many people like her do it before. She hated that feeling.

Susan released her grip on John's arm to hold his hand instead, and with a slight jolt of shock, Tatiana noticed their hands properly. They were wearing wedding rings. Married? Susan had clearly known more than a human should when Tatiana had seen her after surviving the wolfsbane, but she was *married* to a Were? How could anyone possibly allow that?

While she waited for Tom to return, Felicia came around to the end of the alphas' beds to glower at Tatiana. The move-

ment distracted Tatiana from the human, and she winced in-
ternally when she noticed that in wiping the blood off her face,
Felicia had missed a streak in the hairline in front of her ear.
Perhaps it had been foolish to make the young woman angrier
by hurting her more than necessary. But it had seemed necessary at the time. Tatiana dropped her eyes to look weak. She
could at least try not to antagonize her now.

Felicia's lip curled in an unvoiced snarl. "There's some of
the wine left. I suppose you all don't want to execute her, so I
think we should give her enough she's sharing their experienc-
es properly." She gestured back in the general direction of the
alphas.

"That would be the same as an execution." Tatiana didn't
mean it to sound as dire as it came out, but if they meant to kill
her, better they intend to. She'd hate Death to gain her voice by
a simple miscalculation. She saw the new, older Were react to
her accent now she was saying more than a few words. She gave
him a thin smile. She didn't have the humor for a Bond joke at
the moment.

Felicia growled. "So you say. All we have is your word for
it!" She rocked forward, then strode for Tatiana.

John dropped Susan's hand and put out his arm so Felicia
tangled with it before she reached Tatiana. "Felicia. Stop this."
He put enough authority into his tone that she stepped back,
but she kept glowering, not accepting the order gracefully.

"What if she is not lying, and more wolfsbane will kill her?
You need to fully consider that outcome. Does she deserve to
die? Your parents are not dead, and may yet recover." The older
man's voice was just as level and considered as Tatiana would

have predicted. At least he was arguing on her behalf. She thought. Her alpha was usually three turns of the trail ahead of everyone when he spoke.

her breath. Tom smiled hopefully at her when Silver swallowed a whole can without incident, but she seemed too tangled up in her own emotions to notice.

Tatiana eased back toward the wall as much as Pierce's grip on her arm would allow. Felicia had plenty of people in the room to vent her anger on. Hopefully if Tatiana kept a low profile, Felicia would focus on the others for a while.

"I suspect you can figure out part of it yourself, with some consideration," Boston said with a probably calculated degree of disappointment. He folded his hands together. "With their envoy's knowledge or not, Russia has moved against us. Our response is our next move. Do we kill their envoy? Perhaps that is the excuse they wish for pack war. Do we threaten to kill their envoy to force them instead into an action we prefer? Roanoke is large, and Russia is large, and far, far more is at stake than one life, girl."

Felicia looked up, mouth slightly open as her immediate response died on her lips. She did see when she thought about it, Tatiana could read that in her expression. But she didn't like seeing it. Tatiana saw something else: if Boston decided, after careful consideration and discussion, that Tatiana needed to be killed, he would do it without hesitation or regret. Not a good thing for her continued survival, but at least he would consider.

Felicia shoved away from Silver's bed and came to stand, metaphorical hackles bristling, in front of Boston. Her volume ratcheted up with each word. "One life? The Russian's life? How about two? How the two most important lives in Roanoke? You're playing political games while they're dying!" She screamed that last, hands clenched at her sides.

Boston showed no reaction. "If they are dying, as I understand it, there is nothing to be done about it at the moment. Thus, I am tracking political possibilities in the downtime. You are welcome to use it to fret, or throw tantrums, instead."

Felicia growled deeply and launched herself at Boston. Or tried to launch herself, but Tom caught her from behind. Silently, he got a good hold on her shoulders and twisted her around to face the stairs. He propelled her firmly toward them. Felicia could have pulled away, but she seemed too surprised to do it yet. "Tom, what are—? I'm not done—" She switched to angry Spanish, clearly swearing at him as she twisted back. Tom blocked her with his body, turned her shoulders back around, and calmly guided her up the stairs.

Tatiana stared after them until a choked laugh jerked her attention back to Boston. "Lady, if only someone had thought to do that to Dare when he was her age."

Susan covered her curving lips with her fingertips, and even John cracked a smile. "They've been roaming together for six months. Guess he's picked up a couple tricks."

Tatiana twisted to stare at the door at the top of the stairs.

That was one way to deal with a tantrum, she supposed. She wouldn't have thought of it herself. The swearing trailed off to be replaced with voices at much lower volume a few minutes

Boston nodded once, somehow respectful of Felicia even in his acceptance of a well-deserved apology. "We need to consider our move carefully."

Sacramento looked in from the top of the stairs, presumably attracted by all the shouting. She looked concerned and trying to hide it. When no told her to chase her tail elsewhere, she jogged down the stairs to hover at the edge of the gathering. "Do you really need the envoy down here for this? Pierce and I could take care of her upstairs."

Tatiana would have liked to heartily second the idea, but she doubted that would make the outcome more likely. She supposed she should have tried to stay to argue her case, but she'd been doing a shit job of that so far, and it had to be weighed against the rising emotions her presence seemed to evoke.

Boston raised his eyebrows at Sacramento. "And if we need to ask her something?"

Sacramento threw him a thin smile. "You'll have time to craft your questions to be as sneaky as possible by the time you call her back down. Let her take a shower or something. We'll make sure she's secure afterward." She sounded almost protective. Tatiana wished she wouldn't be. It made everything too complicated.

"And you'll accidentally let her escape one more time?" John said, moving a little closer like he was afraid Sacramento would jump Pierce to free her immediately. Pierce himself, at least, remained calm, no tightening of his grip.

"Pierce will be there. She can't get away from two of us. I'll have my eye on her the whole time." Allison held her hands up and wide to show how she wasn't trying to get away with anything.

"I'm sure you will," Felicia muttered behind a hand she brought up to rub her nose.

Susan looked pained, but John ignored Felicia. He faced Sacramento squarely and crossed his arms. "Fine, Pierce can go lock her up. I don't think you should be involved—"

"I don't think you get to be the one to make that decision. A sub-alpha's equal in rank to the Roanoke beta, or had you forgotten? I'm not yours to order around." Sacramento stepped closer to John, volume rising.

"Maybe normally, but when I'm standing in for the al-pha—"

Boston cleared his throat loudly. Sacramento and John both fell instantly silent. "Let's not get distracted by abstract arguments of dominance." Nothing about his tone was harsh, but Sacramento and John both hung their heads. "My under-standing was that our guest is in very little danger of escaping at the moment." He gestured for Pierce to turn Tatiana to show her bound wrists, but she moved of her own accord first. Her wrists Lady-damned *hurt* at this point, her reserves of healing—if she had any after the wolfsbane—long drained away. If they did allow her that shower, they'd have to cut the tie, so hopefully her overall weakness showed in obvious bruises

Sacramento a meaningful look that clearly said, "Don't screw this up." Sacramento took a good grip on Tatiana's arm and nodded. Tatiana didn't understand why he was going on ahead alone, but she got it after a moment. He'd seen her with the knife, and the kitchen had too many of those to hand once she was free.

"I won't let them kill you," Sacramento remarked to the air. Again.

Tatiana sighed. She thought about saying, "How?" but didn't bother. Sacramento likely didn't know. She chose another question instead. "Why? Everyone thinks I'm manipulating you, I'm sure."

"You deserve better than being treated as a political pawn." Sacramento was looking away, so Tatiana edged around in her grip to face her. Her face and scent told a different story: she was doing this out of kindness. Even after everything Tatiana had done. An impulse to thank her properly surged up, and Tatiana leaned in, a little off-balance, without her hands free, and kissed her before she questioned it. And maybe she'd die in a vision sometime soon, so why not kiss the beautiful woman?

Sacramento didn't even hesitate. She melted into the gesture, pressing her body into Tatiana's without apparent thought for what she was doing.

That's what stopped Tatiana. Someone in this situation needed to be thinking. If it wasn't going to be Sacramento, it would have to be her. She tipped her head aside. "Sorry," she said, the niceties of her English phrasing suddenly escaping her. She didn't want to insult Sacramento accidentally. "We can't—"

Sacramento jerked back and only seemed to remember to keep hold of her arm at the last moment. "No. No, of course, I'm sorry—"

"I can't take advantage of you—" The phrase Tatiana had been looking for finally rose to her lips.

Sacramento exhaled in an incredulous rush. "You—of me—? Who's tied up here?"

"And who's manipulating whom?" Tatiana could hear Mikhail's voice in her mind, berating her for pointing that out to the prey, advising her to manipulate for all she was worth. But Tatiana was too tired for that, and Sacramento had been too kind. "Sacramento—"

Sacramento huffed an awkward laugh. "At least call me Allison."

"Allison," Tatiana murmured, feeling out the name. She'd never have guessed it, but it was very pretty.

Allison repeated the name, trying to imitate Tatiana's pronunciation. "It sounds a lot cooler all Russian." She leaned close, as if thinking about kissing her again, then pulled away. "Lady damn it!"

A cough made them both start. Pierce stood in the entrance to the kitchen, a pair of scissors in his hand. Tatiana had no idea how long he'd been there, but she got the ~~~ he'd been waiting th   ᵕ

When Tatiana got out of the shower—the single bathroom window was much too small and high for her to wiggle out of, as she'd expected—she found Pierce waiting for her alone. He didn't bother taking her arm this time, but he kept himself always between her and the path to the stairs. Tatiana judged that whichever way she ran, he was close enough to drop her before she got anywhere.

He showed her to a tiny bedroom. The window didn't need bars, as it was too small for an adult to fit through. Tatiana suspected the room had once been a closet, and when adding a window, the pack had chosen one suitable for a rebellious teenager. No trace of possessions or personality remained except traces of scent from a female Were. The only things in the room were a bed with clean sheets and a very heavy dresser with layer upon layer of drink rings on top. Probably bolted to the wall. The venetian blinds were cranked half-open, so at least a little light made it in.

Not bad, for a pack that presumably hadn't been expecting a prisoner. Tatiana let Pierce close the door on her before she remembered that she hadn't asked about fresh clothes. She really should have scooped up her dirty ones from the bathroom floor, but she hadn't wanted to hold them against her clean skin. She sat on the edge of the bed and brought her hair over her shoulder to dry the tips with the towel for now.

A knock sounded on the door and it opened without waiting for a reply. "I pulled some things from your suitcase," Allison said, entering holding out a pile of neatly folded clothes. Better folded than Tatiana had left them, even. She hissed when she saw Tatiana, and it took Tatiana a moment to figure out what she was reacting to. She looked down at herself, and saw the ugly blue-green spread of various bruises anew. The fight with Felicia and the rough treatment she received while returning here lingered still.

"I'm fine." Tatiana took the pile, sat down on the edge of the bed, and looked at it rather than at Allison. "Thanks." Her Tooth training was jabbing at her again. If she could entice Allison into staying, get her to let down her guard, and disable her, that would make Pierce easier to surprise. He'd expect Allison to be the one opening the door. She could use the cord from the blinds to garrote him, knock him out. Then she'd just have to walk downstairs and pick up a pillow to carry out Father's orders . . .

Assuming no one was downstairs with the alphas. Assuming she could make it out of the house afterward without anyone noticing.

Assuming that she wanted to kill Andrew.

To fill the silence of the pause, Allison freed her hair, snapping the elastic down around her wrist so she could run both sets of fingers through it to smooth it out again.

"You look pretty with it down." Tatiana set the clothes aside, and put her palms flat on the bed.

back. Her scent must have been clear enough, because Allison grinned suddenly and took her hips. She kept going back until she hit the bed with her legs and sat down too fast, making Tatiana more or less tumble into her. She laughed and slipped her hold to the small of Tatiana's back.

"Having it down makes you look relaxed. Not afraid to be pretty." Tatiana smoothed a lock along Allison's cheek.

"So you say. Maybe they like things all upside-down and crazy in Russialand." Allison leaned forward and almost kissed her, but at the last minute she looked at the door. Pierce was undoubtedly standing there listening. He hadn't burst in to intervene yet, though.

"*Raise your voice in song, for tomorrow Death may howl with it instead,*" Tatiana murmured in Old Were. She translated when Allison looked confused. She closed the kiss. Her body might be bruised and weakened, but that didn't damp the heat swelling up from low and spreading out. She'd never felt the truth of the proverb so keenly before. Forget Father's orders. Tomorrow Death might have the alphas' voices, and hers after, so why not allow herself a little pleasure with a beautiful woman who would be enjoying it just as much as she was? Allison cupped her breasts, rasping the sides of her thumbs along the nipples, and Tatiana threaded her fingers into Allison's hair at the sides of her neck.

This kiss she savored, slowly. She wanted to truly taste the woman, and remember it afterward, remember her jerk of surprised pleasure as she caught Allison's lower lip between her teeth and held it so gently. They had no space in this closet of a room to chase or be chased, but she knew from experience one could do well enough with subtle touches. When Allison would have pulled back, Tatiana tightened her teeth and Allison laughed, acknowledging that she was caught—for now.

Tatiana gasped and lost her grip when one of Allison's caressing thumbs against her breast turned into a pinch at her nipple. Freed, Allison nipped at her earlobe, the side of her neck, dropped fingertips to caress lower, gently as befitted a first encounter, until Tatiana gave her own pleasurable jerk when a slightly clumsy, harder swipe lit her up.

"I lost track," Allison breathed on a laugh. "Who's taking advantage of who again?"

"I will if you will," Tatiana said, and pushed her back onto the bed. Allison laughed and helped pull Tatiana with her.

This time the vision came when Tatiana dozed, after exertion. Perhaps that was why she felt the transition, stepping from the warm swirl of drying sweat and Allison's body heat and the sheets beneath her, into the chill air of the common room of the Lady's Jaw. Winter, Tatiana decided. It must be winter, in this vision.

The room was comforting in its familiarity. Technically
the Teeth did not have a common room—they were a collection of individuals doing Father's will, not a unit or an army

juries. And so, in the end, they had a room: a rough addition
to the gym, with the logs of the walls still showing, with odd
furniture and a refrigerator and oven and plenty of pillows to
lie on.

This time, it was filled only with the Teeth she would expect to find at home, perhaps twenty people, all at ease. Alexei
bent to open the oven door, releasing a burst of delicious odors
so strong Tatiana could see the crackled skin of the roast in
her mind even with Alexei in the way. Mikhail rose from his
lounge on a pillow on the floor, so smoothly that the surface of
the wine in the two glasses he held didn't even waver.

"Congratulations," he said, and held one out to her. He
laughed when she smelled it, swirled it, and smelled it again.
"It's just wine. You can't have a vision in a vision."

"If you can, I'd be the lucky one to discover it," Tatiana
said, but sipped anyway. It tasted like just wine. A good vin-
tage, too.

Alexei made her wine slosh as he came up and enveloped
her in a huge hug. "You did it. I don't think any of us could have
managed the North Americans with the finesse you did."

"But I didn't." Tatiana wasn't sure why she protested. This

vision was nice, and she didn't really want to fight it. It was heavy, almost, like the security of a thick blanket wrapped around you when you were a child in bed. Perhaps she'd been right to stop worrying the visions would kill her.

"You will," Mikhail said, and looked knowing for some reason.

"Tatiana!" Everyone chorused it together, cheering her, and Tatiana beamed. Finesse, Alexei had said. That's what she'd wanted to cultivate. Anyone could kill, but she had finesse.

"Tatiana." A new voice, accompanying two pairs of urgent footsteps. Two priestesses entered the common room. The older of the pair led, distinguished not just by the beginning of wrinkles at the corners of her eyes, but a braid so long that she wore it doubled up, the end tucked at the nape of her neck, and it still reached down to her thighs. Very old.

Tatiana froze, and then pushed away from Alexei. She held her wine glass in front of her with careful negligence, trying not to look like she was wishing it was a shield. "Yes?"

The old priestess closed her hands over Tatiana's wrists and kissed her cheek. "We are delighted that you have returned safely. We have need of your skills once more, as soon as possible."

Tatiana didn't want to catch the priestess's eyes, so she dropped her own to look at their hands. The priestess's were stained oddly, all the way up to her forearms. Dark purplish, brownish green, in patches and splotches.

Like she'd been crushing vegetation, squeezing out the remains of leaves and stems until they gave up the last of their liquid.

Tatiana jerked out of her hold but the wine splashed onto the priestess's fingers and caught there, much too thick. It caressed the stains, soaking them up, until it turned fat and pur-

ʃнᴇ ʟᴏᴏᴋ лauanas wine glass from her, handed it to the second priestess. She clasped Tatiana's hands between her own, as if she would bless them for the coming task. The stains were redder now, smearing Tatiana's skin with blood, coating it.

"No." Tatiana snapped it, fast, easy. No need to even think about that choice. She backed up, but then she abruptly couldn't move any farther because the Teeth had tightened in a circle around her and the priestess. A low growl began, sourceless, and quickly spread, surrounding her, enveloping her. Not a choice, this mission.

"You've done it before," the old priestess said, inexorably. "You'll do it again."

"No!" Tatiana shouted it to the sky this time, to the vision. Enough.

"Tatiana?" Allison knelt up on the bed to look down on Tatiana, and Tatiana flopped her head to the side and flung up her arm to block out the sight like she would have bright sunlight. She didn't want to see Allison, link her face with her name, and drag the vision with her into reality. Allison frowned with concern. "Was that the wolfsbane again? You went all limp dead weight."

"I—" Tatiana hesitated, telling herself that she needed a moment to transition from the Old Were in the vision to English. It was half true.

And now she really had to decide. Follow Father's orders or not. This was her perfect moment, Tatiana could see the trail laid out in her mind. Get a choke hold on Allison . . .

But that was fooling herself. She'd known when she first kissed Allison she wouldn't do that. Tatiana had vowed she would never kill again for her alpha, and she was going to keep that vow. Especially since she didn't see how killing one of the Roanokes would make any situation better—the political situation, or the situation of the North Americans who loved them.

Allison let herself back down to the bed. She'd ended up on the side closest the door, whether by accident or design to be between Tatiana and escape, Tatiana didn't know. She propped herself up on her side to face Tatiana, and Tatiana mirrored the position so she could look into her lover's face. "It was a vision. Having them without wolfsbane is only supposed to happen when you're over a century and have been using it all your life." She stumbled into a few of the words, not sure why she was admitting any of this. She could have said it had to do with the wolfsbane and stopped. Deciding not to harm Allison wasn't the same as trusting her.

And yet—"It was my friends, at home. Welcoming me."

"I'm sorry." Allison kissed Tatiana's forehead. "Rest. Later we'll figure out something to stop the visions, okay?"

"Okay." Tatiana was too tired to put her dubiousness into her tone. The vision had dissipated the sense of well-being from playing chase, but left behind the sleepiness. She turned

caresses stopped suddenly. Tatiana prodded her exhausted mind into motion—and then everything snapped into clarity as her heart sped once more. Allison must have found her Mark.

Sure enough, Allison's fingertip traced the curved shape of a stylized tooth at the top of her back, over her spine. "This—this is a silver scar. What happened?"

"I dedicated myself to the Lady." That was true enough, but Tatiana had to pick her way carefully through the rest, separating personal from tactical. "The Lady's Jaw. I'm one of Her Teeth. It's about . . . working together, as a pack. One tooth is nothing much, but a whole jaw of them . . ." A whole jaw of them could help Father keep control over half a continent of Were. Informers, translators, problem solvers, assassins.

"Why would the Lady want you to burn yourself with silver?" Allison sounded quite angry on her behalf, and Tatiana had to smile. She turned over and captured Allison's hand in both of hers.

"Things are very different at home." That was the best Tatiana could come up with, and perhaps it was the truest thing.

Neither side seemed to have a decent "why" behind anything. Things just were, accidents of history.

Allison traced the line of her side, up the curve of her hip. "You'll get home." She sounded so concerned that Tatiana believe that, Tatiana wanted to laugh. Lady grant she'd get home somehow. And then she'd have a whole different set of problems to deal with, finding out who had strengthened the wine and why they were working against her.

"Settle down with a nice, normal girl, and raise a family away from us crazy types." Allison blew out a breath in amusement. "If you're the kind who can stay normal and settled down, of course. Half the crazy comes from everyone who can't around here."

"Nice, normal boy," Tatiana corrected. As long as they were imagining a ludicrously idealized picture, it might as well have a mate in it, rather than a series of lovers. Not that she saw herself as a mate kind of person, but as a Tooth, it wasn't like she could ever settle down properly either.

Allison's scent drifted slightly chagrined for a second, only detectable because of their closeness. "Sorry, I didn't mean to assume." Resignation slipped up to take chagrin's place. "I'm someone who wants to mate same, so. I know there are fewer of us around."

"Mate same?" Tatiana frowned over the phrase. Mate the same as what? Or as whom?

"That you want to find a mate of your same gender. Not just play chase with them. I mean, I can get any number of girls into bed, but it gets frustrating after a while, since I know that most of them aren't looking for anything more than a chase."

Allison's eyes suddenly widened. "That wasn't just a phrasing question, was it? Russians don't acknowledge that?"

"Mating's for cubs." Tatiana let the easy answer take over

ishness.

And maybe she would be right to. About parentage, at least. "The alpha isn't my biological father. That's just a social fiction. All of the pack's cubs are 'his.' " Tatiana was surprised at the relief she felt at admitting that.

Allison jerked sitting, anger sharpening her scent. "Lady's kind light, Russians really do a number on their kids, don't they? Even Europeans aren't that fucked up. How does that even make *sense*? If everyone's cubs belong to the alpha, what does it matter who mates with whom? People want to settle down with—" Allison's words seemed to escape her from sheer frustration for a moment, and she gestured jerkily instead. "The kind of person they want to settle down with. If you mate same and want cubs, one of you finds someone willing to provide a couple chases to help out."

Tatiana pressed her fingertips to her temples. "I don't—I don't know!" Too much, on top of everything else. She didn't want to think about cultural differences, or the possibility of death from a vision, or a pack war, or anything. She just wanted to fall asleep beside a lover. She turned over so her back was to

Allison again, and hugged herself.

Allison hesitated, then slipped to snuggle along her back, bare skin to bare skin. "I'm sorry," she murmured into the back of Tatiana's neck. Tatiana tried to relax for her, but sleep wouldn't come when her mind was too crowded with questions.

Did she want to mate same? And now she'd tossed aside Father's orders, what came next?

20

Selene woke stretched out unnaturally flat on a bed that smelled like her brother and his family, light diffuse on her face as if filtered by curtains. She groaned and turned onto her side in the rumpled blankets, more comfortable, and tried to piece things together. She'd lost to Isabel. Someone must have laid her here to get her out of the way. She felt at the back of her head, but healing had taken care of any tenderness or residual concussion while she was out.

Footsteps entered the room, and Selene opened her eyes to watch without moving further. Lilianne. Her expression was tight, and she ignored Selene to stride over to the closet and start jerking down clothes on their hangers, piling them higher and higher over her arm. She smelled of anger and worry, all congealed together.

"What's going on?" Selene sat up and stepped over to Lilianne. When she would have reached out to smooth her hair, Lilianne pulled away.

"I'm sorry, this has to get done quickly. That woman offered to help, but I don't want her touching—" Lilianne stopped and pressed her lips together until they were white, reassembling her control.

"Isabel?" Selene couldn't think who else would provoke that kind of emotion at the moment, but why—things abruptly snapped together in her mind. Lilianne was moving her and her husband's things out of the alpha's room. That was tradition, after the alpha lost his or her position, so the new alpha could take possession immediately.

"Ares—" Selene swallowed.

"Lady, you missed it, didn't you?" Lilianne flicked a glance to the bed. "He and Dare fought after you were out. He lost." Tears wavered near the surface of her voice and she shoved them ruthlessly back down.

"As if he even wants this room," Selene said savagely, looking around at the small, dingy space. Andrew only wanted the power the room symbolized, and this dream seemed determined he should have it. Lady. She'd fought Isabel for nothing. Nothing she did worked. "*I'll* help," she told Lilianne, and reached for the mound of clothes in the woman's arms.

Lilianne pulled away a second time as Andrew appeared in the doorway. She shoved past him, leaving Selene to frown at him in uncomfortable silence. Surprisingly, Andrew had the grace to look slightly embarrassed. "I take it you've heard."

Selene lifted her lip in the beginnings of a snarl, but didn't voice it. She dipped her head. "Vancouver Island."

"Or perhaps Seattle. I haven't decided yet." Andrew shrugged. "We can all move back to Washington now, if you

really wanted: the right—that you claimed we didn't have—to the territory. You wanted to challenge, to take over this pack, take over that legitimacy. One stroke, and you're alpha of the remains of an entire continent. So much easier and cleaner than taking over gradually through a bad deal."

"Would have been even cleaner, politically, if he'd challenged me, but . . ." Andrew shrugged. "Needs must." He wandered closer and searched Selene's face, letting some of his surprise show. "Well read, by the way. You're an extraordinary woman."

Selene snarled right in his face. "You're married." It was unfair—she smelled nothing more from him than the normal attraction of any adult standing next to someone who fitted his or her sexual preferences, but the urge to lash out and wound *somehow* was overwhelming.

Andrew rocked back a step, and his expression hardened. "It's not just for the power. Your brother was the leader they needed, when they needed to run from the Tainted One, but now that's over. He could never hold so many packs together for very long, especially in so small a territory."

Selene clenched her hands. Oh, she would love to hit him. Hit and kick and gouge. "But you've decided you can. The D—" She wanted to say, "the Dare I know," but she stopped herself in time. "The real kind of leader would do it because it needed to be done, and no one else could. Not because he was sure of himself and wanted to show that off."

"A real leader will punish you for that kind of insubordination, if it happens again." Andrew turned his back on her and strode out of the room. "Go outside, cool off. Come back when you can give your alpha the respect he's due." He stopped in the hallway and looked back over his shoulder at her. "And while you're fuming, remember this: you didn't do any good, trying to stop this. Annoyed my wife, hurt yourself. I wouldn't go making any more grand political plans."

Selene waited until he was out of sight before she kicked one of the bed's legs viciously. Damn that cat's bastard. She'd remember that, certainly. Remember it to keep herself motivated until it was time to act again. Because she would take him down, if she had to challenge him herself.

She slammed out of the front door and strode for the woods, but slowed when the shadows cast by the edge of the trees caressed her skin with chill. Andrew couldn't stop her from helping Ginnie. Perhaps this was the dream's way of telling her that the girl was the important thing, not political position or personal pride.

Well, then, Selene would help the girl.

She walked as silently as possible this time, tracking. She doubted the girl would particularly want to be found, not after what happened with Arturo this morning, so Selene would need to stalk her. More than anything else, that process calmed her, focused her mind. This was her goal, and it was a goal she was suited to, more than she was suited to straightforward

it. Selene hoped she wasn't doing it because she was thirsty, but she thought not. The task had the same slightly misdirected sense of effort as all of the things Selene had seen Ginnie doing. Time-consuming to no real purpose.

Selene walked to where the grass turned into bare earth, before the dry part of the rocky bed began. Wind tossed the trees so that dappled light kissed Selene's feet and skittered away again. She sat down and waited for the wind to change and Ginnie to notice her.

Ginnie froze when the breeze shifted. Selene stayed where she was. If the girl was going to run, she'd run. Selene could track her. There was no point frightening her by grabbing her.

Ginnie turned to frown at Selene, annoyed, then finally sighed. She selected a fist-sized stone, waded out of the water, and dropped it unceremoniously in Selene's lap. Selene gathered that as long as she was hanging around, she was supposed to help. She picked up the rock and followed Ginnie back out to the dam, wobbling a little as stones rocked under her feet.

They worked in silence for some time. Ginnie occasionally pointed where Selene was supposed to place her stones.

Selene judged her moment was as good as it would ever be. "Shifting will make you feel better."

Ginnie hefted her next rock like she was thinking of throwing it, and her scent sharpened with anger. Selene continued anyway. "I know it feels like it's better to shut it away, but you'll feel better once you let your body do what it's made to do. Even if nothing else is going right, that's right, and you can feel it."

Ginnie shook her head violently, and threw her stone down onto the center of the dam. The other stones tumbled, and the water gushed happily over top.

Selene got her shoes wet stepping close enough to replace the largest of the broken dam's stones. "I can't make you. No one can. It will help." Maybe now was not the time to push, but Selene's instincts told her it was. If Ginnie was working so hard at unimportant tasks—like Selene herself was working so hard at whatever tasks she could find—she was ready to work just as hard at what she needed to do, which was shift. And heal.

Selene hoped.

Andrew offered to skip the afternoon Convocation session to stay with Allison, but she shooed him off, saying she just wanted-ed to sleep. He spent the whole session on edge, waiting for the other metaphorical hunters to come out of the woods from the other direction, but Rory seemed as calm as Rory ever was. Apparently he was willing to believe that Allison had concocted the story all on her own. Or maybe his ham-handed attempts to influence who ended up as Sacramento now had him too distracted to care. Either way, he left Andrew alone.

After taking her dinner, Andrew escorted Allison to stay with Portland, while questions continued to gnaw uncomfort-

he returned to his cabin in the dusk, trying once more to find a calmer, contemplative state in the cooling air and the softer sounds of animals coming out to forage or hunt. But scenery couldn't hold him when there was so much left unsettled about his own life, and those of people he cared about.

Someone was sitting on the front steps, and Andrew's heartbeat picked up for a moment. Rory? No, a few steps more and he recognized John. The downward slant of his shoulders, of his head, spoke of someone very tired, but it was different than Andrew had seen him before in some way. This was a man brought very low, yes, but one who was looking up to the sunlight now, and planning an escape, not one who was still digging. "I suspected you'd be back to try to convince me again, so I figured I'd save you the trouble." John's voice rumbled low, and he didn't look at Andrew.

Andrew gave a brief grimace. He had considered it. Too much to hope for, that John would have had a change of voice. "Where's Edmond?" he asked, rather than gnaw at dry bones by doing what John expected.

Besides, maybe he needed to think about what would be

best for John, not best for him, or best for his grand plans. The slight improvement in John's manner highlighted how far the man still had to go. Andrew abruptly realized that he wanted to concentrate on that, not on finding a way to get John to agree to help him. He'd see if he could help John first, and go from there.

"Edmond's with my cousins for the evening." John rolled his neck, like tension had made it ache, and stood. "Think I've been smothering him too much, since his mother died."

Andrew raised his eyebrows. That was new, and matched John's body language: the man had finally found a wish to *try* once more. Good. Several platitudes came to his lips, but he cast his mind back to when his wife Isabel had been dead for only a few years. He'd wanted to punch anyone who told him things would get better with time, or she'd have wanted him to be happy.

So he didn't use them on John. The silence stretched a little, but not uncomfortably, until he found something better. "Did you give her voice its color?" In modern times, Were didn't always bother with the ritual's most formal aspects, but the spirit remained the same: tell the story of a Were in others' voices, many voices, until the voices of those she had touched colored her voice as Death carried it back to the Lady. Andrew didn't believe in the Lady, but he believed plenty in the power of memory voiced.

John stiffened in shock, but the strength to his posture didn't fade when the surprise did. "She was human, not Were."

"So? She had a Were's voice." If that was only a false memory, so be it. It was what John needed to hear. Andrew looked around them, but the cabin's porch light and the reflections off windows and parked cars along the row of cabins made this space feel too sharp and human for the Were ritual. He nodd...

to the trees. "I ..."

...ess.

"Yeah." Silence stretched, Andrew started to wonder if John was ready to talk. "She had this . . . glare, whenever I slipped up and tried to order her around." Tears roughened the edges of John's words, and Andrew ignored them completely. He had stars to count.

"Edmond was just an accident. And when she told me, I started thinking about custody battles or making it appear he'd been stillborn, or all the things you're supposed to think about, and then I thought—" John swallowed back the tears enough so his words were still understandable. "What if I told her? And I looked at her, and thought, I bet she could handle it. I bet she's strong enough, smart enough to understand the secrecy."

John's hands clenched. "And she was. It was working. But I screwed it up, I didn't tell her *why* she couldn't be around Were outside the pack. She got stubborn, and showed up when Portland was visiting even though I'd told her not to, and it was just . . . so obvious, in the end. A dozen different things about her scent when Portland scared her, and words she knew . . ."

The tears started winning. John said something else, but Andrew couldn't understand it, choked off by the sobs surrounding it. He stopped walking, and clasped the side of John's neck, made soothing, meaningless noises. He embraced John, and the man cried and shared disconnected little pieces of memories until his voice was hoarse and eyes dry.

When the moment felt right, Andrew stepped back. He examined John's face, hoping to find peace, perhaps. He wished there was more he could do, so he kissed him. Maybe it wasn't the smartest idea, but John seemed to need intimacy, and Andrew needed—something. An escape from memories of a woman who didn't exist.

It grew much faster than he'd realized. Andrew needed, needed badly and he devoured John's willing mouth and pressed himself against his solid, muscled body. Andrew had to pull himself back with a jerk. This wasn't about him. This was about John, and if Andrew remembered anything about the time after Isabel, it was that sometimes he wanted to play a meaningless game of chase to forget her, and sometimes it just tore his voice worse. Only John would know.

John stared at him—not angry at least, but then, he'd kissed back. Bemused, perhaps. Suddenly he laughed, a soft, hoarse sound. "Yes," he said, simply, and shoved Andrew, shoved him and kissed him until his back hit a tree and John fumbled at the button of his jeans. Andrew was more than happy to return the favor, though they did have to stop kissing while he dragged John's shirt up over his head. John closed the distance immediately when Andrew tossed it aside and nipped at his jaw, his neck, his collarbone as Andrew worked by feel below, making

him moan. Andrew grinned and kissed his way down John's
chest as he knelt.

Afterward, when the urgency had mellowed into sleepiness and the

, ... sleepiness banked but linger-
ing. It was full night by now, and the comfortable quiet lasted
them into the cabin and into bed, curled up more on top of the
sheets than under them.

Andrew closed his eyes and let himself drift closer to
sleep. For the first time since he'd woken with his memories
awry, he felt right. It wouldn't last, but he could treasure it for
the moment. Warmth, another Were nearby, and the full moon
above—

Andrew jerked to a sitting position. It was the new. Convocation was held in the new, he'd been outside, seen the empty
sky. But deep inside him with a set of senses deeper than sight
or smell he felt the full, felt it and knew it in his bones. This
wasn't real. The new wasn't *real*. He concentrated, discarding
sight and scent and trying at least for touch, since his sense of
the moon felt most tied to that. What did he feel? He tried to
jerk his body, felt weight and resistance like somewhere else an
entirely different body moved only reluctantly.

"Andrew! It's a dream. You have to pull yourself out of it."
A female voice, coming from nowhere Andrew could see, set-

tling into his ears more deeply than the sound of John's snores. He closed his eyes to listen. A Russian accent. Russian. Why did that tug at his memories . . .

His real memories. Not false. Silver was real, and his time with his daughter, and Susan, and—everything. When he stopped focusing so hard on his goal, the goal he thought he'd needed, everything came rushing back. He knew people too well because he did know them, and he should have trusted that, instead of thinking that he had to win back his alphaship to act like an alpha.

And since this wasn't real, he damn well was going to wake up.

He opened his eyes and tried to look at everything from the corner of his eye, to catch it moving, or wavering, or fading to something else beneath. He'd felt the moon, there had to be other inconsistencies, things at the edge of his senses that would lead him to the real world. In the doorway, a shadow shivered, then stretched, filling out into the forelegs, then head, then body, and finally tail of a wolf silhouette.

Andrew's attention snapped to Death, and for once he didn't disappear just when it was most inconvenient. "This isn't real. I need to get out. Where am I?"

"Stumbling around in a drugged vision like a moron." Death gaped in a sharply toothed grin, then turned around and flipped his tail. "Are you coming or do you want to stay and fuck around some more?" He vanished through the door.

Andrew ran after him, focusing on the loping shadow while the world slipped away around him.

21

Tatiana couldn't spend the whole night sleeping beside Allison, of course. A light tap on the door warned them that Tatiana was wanted. Tatiana was sure it was only in her imagination that the tap sounded sardonic. Taps couldn't carry emotion that subtle.

They got dressed quickly, and Tatiana wasted a few moments wishing she could shower again before everyone smelled her, before she remembered that the whole house probably knew anyway. On the way downstairs, Allison hung back from her a little, at least.

John and Boston were gathered once more, still deep in some conversation. On their beds, the alphas lay motionless, at least until Andrew grunted and jerked in his sleep.

No one else looked over, but Tatiana froze. His movement

would have been perfectly normal in someone who was really asleep, but she had more experience with seeing those in Vision Ceremonies than any here. They didn't move.

She darted to Andrew's bedside and grabbed the side bar to keep her hands visible for the others. "Andrew! It's a dream. You have to pull yourself out of it."

Pierce grabbed her shoulders to jerk her away, but Andrew grunted again and thrashed. Pierce froze. Tatiana focused on Andrew tightly. Please, Lady. Let him wake. "Andrew—"

He surged to a sitting position, and gasped like he'd been drowning. "Silver! Silver, is she here?"

Tatiana laughed with a hint of hysteria from the sheer relief. "She's in the next bed." She opened her mouth to tell him more, but he knocked her aside to climb out. She tumbled into Pierce, but he managed to keep both of them upright.

Andrew bent over his mate, stroking the side of his hand along her cheek. "Silver, love." He leaned to breathe into her ear, giving his order all the authority the alpha of a continent possessed. "Find Death. He knows the way out."

Tatiana's breath caught. He'd barely escaped with his life, and now he was advising his mate to seek Death? That couldn't be right. There was something here she didn't understand.

Selene smelled Isabel coming five minutes before she arrived, but she ignored the woman, even when she came to stand on the bank and watch them. Ginnie kept glancing at the woman, and finally Selene gave in and went to try to chase her off. She didn't want Ginnie running.

Isabel smoothed a heavy black lock of hair behind her

shoulder, and considered Selene. It annoyed Selene how clean and beautiful she looked after their fight, like the effort had been nothing to her. "What are you doing?"

several united packs, to saving one little girl?"

Selene pressed her lips together on her first automatic reply for Isabel to go bite her own tail. She should be polite to her new alpha's wife. "Maybe I should have been focusing on her all along, not prey-stupid political games." Or mostly polite, at least.

Selene glanced back at the girl, and tried to recall her voice from memory. In the real world, Ginnie's father had been exiled, so she'd seen the girl only a few times over the past few years, talked to her on the phone a few more. Taken together, stuck here in this dream, it wasn't enough to call her voice up.

Isabel snorted. "Well, something needs to be done about her. After what she tried to do to my Arturo . . ." She glanced too, but back the way she'd come, probably thinking of her son back at the house at the end of that path.

Ginnie didn't need to hear that discussed, so Selene changed the subject as quickly as possible. If people said too often in her hearing that the violence had become an inseparable part of her, she'd make that so. "Arturo was your brother, wasn't he?"

Isabel's attention snapped to her, like a wolf form's ears to a prey's rustle in the bushes. "Who told you that? He died years ago."

A connection sparked, and Selene smiled at the feel of it, before she remembered that a smile was really not in order. "About fifteen years ago, wasn't it? When Felicia was three. In a fire, perhaps?" That's when Isabel herself should have died. It followed a strange sort of logic that someone else should have died in her place.

Isabel reached Selene in a single stride, pressing close. "How did you know that? Andrew would not have told you." Her accent oozed into her words like honey, smearing them and making them hard to understand.

Selene backed away, picking a new spot along the bank to watch Ginnie. If that made her appear weak, she didn't care. She didn't need another fight with Isabel. "I know it because you're not real. My Dare, the one that's real, he told me lots of things." She rubbed at her empty ring finger. Maybe if she concentrated, she'd be able to feel the cool metal weight outside the dream.

Isabel barked a derisive laugh and gestured widely, to the trees, the trickle of a creek, the tumbled dam stones. "If this isn't real, why are you trying to save a girl who isn't real? Why aren't you trying to get out?"

"Because—" Selene closed her eyes tight, opened them again. Still stream, still Isabel. "Because I have tried! I can't." Her tone was getting away from her, showing her desperation, but she couldn't stop it. "And if I can't get home, maybe I'm supposed to do something here. Maybe I can get out when I save her." And maybe that would be a long time. Ginnie was crouching now, curled up with her hands over her ears.

"Maybe you haven't tried hard enough." Isabel's lip curled into a sneer. "If you can't get out of a dream, why not end it per-

‑‑‑‑‑ ‑‑‑‑‑‑‑‑ ‑‑ ‑‑‑‑‑ ‑‑‑ ‑‑‑‑ of person he's married." She turned to stride away, then hesitated. She couldn't leave Ginnie alone with this woman, not now.

"Silver, love. Find Death. He knows the way out," Isabel said.

Selene didn't hear it at first. The repeated suggestion to find Death fanned the heat of her anger, and it took several seconds for her mind to review the rest. "What . . ." the words got caught, a struggle to get out, "did you call me?"

"Selene," Isabel said, flipping the word like she thought Selene was objecting to her accent. But Selene knew what she'd heard.

"Death?" Selene whirled, searching every shadow she could find, then the sunlit stretches of ground, everywhere. "Don't you want your chance to come out and laugh at me, trapped here?" He'd been missing all along, and she'd never realized it. She didn't see Death when she was Selene, but was she properly Selene now? Why should this dream world conform to any such rule? Death would have loved to be here, taunting her.

Silence, but for the noises of this dream world: trickling water, breeze through growing things. Isabel stared at her with such contempt it was almost audible as well.

Fine. If Death didn't want to come for her, she knew someone who needed him even more desperately. Selene strode into the creek, ignoring the renewed shock of the cold water wicking up her pants. "Ginnie. Ginnie, look at me." The girl wouldn't, but Selene caught her wrists, pulled her hands from her ears, and jerked her up. Ginnie seemed too shocked to struggle yet, so Selene spoke quickly. "Virginia. Understand me. You belong to Death. I should have seen it before. It is not time for him to take your voice to the Lady, but he knows your voice. Because he does not take it, he protects it."

While Ginnie stared at her, and didn't run yet, Selene stooped and smashed one stone against another to create a sharp edge. She gashed her hand along the meat of her thumb and smeared it from Ginnie's cheekbone into the hollow of her cheek, repeated the motion on the other side. The Were had no such ceremony—why would anyone be dedicated to Death?— but Selene could damn well make one up. "You are his. Never doubt it." When Ginnie had no one else, she would always have Death.

Understanding filtered into Ginnie's eyes, turning into— peace. Yes. Selene released a breath she hadn't realized she was holding.

"As are you, Silver." Death's voice. Or rather, the one she knew him best by, for he had none of his own. Selene closed her eyes on tears at the sweet relief of hearing it. "If extremely determined not to see what's in front of you." Death's particular

brand of jabbing humor colored his tone, and Selene turned
around to find Isabel smiling at her, no one else.

Isabel held out her arms, as if to welcome a child loved be

Isabel dipped her head, smile turning the respect for Selene figuring it out into something sardonic. "Come, puppy."
She lifted Ginnie into her arms, and in the embrace, Ginnie
grew younger, years falling away until she was once more the
child Stefan would have found, not the broken young adult Selene had.

"You know the way out," Selene said, slow, thoughtful. Of
course Death would not show her simply because she asked.
Isabel's shadow was that of a woman, but when Selene looked,
really looked, she could see layers within it, shadow on shadow.
One was a wolf, a wolf that belonged to a place not here, and
Selene kept staring at that layer until the edges pulsed in her
sight like the intersection of two overbright colors. Then she
walked, in time with that pulse.

Isabel walked with her. The trees moved aside to make
way for them until their colors ran together, and darkness stole
among them. Isabel's feet were bare, and she padded along
the darkness of the path and her skirt trailed out behind her,
caught like silk in an invisible wind, black silk merging with
black darkness.

Selene stopped, at length, when she could find no hint of the real world to send her steps toward. The substance around them held no form, just darkness and slight chill, but the woman and girl stayed stubbornly as they were. Selene lifted her hands, and both answered her will, turned palm up. Still Selene. She nodded to Ginnie. "She belongs to the dream. She's keeping me here, isn't she? She's not real, so she can't come with us."

"If you think this girl is just this girl, you're as dense as your mate." Death smiled with slightly too much teeth.

Selene lifted her hand as if to smack him. Smugness. That part she hadn't missed. "She's me, I suppose. Broken, and no one understands. Only I'm not broken, and some people do understand. I refuse to have a dream discount the five years of living I have done since Stefan took my wild self."

"If you insist on edging only a step or two away from the literal." Isabel shifted her grip on the girl to pet Ginnie's hair, and kissed the top of her head. "You can think on it as we wait, if you like."

"I'm not waiting. I'm waking *up*." Selene clenched both her hands in frustration. In one, in her bad hand, tightness gathered beyond what belonged to her muscles. It pulled her back, back to the dream.

"You cannot go back as you are, Selene." The smugness in Isabel's expression smoothed away, became slightly sad. "You know that. You must decide."

"Decide what?" Selene lifted her left hand, her bad hand, and flexed the fingers. She knew what she was returning to. "Is Selene an option?"

Death regarded her, silent. His answer needed no words: of course not. Here, the dream had blunted Selene's knowledge and memories, but in the real world, they would be as sharp as

~~~~~ ~~~~~~ y, just out of reach: accident. "An accident did not make me. It didn't change my fundamental nature."

"It did not." Isabel dipped her head.

Selene relaxed her bad hand, trying to find the deadness of the weight of it hanging there when no muscles would answer her. She tried not to think of everything she could see that Silver could not, but the effort of thinking only brought everything closer. "Help me pull Selene away?"

"If you insist." Isabel circled around Selene, and Ginnie must no longer have been in her arms because she gently pushed Selene to her knees, palms on her shoulders. She stood behind Selene, her touch a kind of blessing, and the black silk of her skirt billowed around them. Then Selene felt as if Death had slammed a dagger into the base of her skull, because the memories of her brother, her brother dead, Lilianne dead, Stefan laughing, were sharp, sharp as that dagger, then the wind that pulled the black silk caught her up and—

Dare. Dare was there, and he was crying and Silver only got one arm around his neck, but that was more than enough to breathe in his scent and she was crying too. She thought about pulling back, searching his face and his eyes for the strange not-Dare lurking there, but she knew her Dare in his every touch and every nuance of his scent. "I found Death."

Death jumped down from her bed. "The dense one still beat you out. Ironic, isn't it?"

Silver laughed weakly, and ignored Death. It felt oddly wonderful to have him there making smart remarks *to* ignore. Dare laughed too, probably from the sheer relief.

22

It took a while for Andrew to really believe that Silver was real. Selene and Rory and everyone in that twisted dream had felt plenty real too. But here was different. Here made *sense*, without missing time or false memories. Well, time missing other than between drinking with the Russian and waking up without clothes, in bed. In—Andrew finally looked around—the basement. For some reason.

So maybe here didn't completely make sense. But at least there was someone to ask. Andrew reluctantly disengaged from Silver and stepped away from the bed. The room seemed stuffed with people who'd just arrived: Felicia clinging to Tom at the foot of the stairs, like if she didn't she'd throw herself on her father; John hovering worriedly beside them; the Russian pressed against Pierce beside Andrew's bed; and Sacramento holding up the wall. Andrew held his arms open for his daughter and she did throw herself on him, and he held her. Because in the real world, she was here, with him.

He lifted his head, and focused on his beta. John looked so healthy in comparison to the man he'd dreamed sleeping next to. Grounded. "John? What happened—?"

"She poisoned you." John gestured for Pierce to pull Tatiana farther away from them. Sacramento growled a protest, and Tatiana waved her away. Andrew's head started to hurt. How much had he missed? "And herself, to be fair. You've been dreaming, the two of you, for days."

"Ginnie." Silver pushed herself out of bed and looked around a little wildly. "I want to talk to her. Please. Right now."

"Ginnie?" John blinked at the non sequitur.

It was just as much one for Andrew, but the tone raised echoes in him. "Don't ask, just get her on the phone. And Susan. I need to talk to her—" Needed to know she was *real*. Not dead. Something told him that was what Silver needed too.

"Oh, thank God, they're awake." Summoned probably by the commotion, Susan looked them over from the doorway, then shoved Tom out of the way so she could enter. She was definitely alive, cheeks a little flushed with excitement, brown hair fluffed up on one side like she'd been leaning her head in her hand.

Andrew pulled away from Felicia and strode to Susan. He hoped Felicia wasn't hurt by the abruptness, but he had to touch Susan. He drew her into a fierce embrace. He was embarrassing himself, he was sure of it, because she was his beta's wife, but she was real.

"Andrew? Andrew! Too tight!" Susan shoved him away enough for his grip to ease, but she didn't step away entirely. "Bad dreams?" The understanding in her expression allowed

 naps, but not angry that hed pulled away from her earlier.

Dimly, he registered John speaking on his cell phone to Ginnie's mother—that took a while, probably from confusion rather than resistance—then John's voice gentled for a second greeting, and he held the phone out to Silver.

Silver clutched at it with her good hand. "Ginnie, puppy? How are you?"

Ginnie's voice came out distorted, by the phone's speaker and probably the connection up there in the Canadian wilderness, but recognizable. "Roanoke Silver? I'm okay. In two weeks, my human class is going to Montreal. We're going to go to all kinds of museums and stuff." She rattled on in that vein for another minute before she remembered herself. "Did you need me to do something, Roanoke?"

Silver had started crying silently again at the sound of Ginnie's voice, so she had to clear her throat before speaking. "I hadn't spoken to you for a while, that's all." She hesitated, clearly groping for a way to make everything sound halfway normal, when Tom made a grabbing motion at the phone. She breathed a sigh of relief. "Tom wants to talk to you."

She handed over the phone, and joined Andrew again, sliding her arm across his back, so he could keep Felicia pressed against his other side. Thus supported, he focused on tracking things properly again. Nearly everyone was staring at Silver with varying degrees of wide eyes. She didn't cry often, Andrew supposed. If her dream had been anything like his, he didn't blame her. John and Susan rocked off balance as if they wanted to come forward to comfort her, but both restrained themselves.

Andrew widened the sweep of his attention. Tatiana stood calmly in Pierce's hold, watching everyone with intense focus. Poisoned them.

Something in the wine. But she'd been drinking it too, and she didn't look exactly healthy at the moment, either. Bruises peeked out from under her clothes, the worst at her wrists, which meant something else had used up her energy for healing.

"I think I need to hear the full story." Andrew looked down at himself. "After a shower. And some clothes." And then they'd have to figure out what to do about Russia. Dammit.

John gestured in invitation for them to head upstairs while he lifted the collar and chain they had bolted to the wall for any of the pack members in wolf who needed to calm down for an evening. He gestured Tatiana over and fastened it around her neck. Felicia peeled herself off Andrew and went to join Tom, who was having an argument over what Andrew presumed were TV characters with Ginnie.

Sacramento moved to block the stairs when Andrew and Silver approached. "Roanokes—"

John growled her down. Andrew held up a hand forestall his beta. "We'll—" He caught himself and closed his eyes briefly to reconsider his words. He didn't want to say "debrief" ~~~'¹ the subject right th~~~ ¹'

~~~ wasn't the dream. He was sure of that. Benjamin held up his hands calmingly, however. "John called me in to help, with you both trapped, dreaming. Your daughter was being a handful."

"I can believe that." Andrew threw a glance behind him, though the angle hid anything other than the descending stairs. Poor John, having to deal with an undoubtedly emotional Felicia unassisted. That settled events back into something more even and understandable. He and Silver made it up to their room and into the shower without further interruptions.

It took a while to get washed and dressed, though not for the usual reasons. Andrew was too exhausted—though strangely restless at the same time—for anything fun, but he didn't want to let go of Silver at any point, like she'd disappear if he did. She seemed to feel the same way.

When he was dressed, he left off his shoes, and gathered Silver up for one last tight hug and kiss to her hair. "Guess we'd better go find out what in the Lady's name has been going on, huh?"

"And then decide what our response will be," Silver said,

dry. "You were right about Russia. I just wish we did not have to decide while the dream still lingers."

Linger was such a light word. Andrew shuddered.

As it turned out, John spoke first. He, Sacramento, and Benjamin clustered with Andrew and Silver in the living room, arrayed before the couch where the two of them sat. They all stood so formally Andrew wondered if he should have given up on the hope of keeping the meeting casual and set himself and Silver up in state at the dining room table as they usually did for official business. The living room was comforting, though, with worn furniture filled with the smells of the whole pack and their daily lives.

John presented events levelly and succinctly, what they'd observed from the outside, what Tatiana had told them about wolfsbane, what Tatiana had done. When he described how Andrew had to heal from violence in the dream, Andrew lost himself for a moment in trying to trace when that would have been in the events he'd experienced. But losing himself down that trail did no one any good at this moment, so he yanked his attention back to the real world. He gritted his teeth when he heard about Silver's seizure. They were already holding hands, but at that point she squeezed his so hard her nails dug into his skin. The minor pain helped him focus.

"Sacramento? Anything to add from your observations about the envoy?" Andrew asked. John shot Sacramento a narrow look as he stepped back, but he didn't say anything.

Sacramento drew a deep breath. For a moment Andrew saw her face in the dream, smashed but resolved, and he smiled encouragingly, which seemed to surprise her. "She's definitely well-trained. She wasn't going to stop searching for a way out and throwing herself at it until she was dead. I think I got her to trust me a little and talk to me, but mostly what I found ~~~

is that Dec~~~

~~~ ~~~~~~ on him, flushing. Andrew winced. Once Sacramento got on the defensive, they'd be mired in argument indefinitely.

Silver interposed a smooth question, probably with a similar thought. "Sacramento, do you think she was telling the truth about poisoning us unintentionally?"

Sacramento turned back and loosened hands that had been starting to clench. Benjamin took the opportunity to casually shift his position to block her view of John. "Yes." Sacramento looked into the middle distance, probably searching for words to back up her confident assertion. "She's scared. *Really* scared, about whether she's going to heal or not. She didn't do that to herself."

"Well, whether she trusts you or not, the fact that you two played chase is something to keep in mind. Might be useful." Or it might not. Andrew pinched the bridge of his nose, trying to assemble all the events to point to a course of action through the fog of the dreams. He still felt like he should be planning ways to deal with Rory.

"The question is, do we believe her that it was an attack

against her, not against us? That changes our response, because it changes what we're responding to." Andrew was thinking out loud, but three Were in front of them nodded like they'd already discussed that very question.

"If we were playing by Russia's reputed rules, we'd probably kill the envoy, regardless of whether it was an attack," Silver noted. Sacramento jerked, but controlled herself. Everyone in this room knew that wasn't how Roanoke worked. Besides, neither he nor Silver had ever been ones for playing by old rules.

"That's all about the appearance of strength, anyway." Andrew spoke to Benjamin most directly, because he hoped of anyone besides Silver, he'd be the one to understand what was only just now crystallizing in Andrew's mind. "We can't act based on what kind of alphas it will make us look like. We are, or we aren't. It's internal, and you can't broadcast that in snarls that will carry across the globe."

Benjamin dipped his chin in a slow nod. "Sending her home regardless of whether it was an attack would show confidence, if they choose to interpret it that way."

This time Sacramento couldn't contain herself. "And what if she's right, and someone at home was trying to kill her with that wine? We'd be sending her back right into the jaws of whoever it was."

Silver smiled thinly. "You're not saying it's better we kill her ourselves?"

"She could stay—" Sacramento broke off when Benjamin's hand fell on her shoulder.

"Everyone here trusts you to not let chasing go to your head," he said, without emphasis, but she flushed anyway and fell silent. Even with years of experience as an alpha, Andrew still sometimes envied Boston's ability to avoid conflict with one carefully tailored comment.

23

When everyone had trooped out in the wake of the alphas, Tatiana sat warily on the couch on the same wall as the chain. It was a bit of a stretch, but doable if she sat upright. So. The alphas were awake, which at least removed one point the North Americans were holding against her. It in no way got her closer to home, however. She prodded at the bruises on her wrists, stopped when the pain flared especially high. Humans must hate bruises; they were tremendously frustrating.

She didn't have to consider long before discarding any strategy of attempting to frighten the alphas into releasing her. Better to try to broker the two sides into talking to each other. For all she'd had only a little time to interact with them, these alphas seemed to prefer talking.

But talking depended on everyone feeling relatively secure and not finding out, for instance, that the envoy they were negotiating whether to release had been fully aware of the plot to send them dreaming. Tatiana knew she could be

and tipped her head to give easier access as Susan unlocked the collar. If North Americans had formal councils. She was sure they had some equivalent.

Susan gestured politely for Tatiana to precede her. "So you can add information to the discussion," she said, slightly dry. "There's a great deal to consider."

"*Yes*," Tatiana murmured, and the Old Were word was near enough to the Russian one that Susan seemed to catch her meaning.

They were gathered around the dining table, where Tatiana and the alphas had drunk the wine. It seemed so long ago now. Andrew and Silver sat at the opposite end of the table from their seats then—whether by chance or purpose, Tatiana couldn't tell—and the rest of the Were she'd been dealing with over the past few days were arrayed down the sides. The beta and Boston were nearly equal in rank, if their positions were to be believed. The daughter and the boyfriend were lowish, of course. Allison was in the middle, and kept shooting the beta throat-tearing looks while he ignored her pointedly.

Susan pulled out a chair for Tatiana, then seated herself

next to her husband. Tatiana didn't scoot the chair in, as leaving herself at a little distance from the pack gathered around the table felt appropriate.

Best to begin herself and set the tenor of the meeting. "No pack is entirely without factions. I had no idea that those who disagreed with my alpha were so powerful, but clearly they are. In one snap of the teeth, they thwart his goal and draw him into a fight he did not choose. One he does not want, I assure you." And she smelled like the truth, because that was the truth. Mostly. She assumed her alpha didn't want a fight because he'd sent her to defeat the North American alphas without attacking them.

"And what was your father's goal?" Silver was the one who spoke first. She watched Tatiana narrowly, then her eyes drifted to the floor at her feet. Susan must have returned her silver chain, as it was coiled neatly on the table in front of her. Her good hand had been in her lap, but she lifted it to the table now, Tatiana's ceremony cloth in it. She smoothed the deeply blue silk, tracing the circle of a star here or there with a fingertip. Tatiana wished she dared take it back. That was *hers*.

"More than finding an icon, certainly," Andrew said, dry. Tom twisted in his seat, and Susan coughed, pulling Andrew's attention to each in turn. He raised his eyebrows at Susan first in a silent question.

"Actually, Tom has something that might clear that up." She nodded to him, and he bounded to his feet.

"After you guys were talking about Russian immigrants at dinner, I was going to show it to you, but then . . ." He winced, eyes flicking downward, probably toward the basement. "So I showed it to Susan. I think you'll see why. Just a sec." He disappeared down the hall nearly at a run. Tatiana concentrated on looking nonchalant. What in the Lady's name could he have?

antique store in the town next to the cemetery I found. The one with the wolves and stuff on the stones." He pointed to the object. When Andrew picked it up and popped it open, Tatiana realized it was a pocket watch.

Andrew's eyebrows rose. Silver leaned over to look, then quickly twisted her head away and pressed the watch's lid shut. "Blasphemous." She slid it along the table in Tatiana's direction. "It's worse than you described earlier."

Tatiana took that as an invitation to pick up the watch. She couldn't imagine what it showed. She cradled it in her lap for a moment before opening it. The outside of the bronze-colored case had an etched pattern of circles undoubtedly to do with the Lady, though Tatiana didn't recognize the exact meaning.

"You've had this all this time?" Andrew asked Tom.

The young man shrugged, flushed with embarrassment after Silver's reaction. "Well, it is blasphemous, but I couldn't leave it for the humans. And then Felicia and I left to roam so soon after I got back. I kind of buried it at the back of my closet and forgot about it."

Tatiana finally found the right angle to push the stiff

button, and the watch popped open. The painting opposite the dial inside was exquisite in its detail. Death and the Lady walked together in Her garden, She a shining white wolf, He pale-skinned and black-haired, one hand slightly raised as if to argue the point that went with his slightly sardonic smile. Not blasphemous at all. Beautiful.

Tatiana closed the watch and held it to her core. To think, her excuse had been true. She and the other Teeth had done their research carefully: there had been an immigrant family, a century and a half ago, and they had moved to Washington. They'd clearly built the cemetery Tom had found. But she'd had no idea any of their possessions would be left. And this one had been found by North Americans who didn't want to even look at it.

"It offends you because . . ." Tatiana picked her way carefully through the jumbled mass of differences she'd encountered on this continent. "It is an image of the Lady?"

"In the wrong form." Silver's voice carried more intensity soft than it would have if she'd been screaming. "She and Death are trapped in their current forms—to depict them any other way is simply—" She snarled. No one else made a sound, but everyone besides Andrew and Tom looked like they were close to such a noise themselves. Tom, presumably because of familiarity with the object, but Andrew's continued religious indifference was interesting.

Andrew laced his fingers with Silver's, squeezing until she calmed a little. "Of all the things we might soon be going to war over, I'd rather religion not be one of them, love."

Silver drew a deep, slow breath. "Agreed." Tatiana kept

the watch hidden in her hands. She agreed with Andrew. She'd rather they didn't try to destroy the watch, because then she'd have to defend something so beautiful, and that wouldn't help

tion, but Tatiana avoided looking that way. She doubted the young woman herself felt so sanguine. Tom or Pierce must have related his perspective. "Were your actions not a possible act of war between two continent-wide packs, a decision would be easy."

Tatiana's dipped her head in acknowledgment. That was something, at least. Those who were still deciding could still be persuaded. "Killing me would be more of an act of war. And if you let me go, I can counsel my alpha that he does not wish to fight the North Americans."

"She howls directly to the alpha, not just influences him as a daughter." Andrew murmured, raising his eyebrows in mock surprise. "What rank are you?"

"I don't know if we share enough of the same terms to even explain," Tatiana said with a thin smile. Time to unbury a few of her cached pieces of prey, let everyone share the meat. "Below Father's betas. Not by much. I have some status, as one who goes out to do his work." She tipped up her chin. "Before you ask: information. He knows nothing of you. That was my real purpose here."

Throughout the room, everyone sat up straighter, except for the alphas and Boston. They relaxed, which told Tatiana the kind of leaders she was working with, if she had not already guessed. They'd never have believed any story until they found out what was behind it.

"You could speak to Father yourselves and see what he has to say." Tatiana doubted her alpha would like it, but she didn't have many other options. "He can assure you he intended no attack."

Silver laughed, breaking the tension that had seized the room in its jaws at Tatiana's words. "By all means. If only we could have done that days ago."

Andrew frowned, the steady tap of his fingers on the tabletop betraying his continuing tension. "I suppose since the benign avoidance prey has bolted . . ."

"If nothing else, we could use the measure of the man." Boston watched his alphas, and when he received nods from both, the room's attention transferred to Tatiana, even heavier than before.

Tatiana kept her shoulders down, relaxed. "Do you want his house's direct number, or that of the home settlement? He will not answer the latter, but it is more formal. Once you've made it through everyone on the way up."

"And much better propaganda. Gets rumor fodder into many more ears." Andrew flicked his fingers at Tom. "Go get her phone." Tom nodded and disappeared into the house.

While they waited, Tatiana tried to map the conversation in her mind. At the end of the chain, before the alpha, would be a couple of her fellow Teeth. "Not all of them will speak English. And fewer good English, you realize."

"I'm sure we can manage with a little translation help here and there." Andrew raised his eyebrows at her, and she could

when it came down to it. Silver would never have been on the front lines of a fight, and she had plenty of ability to inspire others to fight for her.

Tom bounded in and set the phone on the table. Tatiana scooted her chair forward to reach it, and set it to speakerphone after she dialed. The ring blared out of the tinny speakers, and she slid the phone down the table toward the alphas. The girl who answered spoke so quickly Tatiana didn't recognize her voice for a couple seconds. Natasha, one of the siblings she'd watched when the girl was young, leaving her with a little hero worship. *"Tatiana, are you all right? Alexei said you might be captured and everyone's been saying you must be dead by now, but no one's telling us anything."*

"Natasha." Tatiana pressed her lips together as the only sign she would allow herself of her frustration. She wished someone less likely to be emotional had answered the phone. "We have to speak in English, okay? Things went a little wrong, yes, but I'm with the North American alphas now, and they want to talk to Father. Is he there?"

"They haven't hurt you, have they? What do they want—?"

The flow of Old Were continued, unsurprisingly.

"English!" Tatiana snapped, and lifted her head to check the alphas' expressions. Andrew seemed the most suspicious, so she spoke to him. "She's worried about me; that's all. Am I all right, they thought I might be dead by now—"

"I think . . ." Natasha's English was painfully mangled. "Father hunts. I go . . . go . . ." She gave up, and the sound of the handset being put down came through the speakers. Her footsteps pounded off.

Time stretched painfully, long enough that Tatiana was sure that someone was in conference with a beta, or maybe even a couple. It didn't take that long to find someone in authority around the settlement.

Finally someone picked up the phone. "Your young sister is very worried North Americans have knife to your throat right now," Mikhail said. She almost wished it had been Alexei, but then keeping her calm in front of the North Americans might have been too hard. Alexei could no more magically deliver her from this situation than anyone else, but the remaining voice tones of a gangly teen might have wanted to ask him to try.

"No." Tatiana flicked a glance to Felicia. "No knife at the moment. But they are angry. They need reassurance that the gift I brought was not poisoned with my knowledge, at Father's orders. They want to speak to him."

Silence for a beat. "And with that reassurance?"

"Perhaps they'll let me go." Tatiana suppressed a sharp laugh. Strange to say that out loud, but everyone knew that was the point here. "At very least, they want this resolved with less than a declaration of war." She gave that emphasis.

"Ah." Mikhail sounded relieved—as well he should, as all the Teeth would be deeply embroiled in any fight—and a mo

...ow all three had only listening expressions, the calm of a skirmish coming soon, even if only verbal.

"Tatiana." Father's voice, resonant. "I am glad to be able to speak to you directly. What has happened to you?"

Tatiana didn't answer for a moment. Was that how he wanted to call the hunt, like they hadn't spoken earlier? Fair enough. And, distractingly, how was his English so accentless? She'd never—well, she'd never heard him speak English before, so she supposed she shouldn't be surprised. He was old enough to have learned dozens of languages perfectly.

"Someone poisoned the wine I brought. You should be careful, I was almost killed. The North American alphas could have been badly hurt."

"My deepest apologies." Father sounded sincere, but then he generally always did, right before you woke up on the ground with an aching head and no memory of how he'd smashed you there.

"Whether your spy was meant to poison us or not, the fact remains that she is a spy." Andrew looked into the middle distance rather than at the phone as he spoke. "We would be within our rights to kill her."

"You're welcome to, if you'd like. Consider it a gift, to balance what she did to you." Tatiana could imagine Father's kind smile, with the ice beneath. "If she is going to set us at odds by ill-considered actions of her own, she has served her purpose in this pack, and there is no need for her to return."

But be warned: your purpose in my pack will change.

Time had blunted those words in Tatiana's mind, until the vision. Years ago, forced to give up the human woman's Were child she'd so desperately hoped to raise to atone for what she'd done, Tatiana hadn't even really listened to what her alpha said. But the vision had brought it back, pressed the words into her mind. Purpose.

If she would not follow her alpha's every order without question, it seemed her new value lay in dying. Dying unknowing so the Roanokes would trust the wine and die too, leaving their continent-spanning pack in ruins, and Russia secure in its strength. The priestesses had made the wine, but Father would have told them to have it ready. Maybe he hadn't added the extra wolfsbane with his own hand, but the priestesses would have followed his orders. It made little difference. Tatiana should have seen it all along.

And now that the Roanokes had not died, she had another purpose. Nested, as Father so often created his plans. She could remove all responsibility from Russia, leave Father free to continue with subtle strategies a little longer, rather than a direct fight. He'd certainly prevent any rescue.

Tatiana's emotions felt whited-out, like standing in a storm so vast she could see nothing and her position assumed a false sense of peace. She recognized the feeling. She'd lit a body in a car on fire once, in that state, after a chase that was too long, after a woman who begged too, too much. She looked over at Susan, remembering again.

No. She might be too slow, the chain might snap, but more than that, she would not kill for her alpha. She would not kill for him before, and she would not kill for him now, when he'd proved just how little he valued her. Tatiana sat back in her chair and pressed the back of her hand to her lips, like that could hold back the reaction that must be written all over her body.

And Andrew caught her eyes. He must have seen her lean forward, smelled her calculation, because he flicked his eyes to the chain and back up again, just as she had. Her voice felt like it dropped away from her. If she couldn't go home, and the alphas thought she was a danger to them . . .

The alphas had ended the call while she was distracted, some stiff exchange of good-byes she half-remembered when she tried. Tatiana shoved to her feet using the back of her chair for support, paused to push her mind into English again. "I will leave you alone. To make your decision." Now they knew her alpha's play. Maybe she could get out. Somehow. While they were talking.

Allison stepped forward to support her, expression crumpled into concern. "I can't believe your alpha just—pushed you into the leg trap like that."

"His own *daughter*," Andrew rumbled, low.

"My alpha is father to all the pack's cubs." She stated it less baldly than she had for Allison, so Tatiana got to see it come together in people's faces, over a slow beat. She presumed sharp observers like Silver were slotting her initial confusion over Edmond into place as well.

"Ah," Andrew said, and his gaze sharpened on Allison. "You're not surprised, Sacramento, are you?" His tone promised words, later, about what other things she might not be surprised about, should they come up. "That certainly gives his voice a different tone." Silver grimaced in agreement.

Tatiana felt a sudden savage impulse to shout at all of them, for the suspicions she knew must be forming in their minds, as they set her parentage aside and returned to the preceding subject. She managed to keep her voice mostly even. "My alpha's lying, by the way. This was no plan of mine." Allison whined a protest, and Tatiana contemplated pushing away from her. "They want to believe him. It would be easier."

The clogged blizzard of her thoughts cleared for a moment, offering up a solution to one problem, at least. She could get the space alone she needed to think. "Stay and argue for me, would you?" Tatiana forced herself to wait until Allison nodded emphatically, then turned to go.

Of course, John got up to follow her. To make sure she was securely chained once more, no doubt. Lady damn it. Perhaps it was for the best, to make them feel secure about her while she tried desperately to think straight, for the storm to catch her up and grind her to pieces and pass.

24

After John left, Tatiana barely had time to try to regather her thoughts before new footsteps approached the basement doorway. She looked up from her slump over her knees to see Susan there.

The human came down, settled herself on the bottom stair, and looked at the opposite wall rather than Tatiana. "That's a new one on me. 'Pushed into a leg trap.' I'll have to file that away. I kept trying to say 'threw to the wolves' when I first got here, but 'threw under the bus' works as well, generally. Lacks a certain poetry, I suppose."

Tatiana stared incredulously at the woman for her chatter, but when Susan turned to meet her gaze, she was smiling sardonically, not looking nervous. "Humans actually talk about throwing each other to wolves?"

"Well, it's an American English idiom. I don't know about anywhere else." Susan allowed herself a small laugh. "You left the room, and you know the first thing Felicia said? 'If she doesn't know who her parents are, how does she ever know who she can play chase with?' "

"Everyone knows their mother. All the children are raised together, yes, but it's a little hard to hide the one who nursed you." Providing an answer to such a silly question was easy enough, at least. Tatiana could speak without thinking too much. "And if your mother has a mate, the conclusion is usually obvious."

"And if she doesn't?" Susan waited patiently for an answer, but Tatiana shook her head, and treated the question as rhetorical. If she didn't, you wondered. And worried. "I suppose that's supposed to be like real wolves—true wolves—where only the alpha pair has cubs, but if there's anything I've learned through years of observation, it's that you guys definitely aren't human, but you aren't wolves either. I'm surprised that kind of family structure has survived all the social complexity your human sides layer on top."

When Tatiana didn't comment on that either, silence settled for a beat. Susan's smile grew smaller as her attention intensified. "If your alpha's telling the truth, you're a good actress."

"Go away." Tatiana turned her body completely away from the woman and hugged herself. She wanted to be alone, she wanted to fall apart, and she couldn't let herself do it in front of an enemy; she was too well trained for that.

Well trained by the Jaw, for Father, if not directly by him.

"All right." Susan didn't move, but her voice changed like she was looking at the wall again. "I just came down to tell you that they're not going to kill you. It might not be official yet, but

Only then did the first part register. The human didn't smell of any dishonesty, any trick. Perhaps Susan didn't know the Roanokes as well as she thought she did, especially after the impulse Andrew had witnessed. But if she did know them . . . they'd let Tatiana go? And then she would return home to, what, an alpha who saw no value in her life? She supposed he wouldn't directly try to kill her.

Tatiana clung to the relatively straightforward part of Susan's comment. "How did you know there was a human—?"

"You were staring at me." Susan's voice was colored with another sharp smile, even though she was facing away. "I know that stare, trust me. That's the stare Were use when they're looking at me, but what they're seeing are humans in abstract. So while it could be that you were thinking about the role of humans in this Were political situation, I rather doubt it, so I'm guessing there's one in particular. Who was—he? She?"

Tatiana looked down at her hands. She'd liked it better in the vision, when they'd been covered in scratches, a visible reminder of what she'd done. She'd never actually told anyone this story outside of an official report, she realized. It tumbled out more easily than she'd have expected. "She. Very young. Had a Were baby, by mistake. I was the one to take care of her."

Susan gave a sharp bark of laughter. "Oh, does that phrase bridge Were cultures? I've had some try to take care of me, in my time."

Tatiana twisted around, more than human-fast to catch Susan's attention. Susan stared, eyes a little wide for all her world-wise tone just a moment before.

"She was the last I ever killed, human or Were. It was . . . so messy, everything went wrong, and she suffered, and I suddenly thought: Who was to say that the others' suffering was less for being faster, for being something we didn't have to watch at painful length? Why would the Lady wish this? And maybe it was a necessary evil—my part in the pack wasn't big enough to truly know that—but it wasn't necessary for me. I could refuse to kill anymore."

It was more than Tatiana had meant to say, but the momentum was carrying her along and her former calm had gone and her emotions were tearing at her voice with sharp teeth. "And when I told Fa—the alpha that, he said that he understood, but my purpose would change. And apparently now my purpose is to die."

"I'm sorry." Susan stood and came into reach to touch Tatiana's shoulder. Even with only human strength, her squeeze was firm. "You can't choose your family. And your pack seems more like family than most around here in that sense."

Tatiana shook her head, not sure how to respond to that. She hadn't chosen her pack, but she did have to choose what she did now. She'd told Susan something she'd never told anyone before, not properly. Her alpha had abandoned her, so perhaps it was time she abandoned her loyalty to her pack's secrets. Her knowledge of her alpha and the Jaw might be the

with, and others in the Jaw were so slippery, like Mikhail. Perhaps they'd understand her motives. Perhaps they wouldn't and she didn't care. But Alexei . . . he was what was best in the Jaw. Perhaps her mother might understand, stretch her implicit assurances of love and support to encompass even such a betrayal, but Alexei was too solid. He had no stretch, and that was the best of *him*, that he'd never stretch away from her.

And now she was pulling away from him. Because she had to.

She believed Susan when the human said they wouldn't kill her, she realized. She'd return the favor, trust them with the information they needed to protect Allison, and Edmond, and everyone else she'd met here. And if Alexei and the others couldn't bear to listen to her voice when she returned home, so be it.

"Your alphas are impressive," Tatiana said. It seemed like it almost followed from what Susan had last said, camouflaging her racing thoughts between. "They don't seem like they could hold power for more than a moment, yet they do. And wield it well."

"Back when I first interacted with them for any length of time, my husband said that Andrew—though it applies just as much to Silver—was driven to protect the world, one person at a time." Susan shrugged, and ran a hand through her hair so it fell back with more body. "It's how they're built, I think."

"*No accident,*" Tatiana whispered in Old Were. Had she given the alphas only as much wolfsbane as she'd planned, the suggestion wouldn't have worked anyway, she'd bet. She touched her collar's lock. "There's something else they should know."

Susan gave her a sharp look, entirely too intelligent, like she guessed the gist of what Tatiana had to say. She didn't say anything, though, just dug the key out from deep within a pocket and unlocked the collar. Tatiana didn't even bother assessing whether she could overpower Susan. There would be someone like Pierce waiting upstairs.

The connection floated into Tatiana's mind on the way up the stairs, so obvious she wondered why she hadn't seen it sooner. And so beside the point, she wondered why she was thinking about it now. "Edmond's your son, isn't he? He's the beta's son, and you're his wife. You got—" As Tatiana's voice failed briefly, she realized why she was thinking it now. "You got to keep him."

"I did." Susan paused and gave her a sharp, sideways smile. "And my alphas have had no cause to regret it, if I do say so myself."

"I'll bet they haven't." Tatiana paused too and searched her memory. If she was honest with herself, she'd admit she was stalling, digging through ancient history for facts that didn't matter. But she needed a little stalling at the moment. She'd made her decision to betray her upbringing, and everything in her subconscious kept protesting. But it had to be done.

Tatiana nodded. Rasputin had been grooming her and her siblings, before the humans killed him, in hopes of using royal influence for Were purposes. The pack tried to rescue all of them for the same reason, but only managed to save her. In the end, they kept her hidden. I suppose it amused Grandfather to think of bringing human royal blood into the pack."

Susan shook her head this time, smiling. "Of course Rasputin was . . ." She held up a hand. "Never mind. You'll have to tell me more about it later, if we have time."

Tatiana dipped her head in agreement. Enough stalling. They reached the doorway to the dining room too quickly after that. Tatiana drew a deep breath. She was doing this because it was right.

She pushed away from Susan as the Were around the table fell silent in surprise at seeing her back. She went to her knees, to her hands, then low to the floor until her forehead touched the wood and her hair tumbled to either side, leaving her neck exposed. She didn't know if the North Americans prostrated themselves this way, but the gesture couldn't be that different. She was very low, and at their mercy.

"There is more I must tell you," she said, and paused, but they didn't comment. She smelled the sharp bite of surprise, but could not trace it to its exact sources without seeing faces. Someone gasped. She was fairly certain it was Allison. "Father plans very carefully. Contingencies and backups, but rarely straightforward attacks. I did know there was wolfsbane in the wine, but not that much. I think those were two of his plans: either the vision would have an effect, or the alphas would be killed. Whether you drank enough to kill or not, his ends were served. That is how he plans."

"What effect was expected?" Silver's voice, tight with tension. "How did *that* . . ." She sputtered for a word for several moments, before using the obvious one and giving it a venomous twist. "Dream serve a foreign alpha's plans?"

Tatiana risked looking up, because she couldn't read the alphas just from scent, not when several Were were reacting emotionally together in the same room. Silver looked ready to stab her in a few choice places to mimic blows she took while in the dream. "Wolfsbane visions—they are guided by things you hear a certain time before. If you wish to receive the Lady's wisdom on a certain topic, you have someone suggest it to you beforehand. I was told my mission was to suggest that the burden of being alpha was so heavy that you two would wish to set it down."

"But that's not what you said." Silver smiled, thin-lipped, and pushed away from her mate to stand over Tatiana. She bent to take the other woman's chin, lifting her head enough to face her directly. "You told us it was an accident. And so it was, it seems, but I was no less alpha when that accident had not occurred. I would have killed myself for it still, and now your alpha has allowed the Lady to show me—" she glanced back at her mate and must have read something in his ~~expression~~

he does not share his motives with me, but—" Tatiana drew a deep breath and looked straight at Silver again. A white lock had slipped forward over her shoulder, but otherwise her hair was along her back, minimized. "We hear rumors of a Lady-touched, and he suddenly begins seeking visions. We have strength of numbers, of trained fighters, but to have as your leader a woman who whispers say rose from the dead with the Lady's spirit inside her . . . that is a religious strength we cannot touch. I think he fears it."

Silver made a strangled whine and pressed at her throat like she could prevent the sound like damping a resonating piece of metal. "I am not—!" Tatiana had never heard anyone sound so lost.

"And that's why Russia is interested in us, far across the ocean." Andrew's low laugh was formed entirely from bitterness, no humor. "And you are more loyal than you would have had us believe. You did know of the first plan with the wolfsbane. I suppose the other was only kept from you because you couldn't have played your part convincingly if you'd known the danger to yourself."

"I am less loyal than you think. He risked my death, tried to abandon me here because I told him I would not kill for him any longer!" Tatiana couldn't keep her voice from rising with tension. Let them make their decisions based on the truth, but not on evils that did not belong to her. "I have kept that promise since I made it to him, and to the Lady."

"I believe her." Susan's voice. Tatiana didn't turn, keeping her eyes on the two Roanokes, but she was sure her surprise joined the general scent of the room. "She told me about it, and I believe she has kept it, and means to keep it still."

"I advised someone once—" Silver turned a glance down the table, though Tatiana couldn't pick out her target until Felicia flushed. "To judge someone's character by those who follow that person. Or argue on her behalf, perhaps. You've gathered support in interesting quarters, envoy." Allison hunched her shoulders, looking guilty under the increase of attention from everyone in the room, but Susan bore it calmly.

Andrew made a low, agreeing noise in this throat, and then silence fell as the mates communicated through looks. "It strikes me"—he flashed a smile to Silver, then focused on Tatiana—"with less poetry than my mate would use, maybe, that we discovered that we would be alphas with or without the position, but more than that, we have before us someone who is no killer, even with the position thrust upon her."

He slid tented fingertips along the tabletop near, but not touching, Silver's chain. "You were considering it, were you not? And you didn't."

"Instead, you persuaded others to your cause. Perhaps without even intending to?" Silver picked up her chain with a quiet metal shiver noise and tucked it into her pocket.

Tatiana grasped after responses like retreating prey. Andrew did not seem angry she'd considered attacking them

nostage?

"That's what we'll tell your alpha, certainly. And he'll presumably consider us foolish for trying to keep someone hostage who has no value. To him." Andrew's expression was suddenly slashed with a grin. Tatiana could tell he was thinking of the value she'd just given them by revealing Father's probable motives.

Silver exhaled as if in amusement at a joke no one had made. "While this offer is not dependent on what you can give us, do not think we won't at least ask for what information you have, and what you might be able to find out from your friends who remain in Russia."

Whether Andrew had intended that or not, when he made the offer, he followed his mate's lead smoothly enough and nodded. "And you'll need to swear on the Lady that you not try to escape to Russia or work against Roanoke." He stood and crossed to help her up. "Do you accept the offer of asylum?"

Tatiana searched desperately for the word in her English vocabulary. Wasn't that a method of locking away? For those who were crazy?

Andrew must have read her confusion. "Refuge," he said, formality of the original statement easing. "From a political enemy."

"Different than being a hostage?" Tatiana asked. She could hardly process the idea. They were offering to let her stay? Because she didn't want to kill? With considerable self-interest of their own as well, but also because they could see in her something Father had proved he never could.

"Sometimes different," Silver said. "Sometimes not." She laughed, not unkindly. "Let's give it a while and see."

Tatiana tried to test the idea out in her mind, see if her emotions overcame her. Never see any of the Jaw again. Never see Alexei. Never see her mother. Of course, never was a long time that didn't tend to stand up to a werewolf lifespan, but she tested herself with never.

She found that she'd said her good-byes already, when she considered betraying them by revealing secrets. Alexei was already lost to her, but this way she wouldn't have to see his betrayal on his face. And perhaps . . . perhaps she could speak to her mother still, supposedly in search of the inside information the Roanokes wanted. She could see how far that love stretched.

"On the Lady, I swear. I will not try to escape or work against Roanoke." Tatiana almost whispered the promise. She pressed her thumb to her forehead hard enough she must have left a red mark. She gestured for her phone, and Andrew handed it to her.

She composed a text to Alexei with unsteady fingers. *The North Americans are keeping me as a hostage. Please don't let anyone come after me. Better I'm a hostage than dead at their hands, as Father would have preferred.* She paused, lost. That was the business part, but she didn't know how to say anything

Allison tackled her in a hug out of nowhere while Tatiana was still trying to realign her mind. Whatever she was leaving at home, women like Allison were one thing North America had, besides no one asking her to kill or give up her life to serve her purpose. She could focus on that distraction, let the feeling of childhood friends being ripped away trickle back later, to be dealt with slowly.

She wiggled her hands free from the embrace and cupped the sides of her lover's face and kissed her with all the force of her wild emotions. And then she remembered how everyone was watching, and how she wouldn't want Allison to come under too much of the constant guard Tatiana would be under herself, and she pulled away. But Allison was beaming anyway, and she gave a laugh of triumph. "You can *stay.*"

She flicked a glance back at the alphas, apparently asking for permission, because the next thing Tatiana knew, she was being urged toward the back door and the yard between the houses. The sun was low in the sky, casting everything in the yard into deeper contrast, each bush and angle of the guest-house outlined in shadow. "You can go back to your own room if you want, but you can also stay with me." Allison babbled on.

Tatiana twisted her fingers free and stopped on the path. She was so tired, but she needed a few steps on her own. She stepped off gray gravel onto green grass, between two of the stars, unlit now. Staying. She was staying. Here where Were looked ready to snarl in your face when you painted the Lady in wolf; where children knew their parents; where she didn't know anyone properly except a passionate, slightly immature woman she might be able to love. Where everything was different.

"Oh, Lady. I'm sorry. I'm being stupid. You should hit me when I don't shut up." Allison strode to her and gathered her into her arms again. "Are you all right, puppy?"

The diminutive, incongruously used by the younger one, made Tatiana laugh, and from there she couldn't stop the tears slipping out. She wasn't even sure what emotion had created them, not wholly sadness, not wholly happiness, but extreme difference, too extreme for her to handle at the moment. She pressed her face into Allison's neck, like maybe the other woman wouldn't notice. Thank the Lady, no vision, called by the stress of it, pulled her away. The suggestion that the visions were getting farther apart gave her a thread of reassurance to cling to.

"Shh." Allison moved to cradle her more comfortably. "If you pry a couple fingers away from your death-grip on control, I won't tell anyone, promise. It'll be all right." She smoothed Tatiana's hair. "You're all right."

"*Lady grant,*" Tatiana said in Old Were, and let herself cry silently. For now, yes. Things were all right.

25

Felicia's wild self raised its hackles as Sacramento pulled Tatiana from the room. Silver smiled lopsidedly. Better to at least try to explain, rather than let the young woman get sullen. "Relationships bind her to us, and away from her birth pack. I do not think they offered her the ones she most needed." That was true, but the question was whether it would be true enough to keep the Russian from working against them. Still, Silver considered they had a good chance, considering how Tatiana had acted when they'd pointed out what her alpha was trying to do to her.

"We'll be watching her; you're welcome to watch her all you want as well," Dare said, and gave Silver a thin smile, full of all the things they weren't saying in front of the others. One Russian Were under the eyes of the pack was a stroll of a hunt compared to a leader across the sea who feared a religious gift she did not possess. Dare had been right about the Russians.

"And the two of you must carry such a heavy, weighty burden completely alone. How voice-breaking." Death would not lower himself to gestures of affection, but he had not left her side since she awoke, and she could feel his warm weight against her leg now.

True enough. They were not alone in this, and there was no sense in chasing trouble ahead of time. For now, they had dealt with the envoy, everyone was safe as they could be, and Dare and she were here together. Awake and aware.

And Dare was hers once more. Earlier, she'd still been reeling too much for her mind to turn in such directions, but now all the attraction she'd had to suppress in front of his wife in the dream was surging back up.

She grabbed at Dare's hand. "Now that is finished, perhaps we could speak privately." For the sake of politeness to Felicia, she didn't emphasize it at all, or she thought she hadn't, but Boston smelled amused and knowing anyway. Silver pulled a face at him as she dragged Dare past. Not that Dare needed much dragging. He caught her up in a kiss at the entrance to their bedroom and she deepened it, held it, gathering the sensation up and reflecting it back and letting it fill them both up until it began to wash away the memories of the dream's pain.

Then, laughing, she dragged him into the room. He was hers—and she was his—and she planned to capture him all over again. Repeatedly.

Normally they would have dozed afterward, but Silver wasn't ready to brave that just yet, and neither did Dare seem to be. With eyes and fingertips, he traced the scars of the dead snakes on her bad arm where it rested on the bed between

smooth her hair where their exertions had tumbled it all over her shoulders. His tone made it clear that was not a complaint.

"You were in my dream." Silver hesitated on the edge of letting everything tumble out. She wanted to tell him everything, to banish it by putting it into plain words in the harsh light of reality, but would that cause him pain? He had loved his wife. "With someone else."

Dare smiled thinly. "And you were in mine. With . . . no one in particular."

Silver heard something of the tone of her hesitation in his. Perhaps it was better to have everything in the open, pain or no pain. She'd felt pain enough having lived the dream. "Your wife never died. It was her brother, instead, in the fire." She cupped the side of his face. "So you never left Spain, and Roanoke crumbled into individual packs, and the Tainted One—" Silver gritted her teeth against the words. That name for her monster had been of the dream, not this world. "Stefan worked his way through pack after pack in the chaos. My brother was alive, and leading those few who remained."

The skin of his cheek was smoother than it would normally have been at this time of day, so recently shaved after awakening. Dare remained silent and a little still, perhaps while he imagined what that world had been. "My brother was alive, and you had your family. You, and your wife, and Felicia, and you had a son as well, visiting as a delegation. But . . ."

This time the silence stretched long enough that Dare prompted her. "But?"

Silver squeezed her eyes briefly closed. "Spain had made you hard. Of course it wasn't real. It doesn't actually mean anything. But it was so much you, and so much not you—taking power in the name of the greater good, but hurting so many along the way . . ."

"You . . ." Dare swallowed, but he seemed to draw strength, not hurt, from her admission. "Were so self-contained. You had your brother, and your self-confidence, and you didn't seem to realize how much in the end, we all need each other."

"I think I was like that, once, when I was young." Silver drew a deep breath, trying to step outside herself and see truly the faded layers of memories she had from well before Stefan. "To say I might have been like that still, with my brother alive . . . it's not wrong. Just not true, either."

"I like that." Dare settled his hand on the back of her neck and squeezed briefly. "Not wrong, but not true." He blew out a breath. "The rest—it was similar to yours at the core. Because Tatiana suggested everything was an accident, I suppose. Stefan never escaped. I stayed on as enforcer until I'd come to hate Rory and myself for it." He tried to laugh, but the sound twisted halfway through. "Sounds like mine had a lower death count, but . . ."

Silver's turn. She caressed the side of her thumb along his lips, then dropped her hand to his. "But?"

"Susan was dead. It had nearly killed John, too, and he was me that when nothing else is left, I'm still an alpha, and even if as an alpha a single person is all I can save, that person is still worth it."

"If you want," Death said, and snapped his teeth down.

"Ginnie? Is that why you wanted to call her? What happened to her?"

Silver considered refusing to tell him, but she'd come so far already. "Stefan killed her pack first, but kept her. Through the rest." Nausea was rising in her throat, and so she left it there. Dare could imagine. Not as precisely as she could, but well enough.

Dare pulled her close, and that was enough talking for a while. She breathed in his scent until her thoughts had settled once more. She felt when his own thoughts pressed up to the point of speaking again, because he took a deeper breath. "I'm surprised I was the first to wake up. I really did believe it was real. You're the one who's good at the slippery edges of reality."

"Exactly." Death padded over with something unidentifiable, torn and bloody, hanging from his mouth. He sank down to gnaw it. "He is used to things making sense. When the strangenesses piled up too high, it pulled him out. You, on the other hand—" He gave Silver a canine grin. Far too many teeth. "Everything is strange for you. You swallowed all of it whole."

Silver repeated Death's words for Dare, though not without a little grumbling at the end. "I knew it wasn't real, so I would have found my way out eventually, even without help."

"Of course," Dare agreed. Because he knew what was good for him. She laughed, and he joined in, and the dream receded a little more.

When they did sleep, Silver did so only lightly, and woke sometime in the middle hours of the night. Andrew roused as she got up, then settled again, always a heavier sleeper than her. She'd make sure to be back in good time so he did not wake properly without her.

She wanted to feel the Lady's light on her skin, so she slipped outside. They had not much wild land, here among the humans, but it had sky. That was enough. Death joined her along the way, so quiet she couldn't have said just when he did. Darkness was just there, traveling with her. As she had become so used to.

Silver sat in the grass and held her bad wrist with her good hand so she could drape both arms over her upraised knees and no one watching would ever know one was wrong. Death sat tall beside her. She wanted to asked about the Lady's touch, the rumors Tatiana had spoken of, but she knew he wouldn't answer, knew that the question would hurt him. He was barred from the Lady, as she was. He undoubtedly knew the direction of her thoughts, but he still sat beside her, did not slip away into the night. That was enough.

"Did you miss me?" she asked him instead. His ears
~~1 4~ b~~ ~ ~i~~ of surprise, perhaps. If it was, it was the

weight against her skin. "Chalk it up to mortal foolishness. I
would have noticed, given time. I value you no less than I value
my mate." She turned her head to face him properly. She could
hardly find any lines of him, so undefined was he against the
night at this moment. "But perhaps *you'd* rather be rid of *me*."

His answer was so long in coming, Silver thought he was
ignoring her, and her maudlin reflections. He used his habitual
voice, as much a part of him as her poisoned sight was a part of
her, Silver suddenly realized. "Never, Silver," he said.

Silver smiled. Never.

26

Allison found excuses to stay for about two weeks before some mundane crisis or other at home got too tangled to resolve over the phone. Tatiana had expected some whining, but when the Roanokes came to see her off, Tatiana caught Allison frowning like she was marshalling a whole pack of arguments. Lady damn it.

It was nearly midday when Allison had to leave for her flight, but the clouds pressed indeterminate grayness down on them anyway. It wasn't raining, but it seemed a little too cold for everyone to stand out on the driveway beside the car that would drop Allison off at the airport. Everyone stood around anyway.

Tatiana tried to head off trouble before it appeared, though she suspected it wouldn't do much good. "You'll have to visit soon," she told Allison, and brushed away her hair to kiss the corner of her jaw. She'd finally talked her into wearing it down the other day, and Allison looked more relaxed already.

"You could come and stay with me." Allison spoke in the

would screw up what we have now, to make you try to be both simultaneously." She slipped her fingers carefully out of Allison's grip.

Allison frowned, but she at least clearly understood the idea. "Someone else could . . ."

"Like a beta?" Silver draped her arm over the top of the side mirror. "You're not released from the trap about that either, Sacramento."

Tatiana eyed her lover. She'd actually been thinking about that. Might as well make her suggestion now Silver had reminded her, while Allison and the Roanokes were in the same place. "Had any of those applying for the job ever been betas before?"

"Craig," Andrew said, and Allison growled. Tatiana searched her memory. Too many damn North Americans to meet and remember all at once. Andrew tossed her a dry smile. "The one she was yelling at when you first arrived."

Tatiana winced. Well, it had been a good idea. "What's wrong with him?" she asked Allison, who looked at the ground guiltily.

"He tried to force his last alpha to step down while she

was pregnant," Allison muttered. It seemed like a pretty good reason to avoid him as beta, so Tatiana wasn't sure why Allison was acting so embarrassed about it. She looked to Silver for clarification.

"He was the father, he only wanted her to step down during the actual pregnancy to protect the baby from emotion-related shifts, and he withdrew his petition when we convinced him the issue was much more complicated than that." Silver shrugged, and Tatiana got the sense that was another one of those "snap their fingers, just that easy" incidents like their winning of the Roanoke pack.

"And now he's living just outside Portland's borders without a pack, so he can visit the child." Andrew didn't explain further, but his emphasis suggested the rest of the story: *without a pack*. A situation many Were would find deeply miserable.

"And Sacramento is close enough to Portland for him to still visit?" Tatiana said.

Andrew nodded. "Short plane ride."

With each detail added to the explanation of Craig's situation, Allison's shoulders hunched deeper. "His situation sucks, but it's no good me taking on a beta I can't get along with!"

"Maybe you should." Tatiana nodded respectfully to the Roanokes when they focused on her, but she spoke to Allison. "It sounds to me like you need a beta who already knows how to be a beta, and can tell you what you should be delegating to him. You don't need a friend, and you don't need another lover. As long as you can work with him, maybe you need someone for a while that you aren't even friendly with, just have a professional working relationship with." At home, the betas were

certainly never Father's friends. They were subordinates, but ones who knew their duties, and didn't need Father to con-
~~tantly supervise them.

deep, but for where Allison's hand ended up. Tatiana smacked it away, and finished the kiss with her hands very politely on Allison's upper arms. She hadn't had a vision after a chase since she'd been offered asylum, but she'd had two after physical exertion in that time and still didn't have a good feel for what might trigger one.

Besides, the alphas were watching. "You'll be late," she admonished, and pushed Allison to the car.

She watched the car farther down the street than she really should have, considering the breeze held droplets promising drizzle moving in. She would miss Allison for herself, but also because the woman was a force of constant distraction from the problem of how she was going to relate to the alphas now. Her alphas, but not her alphas; her captors, but not her captors.

"Well done," Silver said, and Tatiana couldn't figure out what she meant for a moment. Well done moping about how she would fit in to this pack's daily life? "We'd despaired of getting her to pick a beta."

Tatiana shrugged. "It's what I do." Convinced people that things were good ideas—whether they really were or not.

Hopefully, having recognized that in her, the alphas wouldn't be asking her to persuade people of any bad ones.

"Help people?" Silver laughed, and held up her hand to forestall Tatiana when she would have objected. "Come on, it's going to rain." She led the way inside. "Have you heard from anyone at home?"

Had she gotten any useful information about her alpha's next move, Tatiana knew Silver meant. She might have hesitated, but anyone with a brain—and her mother definitely possessed one of those—had to know where the information was going. Sorting disinformation from good was the Roanokes' job. She thought her mother's information was good, though, since it was coming at all. Since she hadn't disowned her daughter, Tatiana guessed her mother wouldn't hurt the side her daughter's well-being was currently harnessed to. "My mother is of the opinion that his obsession with you as a religious symbol is growing. They might try to grab you, but not yet. They'd need better local intelligence for that."

Silver pressed her lips into a thin line, but didn't otherwise react to the religious implications this time. "Better to rush them into it than wait, perhaps—"

Andrew made a small gesture and she cut off. To be discussed later, not in front of the Russian, Tatiana presumed.

"Speaking of my former pack, I wondered if you could do me a favor, Roanoke Dare." Tatiana stopped in the entryway, and Andrew turned around in the middle of the living room. Tatiana took a deep breath, but couldn't continue just yet. She rubbed the back of her neck instead. "Help me with my Mark? I don't want it anymore."

"Mark?" Andrew crossed to her and looked down at where she'd rubbed. Tatiana shrugged out of her shirt and then ¹ ˡ ~~ ˡᵃᵢᵣ forward over her shoulder so he could see it

Mark of the Jaw, they put it there specifically so you can't get the right angle to remove it yourself." She touched hers, arm twisted back awkwardly. "Is that why you kept your scars? You didn't know?"

"Cutting it out?" Andrew's hand went to the small of his back in turn.

"And it heals clean." Tatiana smiled, wan. "Of course, being Were, anesthetic doesn't work properly. You could always starve yourself until you pass out from the extra injury, but then it doesn't heal properly. It takes fortitude. Few but Father and a few of the betas do their own."

Andrew looked a little white around the lips where he had them pressed together too hard, but he nodded once. "You want it that much? Let's be clear; no one here is asking you to break with your homeland to that degree."

"I will not deliver any of them to harm." Tatiana lifted her chin high. "That doesn't mean I wish to wear the mark of one who sent me to die."

"Fair enough." Andrew gestured for her to follow him down the hall. She kept her shirt off, bunched up against her chest. "I don't think it's something I'd want done to me without a damned lot of thought first."

"Would it work on my arm?" The tentative hope in Silver's voice stopped them both, turned them back.

Tatiana looked at Andrew, shaking her head. She had no idea, and she probably shouldn't answer without a lot more information about Silver's condition. He grimaced. "Well, the damage that's keeping you from using it properly is internal. You'd have to cut pretty deep, and you heal like a human. Humans don't heal clean, so it might just make it worse."

Silver looked down and to the side, like someone had spoken from a sitting position on the floor. She was silent, as if listening, for a moment, then nodded. "True. Something to test in small ways first, to consider all the circumstances to give the best chance of success, in any case." She gestured for them to continue ahead of her. "Now is the time to deal with yours."

When they reached the kitchen, Andrew rummaged in the drawers until he came up with a knife. It seemed so prosaic. A kitchen lit by diffuse, cloudy light and a paring knife, not a chapel grove and a ceremonial blade. Or a quick stop on the trail home, gritted teeth and the slash of a skinning knife, clearing away evidence of injury before anyone at home would see.

Andrew turned a kitchen chair around for her to sit on backward. Tatiana settled and folded up one sleeve of her shirt with precise movements, focusing on getting just the thickness she wanted, rather than on anticipating the pain. She'd done this before, but it wasn't something one got used to. At least she hadn't, with the few scars she'd had in her life. She tucked the bulk of the shirt between her chest and the back of the chair.

"You'll get blood on your bra," Andrew said.

~~— · · 'd feel his hands hovering near, and she gave~~

pain, and Andrew flicked something into the sink.

Andrew's thumb stroked along the patch of new, smooth skin, sliding in blood on one trip, and sticking to the drying dregs on the next. Then his hand settled, firm and protective, on the back of her neck. "Refuge," he murmured, low.

"*Yes*," Tatiana said in Old Were. It seemed North America would be.

Made in the USA
Lexington, KY
26 April 2017